CLIFF HANGERS: MR. & MRS. PLATT

A CLIFF FORD MYSTERY

TERRY TOLER

D1521374

Cliff Hangers: Mr. & Mrs. Platt

Published by: BeHoldings, LLC

Copyright ©2022, **BeHoldings, LLC**
Terry Toler
All Rights Reserved

Book Cover: BeHoldings Publishing
Contributing Editor: Donna Kos

For information email: terry@terrytoler.com.

Our books can be purchased in bulk for promotional, educational, and business use. Please contact your bookseller or the BeHoldings Publishing Sales department at: sales@terrytoler.com

For booking information email: booking@terrytoler.com.
First U.S. Edition: February, 2022
Printed in the United States of America

ISBN 978-1-954710-08-5

OTHER BOOKS BY TERRY TOLER

Fiction

The Longest Day
The Reformation of Mars
The Late, Great Planet Jupiter
The Great Wall of Ven-Us
Saturn: The Eden Experiment
The Mercury Protocols
Save The Girls
The Ingenue
Saving Sara
Save The Queen
No Girl Left Behind
The Launch
The Blue Rose
Body Count
Save Me Twice
Cliff Hangers: Anna

Non-Fiction

How to Make More Than a Million Dollars
The Heart Attacked
Seven Years of Promise
Mission Possible
Marriage Made in Heaven
21 Days to Physical Healing
21 Days to Spiritual Fitness
21 Days to Divine Health
21 Days to a Great Marriage
21 Days to Financial Freedom
21 Days to Sharing Your Faith
21 Days to Mission Possible
7 Days to Emotional Freedom
Uncommon Finances
Uncommon Health

Uncommon Marriage
The Jesus Diet
Suddenly Free
Feeling Free

For more information on these books and other resources visit
terrytoler.com.

Thank you for purchasing this novel from best-selling author Terry Toler. As an additional thank you, Terry wants to give you a free gift.

Sign up for:

Updates
New Releases
Announcements

At terrytoler.com

We'll send you the first three chapters of *The Launch*, a Jamie Austen novella, free of charge. The one that started the Spy Stories and Eden Stories Franchises.

1

Mr. and Mrs. Robert S. Platt walked into the Regency, a five-star twenty-three story luxury hotel in downtown Chicago. They were coming up on their sixth hour as husband and wife. The girl at the front desk was friendly and accommodating.

"We have you booked in the honeymoon suite," she said with a smile. "Congratulations on your nuptials."

Sylvia, the beaming bride, conspicuously flashed her rings at the clerk. They cost just under a hundred thousand dollars for the set. Robert could never afford such extravagance. His wife came from old Jewish money from the North Shore. A source of angst between Sylvia and her parents who weren't particularly pleased with her choice of husband.

Once they realized they couldn't convince her to dump the man they considered a loser, they spoiled the pair with gifts and money. Including an extravagant wedding by anyone's standards and an all-expenses-paid honeymoon to the British Virgin Islands. They'd leave tomorrow after spending their wedding night in the honeymoon suite. Also compliments of Sylvia's parents.

"Would you like some champagne brought to your room?" the clerk asked.

In sync, Robert and Sylvia answered at the same time except with different answers.

"Yes, please," Robert said.

"No, thank you," Sylvia answered.

She thought Robert had a drinking problem and, now that they were married, she was already trying to change him. At least that's how he interpreted her response.

"It's on the house," the girl behind the counter said. "Compliments of the manager. He said to congratulate you both on your marriage."

Robert caught the clerk's eye and gave her a nod of the head. "Since it's free, go ahead and bring it up," he said tersely.

Sylvia let out a huge sigh but didn't protest further.

The clerk called for the bellman who was standing to the side. She handed him the room keys without saying the number aloud for security purposes. The uniformed bellman directed the couple to follow him with a gentle hand gesture.

"You're on the top floor," he said.

"How many floors are there?" Sylvia asked hesitantly. She was afraid of heights.

"Twenty-three," he answered.

Robert took his wife's hand and squeezed it reassuringly.

When they arrived at the room, Sylvia seemed to lose her concern. She ran from room to room like a silly schoolgirl.

"Robert, come look at the bedroom," he heard her say from the other room. "It's simply amazing," she chirped.

"Just leave the bags here," Robert said to the bellman. "We'll take care of them."

The man sat the bags down and then stood at attention with his hands clasped in front of him. Clearly expecting a tip. Robert slipped a five-dollar bill out of his pocket and handed it to the bellman who was unable to hide the disappointment on his face. Probably used to big spenders in that suite.

Once the bellman was gone, Robert hurried into the bedroom when his wife called for him a second time.

Robert felt his mouth fly open.

The master suite was as big as a small house. A large king-sized bed seemed dwarfed by the size of the room and the three separate sitting areas. One was off to the side and had a huge plate glass window overlooking Lake Michigan. The hotel was known for its unobstructed views and the panoramic scenery was more than even Robert was expecting.

Coming from his background he'd never seen anything like it. He could get used to this.

Sylvia was in the bathroom and called for Robert a third time. His mouth gaped open again when he entered it. Everything was marble. The floors. The countertop. The large, walk-in shower with at least a dozen spray faucets. The large jacuzzi marble tub had tints of red and white on the sides and walls.

Lush towels and two seductively soft bathrobes were hung by hooks on the wall near the extravagant shower. The words *His* and *Hers* were monogrammed stylishly with gold thread on the robes. The selection of amenities on the counter was staggering.

How could anyone need so many different kinds of lotions?

Sylvia threw her arms around Robert's neck and gave him a big kiss. He didn't remember seeing her so happy. She gushed as you'd expect from a new bride, but this reaction was over the top even by Sylvia's standards of exaggeration.

"Have you ever seen anything so luxurious?" she asked.

Before he could comment, she was off exploring the other rooms.

Robert went back into the living room, gathered up the bags, and brought them to the bedroom. He didn't dare open them. Sylvia was particular about her things and would want to unpack them herself.

When he heard his name and another squeal of delight, he made his way to the kitchen and dining room area. He found a massive dining room table that would seat at least a dozen people. That struck him as odd since a honeymoon suite would only be for two people. Perhaps couples held after wedding receptions there for special guests and family. He almost expected a butler to appear out of thin air and start taking their food order.

A knock on the door interrupted his thoughts.

Probably the champagne.

The bellman sat the large bucket filled with the bottle and ice on the dining room table and then stood waiting for a tip. Robert pulled out another five-dollar bill and handed it to him.

This could get expensive, he thought. Good thing her parents were paying for it.

Sylvia came out of the kitchen area with what looked to be a menu in her hand.

"I'm famished," she said. "Let's order room service."

"That's a good idea," Robert said.

Sylvia ordered a Gluten-Free Penne with pappardelle pasta. No chicken or shrimp but with wild mushrooms and edamame on top. Robert ordered Cigar City braised bone-in short ribs in a red wine sauce, with onion soup, steamed asparagus, and whipped Yukon potatoes.

By the time the food arrived, Sylvia actually looked relaxed. The first time in several months. At least since they'd started planning the wedding. While they waited for the food, she took a shower and changed to more casual clothes. Robert took his suit jacket off, loosened his tie, and unbuttoned his collar, though he didn't expect the tension to leave his shoulders anytime soon.

He opened the bottle of champagne and poured two glasses. Sylvia even took one sip, much to his surprise. They then allowed themselves to think about the activities of the day. Which still seemed like a blur to Robert.

"I can't believe the Rabbi forgot the rings," Sylvia said, almost giggling like she'd had a full glass of champagne even though she'd only had one small drink.

"I didn't even notice," Robert said, letting out his still-tense laugh. He gulped down his glass of champagne and poured himself another.

"He pronounced us man and wife, and we just stood there," Sylvia said. "I was, like, something's wrong. Did we forget something? Then I remembered we hadn't exchanged rings or said our vows! I couldn't believe it. I mean what was I supposed to say?"

"How old is that Rabbi?" he asked.

"I don't know. But he's been at the synagogue since I was a little girl. Bless his heart. He's forgetful in his old age."

"Something always goes wrong at a wedding. If that's the worst of it, then it's not so bad."

"Forgetting the rings is a pretty big deal. Daddy didn't look very happy."

"You know how he is. If everything's not perfect. . ." Robert said it almost bitterly. The old man was almost impossible to please and a mistake like that would be a pretty big deal to him, even if it wasn't to Robert.

"I'm going to get changed," Sylvia said, after she'd eaten about half of her food. Sylvia weighed a little over a hundred pounds and ate twice as much as Robert had expected from her.

She gave him a seductive look as she stood to leave the room. "I have a surprise for you."

She disappeared into the bathroom in the master suite and closed the doors.

Robert followed her into the bedroom and got out of his suit and into shorts and a tee-shirt. Then he went back into the dining room and downed another glass of champagne. He set the glass down and opened a set of double doors that led out onto a balcony and stepped out onto it. The height caused him to almost lose his balance and took a second to get used to. Being up that high was disorienting, even for him. It felt like the hotel was swaying in the breeze.

A heavily secured steel railing ran around the outside of the balcony and came nearly up to his chest. The bellman said the honeymoon suite and presidential suite were the only two rooms in the hotel with balconies while showing them to their room.

Two chairs and a table were in the small area and Robert sat down in one of them and took in the view. By that time, darkness had set in, but the moon provided enough light to see the waves of Lake Michigan beating against the shoreline. The city lights in both directions delivered spectacular views in all directions except to the west.

After a few minutes, Sylvia called for him. "I'm ready, Robert," she said.

He stood and walked back inside.

"What do you think?" She was wearing a white nightgown with a train. She twirled around in a circle. It was beautiful and sexy. She looked stunning. He imagined that piece of lingerie cost a fortune.

5

"Beautiful," Robert said as he walked over to her and took her in his arms. He kissed her hard and deep. He held her briefly when she found her words.

"Let's go into the bedroom," she said shyly.

"In a second. I want to show you something."

Robert took her by the hand and led her toward the balcony.

Sylvia resisted.

"Trust me. It'll be okay," he said. "I've got you. You have to see the view. It's spectacular. And you'll want to tell your parents how beautiful the views are and how stunning Lake Michigan looks from the Honeymoon Suite."

"I don't like heights," she stammered, clearly uncomfortable.

"I know. It has a railing all around it. You'll be fine. It'll be worth it."

Sylvia was hesitant but finally agreed. She stepped out onto the balcony gingerly, with trepidation like she was scared to death. Which he knew she was.

"Okay. I've seen enough," Sylvia said, as she started back into the safety of the room.

"Just a second! We forgot something."

"What?" she asked.

"I never carried you over the threshold."

Before she could say anything, Robert had Sylvia in his arms. He played linebacker in high school and was bigger than the average guy. He hadn't lost all his muscles and was able to pick up his petite wife with little trouble.

She let out a nervous laugh and looked back at the railing. Her head was precariously close to it.

"You're fine. I have you," Robert said. "Just relax. It's a groom's duty to carry his lovely, new bride over the threshold. We don't want to get off to a bad start. It's bad enough the Rabbi forgot the rings. Not to mention that he forgot our vows."

He swung around so they were facing the doors that led into the room and started to walk forward like he was going to carry her over the threshold of the two double doors.

Suddenly, Robert took two steps back and in one motion flung Sylvia backward over the railing.

He leaned over to watch her fall the twenty-three stories, careful not to touch the railing. He could barely hear her scream with the waves of Lake Michigan muffling the noise.

By the end, she was barely a blip in the darkness. Robert had to squint to even see her hit the concrete sidewalk below.

Without emotion, Robert took the glass of champagne off the balcony table and took another sip. Then dropped it on the balcony floor.

The expensive, crystal, champagne flute shattered.

Careful not to step on any glass, Robert went back into the room, left the double doors slightly ajar, and turned out all the lights.

He went into the bedroom, pulled back the covers on Sylvia's side of the bed, and messed up the sheets. He walked around the bed to the other side, pulled back the covers, got under them, and went to sleep.

2

Cliff Ford arrived at the Regency hotel within thirty minutes of being awakened from a deep sleep. He hadn't expected to get a call. Technically, at midnight, he was off the clock. Tomorrow was his wife's birthday and he'd taken the day off. Now that he was at the scene of an apparent homicide, his day off wouldn't start until he finished whatever preliminary investigation was required.

While his wife was understanding, he felt guilty about her birthday possibly being spoiled by a dead body. He'd never take shortcuts in an investigation, but he was determined to move it forward as fast as humanly possible.

Finding the crime scene wasn't hard. The dead body was in front of the hotel around the corner from the lobby. He walked toward it with a purpose and made a beeline for the beat cop who was clearly in charge of the crime scene.

"Homicide Detective Cliff Ford," he said introducing himself. "What you got?"

The uniformed policeman standing in front of him was a fairly young cop and looked a bit nervous. Perhaps intimidated. A good thing. Cliff preferred a beat cop who knew the situation was way over his head opposed to one who thought he knew more than the detectives.

The dead body lay on the sidewalk behind yellow police tape. A crowd had gathered. Cliff didn't see any reporters which caused him to breathe an undetectable sigh of relief. Reporters were never helpful in the early stages of an investigation. He preferred to call them in on his own terms. When he could control the narrative and use them to help find suspects. If they arrived too soon, they often printed whatever they decided was the truth, or worse, speculated with all kinds of wild scenarios.

It didn't do the deceased any favors nor the detective trying to solve the case.

"Female," the cop answered in his most serious tone. "Deceased. Looks to be in her early thirties. Wearing a fancy nightgown. Severe trauma to several parts of her body. She's a real mess. Sorry, sir... but we just don't see this every day. This is different. Strange, you know?"

Cliff did a quick scan of the scene. He saw immediately what the cop meant. It didn't make sense. Why would a woman be wearing a fancy nightgown, or any nightgown for that matter, outside the hotel?

He didn't bother to ask if she had identification on her. The beat cop would've said so if she did. Checking for a pulse and identification was in the Cop 101 handbook.

"Any witnesses?" Cliff asked. He knew the odds were slim based on his initial assessment, but it had to be asked of the first officer on the scene.

"None that we know of."

"Did anybody touch the crime scene?"

The cop hesitated.

A jolt of concern flashed through Cliff. He never relished asking this question because the answer could make or break an investigation. Good defense attorneys pressed this issue at trial whether it was an issue or not. Most people had no idea how many fibers they left behind everywhere they went. The last thing he needed at a crime scene was one of the beat cops touching something and contaminating crucial evidence. All it took sometimes was one piece of unrelated DNA to create reasonable doubt in the minds of a jury.

"I was the first on the scene," the beat cop explained. "When I arrived, I checked for a pulse. When I didn't find one, I called it in and secured the scene."

The angst left Cliff. The cop had followed procedure. The first on the scene had to tend to the victim first. Even if it potentially contaminated the evidence.

"Good work," Cliff said.

"Thank you, sir."

Some detectives treated beat cops like second class citizens. Cliff tried to endear himself to them whenever possible. His experience was they were more cooperative if he didn't act like a jerk.

Cliff walked toward the body and lowered his shoulder to go under the tape. He squatted down beside the lifeless figure, careful not to touch anything. Just observe. The beat cop stood over his shoulder which was annoying. But he bit his lip to keep from saying anything.

After a good minute, Cliff checked for a pulse even though he didn't expect to find one. The visual was confusing and not just because of the nightgown. The woman had severe injuries and several obvious broken bones. Her right leg was contorted and lay in an unnatural position, sticking out and to the left with broken bones visible. Her arms appeared to have multiple fractures. Both of them.

Cliff didn't remember ever seeing this many injuries on a victim.

Her head was turned to the right in the opposite direction of her leg. It had sustained severe trauma, and the side of her face that lay against the sidewalk was caved in on one side.

Not a pretty sight.

The cause of death could be any number of things.

Strange...

Cliff stood and turned his attention to the surroundings. His first thought was that the woman was attacked right where she lay. Then he dismissed the thought. Not entirely, but he put it on the backburner. The location was not an ideal place to murder someone. If there was such a thing. The area was well lit, and the lobby was just around the corner. As was the parking lot.

Valet attendants would be on duty 24/7 in an upscale hotel like this one. None of them had a direct line of sight to where the body was. But were they close enough to hear a scream?

Probably not.

Maybe it was a better location to kill someone than Cliff first thought. Unless someone had been looking out the window or happened to be walking on the sidewalk at the time of the attack, they might not see or hear anything.

If anyone had, the odds were, they would have come forward by now.

The absence of blood also gave Cliff pause. The injuries didn't seem consistent with blunt force trauma. They were too severe. Something you'd be more likely to see in a torture chamber than in a public place.

No obvious gunshot wounds.

Someone in the hotel would've heard a shot ring out, so Cliff had already moved that down the list of possibilities.

Did she fall?

Cliff looked up in the night sky at the building and scanned each floor as far as he could. The top of the building wasn't clearly visible, but he could see the occasional light on in a room which gave him some depth perspective. From what he could tell, none of the windows opened.

A man suddenly approached, ducked under the tape, and walked up to where Cliff and the beat cop were standing, interrupting his thoughts.

"You're not allowed in here," the cop barked, before Cliff could say the same thing.

"I'm the manager of the hotel," he said confidently.

The man was dressed in an expensive suit. The name tag on his lapel confirmed he was the manager.

Cliff motioned to the cop that it was okay. The cop's shoulders relaxed, while his stiffened. He needed answers, and the manager might be the person to provide them. Any insight would be valuable. The manager could give him access to security tapes. He'd know the layout of the hotel. Could give him the names of the guests. Perhaps even identify the woman.

He'd also be as concerned about a dead body in front of his hotel as Cliff was.

As if on cue, the manager looked around nervously. Probably looking to see if the press had shown up. Cliff saw the relief come over his face when he realized they hadn't.

"What's your name, sir?" Cliff asked even though he could read his name on the gold embossed tag on his suit.

"Gil Hildebrand."

Cliff motioned for the man to follow him. He led him away from the body, still inside the yellow tape but out of earshot from the crowd which continued to grow in size.

"Does this hotel have a roof?" Cliff asked.

The manager chuckled slightly. "Of course."

Cliff instantly realized how foolish the question must've sounded.

"What I mean is, can guests of the hotel access it?"

"There's an observation deck at the top and a bar."

"Was it open tonight?"

"Yes. It closes at ten. On the weekend, it's open until two in the morning."

"Was it crowded?"

"Not like the weekends. It's really hoppin' then. We have live music. Sometimes it's jazz, pop, or whatever, but people really love our rooftop lounge regardless of what kind of music is playing on a particular night. But, even on a quiet night, there would've been a dozen or so people up there along with the staff until they closed. And the closing duties of the staff included making sure all areas are secured, the doors are locked, and all of our guests have left the lounge."

The manager finally took a breath.

While he tried to sound professional, he couldn't hide his concern. Cliff knew from experience that people talked too much when they were nervous. A good thing for Cliff and his investigation. The more the man opened up, the better.

The information was helpful. It made a fall from the roof unlikely. The woman wasn't dressed for a party. The white silky nightgown had a slight train. That made her noticeable. There's no way she could walk through a crowded bar without being noticed.

For that matter, it was just as unlikely that she walked through the lobby without anyone noticing her.

Was she a prostitute, or a high-end escort?

Her nightgown wasn't a cheap throwaway that a hooker would wear. He'd seen a lot of dead prostitutes in his day. He wasn't a fashion expert, but it looked like the lingerie was probably expensive.

Never assume. This was an upscale hotel. Some working girls got several thousand dollars an hour from high end clients. She could certainly afford an expensive nightgown in that case.

Was she married? Cliff walked over to the body and looked at her hand.

She was wearing wedding rings.

That ruled out a prostitute.

Didn't rule out an affair.

Cliff began to consider again the possibility of a liaison gone bad. Before he could get very far in the thought process, the forensics team arrived. One of the women on the team walked straight to the body and began to examine it. He walked toward her and was now the one looking over her shoulder. He moved to the opposite side so he wouldn't be annoying.

She was already taking the woman's temperature.

"I'm Detective Cliff Ford," he said after she finished.

"Roz," the woman replied without bothering to look up at him.

"Do you have a time of death?" Cliff asked.

He knew that's why she was taking the woman's temp. When the circulation stops, the body cools by one to two degrees per hour until it reaches ambient temperature.

She examined the woman's pupils and the bottom of her feet before she answered.

The dead woman was barefoot. Another inconsistency in the crime scene. A woman wouldn't be walking around late at night with no shoes.

"From the looks of it, I'd say... more than an hour, but less than two hours."

Cliff looked at his watch. It was 11:33 pm.

That ruled out the party on the roof. It seemed unlikely that a woman wearing a nightgown could jump or be thrown off the roof without anyone seeing her. The roof was locked after the party ended. At least according to the manager. Cliff made a mental note to check the door.

He stared up in the sky and strained again to see the top of the building.

As if he had read his mind, the manager approached and said, "There's no way she jumped off the roof, if that's what you're thinking. There's a high railing and a security net that goes around the entire building to prevent that from happening. Jumpers are bad for business. Sorry, I know that sounded really crass, but it's true. Plus, we value our clients' safety immensely."

Cliff looked at his watch again.

He'd been there thirty minutes and was no closer to piecing together what had happened than when he had gotten there. So many things just didn't add up. A woman with her head bashed in and both legs broken. Severe injuries. It looked like virtually everything could be broken.

He looked at his watch again. It was clear he wasn't going to be finished by midnight.

If he didn't get answers fast, he might not even be home in time to fix his wife the breakfast in bed for her birthday.

3

12:03 a.m.

Cliff took out his phone and dialed his wife, Julia. She answered on the first ring, which meant she was still up.

"I want to be the first to wish you a happy birthday," Cliff said.

"Thank you," she said through a noticeable yawn. Midnight was about the latest she ever went to bed. Since he wasn't there, he expected her to still be awake. At least until he called. He would've called sooner, once he knew he'd be delayed, but waited until the clock turned twelve so he could express the birthday wishes. Which she'd appreciate, even if she had fallen asleep.

"I'm sorry I'm not there to wish you happy birthday in person," he added.

"If you were here, you'd be asleep!" Julia said.

"That's true enough," he said with a chuckle.

He shifted his weight from one leg to the other. He was standing outside the Regency Hotel several yards away from the crime scene. From the looks of things, he might not be home before she woke up in the morning.

A new murder case always came with time pressure. The investigation could go cold within minutes or hours if clues were missed. The odds of solving a case decreased as time passed anyway. He couldn't leave and go home even if it was his day off and his wife's birthday.

He suppressed his own yawn, even though he wasn't really tired. Normally he went to bed between eight and nine and was an early riser. This was way past his bedtime, but surprisingly, he was wide awake. Dealing with a dead body did that to him even if it was in the middle of the night. Even if he went home now, he wouldn't be able to sleep. The crime scene would play in his head over and over again like a bad movie. That and the adrenaline of the murder case and the second cup of coffee which had his heart racing faster than normal.

"Are you coming home soon?" Julia asked, with a touch of yearning in her voice.

"I don't think so. I'm going to be tied up at the crime scene for a while."

He looked over and saw the coroner loading the woman's body into a body bag, preparing to take it to the morgue where they'd perform the autopsy. From that standpoint, things were moving faster than normal. During the day, the coroner might not get to a scene for hours.

But for Cliff, the real work was just beginning. He needed to find a witness. And an identity. It would help if he knew who the dead woman was.

"I thought you were off duty at midnight," Julia said with a slight groan.

"Technically I am. But you know how it works. If I get a case, I have to work on it until I'm finished. Then I can take off. I don't have to solve it, but I do have to take care of the preliminary work."

"From the sound of your voice, it seems like you have a tough one," Julia said sweetly.

He could hear the sound of what he thought was ruffling bedding in the background. Cliff could picture his wife tucking herself in. A strong desire to be in that bed with her shot through his heart. Even though she was right. If he were there, he'd be asleep.

"It's shaping up to be a tough case," Cliff said. "It's a mystery. I've got a dead woman."

"How old?"

"Thirty-three or so is my best guess."

"Ahh. Is she pretty?"

"Hard to say. One side of her face is caved in, and her arms and legs are broken and pointed in several directions. Not a pretty sight. That's for sure."

"Ouch."

"I would say she's pretty based on the side of her face that's not caved in. Blonde hair. Styled. She's also wearing a nightgown. On the expensive side. White satin with a train. Not that I know much about lingerie. It's one of the strangest things I've ever seen."

"How so?

"Her body is lying on the sidewalk. Outside the Regency Hotel. No witnesses. No ID. No clue if she was killed on the spot or the body was moved to that location."

"Is she wearing a wedding ring?" Julia asked.

Cliff often ran the specifics of cases by his wife. She had a knack for asking the right questions and seeing things he hadn't seen. Although, he already knew the answer to that question.

"Yes. And it appears to be a very expensive set. Her hair's all dolled up too. Like she's been somewhere special today or something."

"She's on her honeymoon," Julia stated emphatically.

"What?"

"Ten to one she got married today."

"Why do you say that?" Cliff asked, trying to follow her logic.

"Think about it. The fancy, white nightgown she's wearing is a dead giveaway. What you're describing isn't a typical piece of lingerie. It's for a very special occasion. Like a honeymoon."

"I suppose. She could be a high-priced hooker."

"Wearing a wedding ring?"

Cliff had already run through this train of thought once in his mind and had come to the same conclusion. He hadn't thought of the honeymoon angle though.

"Remember the nightgown I wore on our honeymoon?" Julia asked.

"How could I forget?" Cliff said. His mind went back to their wedding night a little over a year ago. The image was firmly etched in his mind. Just thinking about it brought a smile to his face. All it did was make him wish he was at home in bed with her even more.

"Have you seen me wear it since?" Julia asked.

"No. I don't think I've seen you wear any nightgowns since our wedding night. You like that old T-shirt and pajama bottoms."

"My point exactly. The woman's on her honeymoon. And they're staying at that hotel. Mark my words."

"Who killed her though?" Cliff asked.

"Her husband," Julia said with an air of certainty. Cliff knew better than to dismiss her women's intuition out of hand. Even though they'd only been married for a year, Cliff had learned to trust her instincts. They'd been right more often than not about a lot of things. Not only in his investigations.

"Why do you say it's her husband?" he asked.

"Because most women are murdered by a husband or by someone's lover. Am I right? And on top of that, she's outside one of the swankiest hotels in Chicago. She's on her honeymoon. Mark my words."

Cliff paused for a moment to let that sink in. Then asked the obvious question. "Who kills his wife on a honeymoon?"

"It happens."

"Most women are killed by their husbands, I'll grant you that," Cliff said. "Unless it's random. It's not quite as simple as that though. Most people are murdered by someone they know. But it could be anybody. The woman could've been having an affair. Her lover's wife might've killed her."

"You said her face is smashed in. She was killed by a man. A woman doesn't have that kind of strength."

He didn't respond right away. He'd already come to that same conclusion even though he was throwing out counter arguments. It helped him to solidify theories in his mind.

"She also might have fallen," Julia added. "Off the roof of the hotel or something. That would explain her face being caved in and the condition of her broken extremities."

Cliff still hadn't ruled that out. But with what he'd learned from the hotel manager, the roof sounded like it was unlikely.

"There's a bar on the roof, but it's closed," Cliff said. "I mean... It was open at the time, but it's closed now. Anyway, somebody would've seen a beautiful lady walking around the bar in lingerie."

"Yep. It has to be the husband," Julia stated again matter-of-factly.

"Oh, that's what you think, huh? You solved that awfully fast," Cliff quipped. He enjoyed their banter when they were talking about a case. "So, Sherlock, why would a husband kill his bride on their honeymoon?"

"I can think of a lot of reasons. You mentioned the affair. Money might be a motive. They might've had an argument. Insurance policy. You know the drill."

"I suppose. I haven't ruled anything out."

"Take my word for it. Find the husband, and you'll find the killer."

"How did she get on the sidewalk?" Cliff asked.

"Do I have to do everything for you?" Julia said in a teasing voice.

"I gotta go," Cliff said, as he suddenly thought of something that popped into his mind.

He was glad he ran the information by her and had been able to wish her a happy birthday, but the clock was ticking. He needed to get to work on the case. It made sense to focus on finding the husband. He wanted to ask the manager if the hotel had a honeymoon suite.

"Find the husband," Julia said, reinforcing what he was already thinking.

"I'm on it. Love you. Happy birthday, Sweetheart."

Julia made the sound of a kiss as he hung up the phone. Cliff looked around and spotted the manager. He was still hanging around the scene. No surprise. It's not every day that a hotel manager has to deal with a dead body.

The deceased woman had been loaded into the coroner's vehicle.

"Can I go?" the coroner asked.

"Yes. You can shove off. Let me know when you have a cause of death."

Cliff could've probed him about his initial reactions but didn't bother. He wouldn't know anything more than Cliff did at that point. Tomorrow, after the autopsy, he'd have more concrete answers.

The manager and the crowd watched as the coroner drove away. Cliff didn't expect the crowd to disperse right away. They'd hang around. Almost morbidly. Hoping to see more action.

The gawkers made Cliff mad. Who wants to stand around and look at a dead body? Even though it was his job, Cliff hated it every time he saw the tragedy of death. Especially one like this. A beautiful woman. With obvious means. Her future, taken from her.

If he had the authority, he'd make them leave. He didn't. He could make them stand at a distance but couldn't force them to leave the scene.

Didn't matter. Cliff wasn't going to hang around either. He needed to come up with a plan to see if the woman was a guest at the hotel. Maybe look at security footage. Examine the roof. Cliff wanted to see it for himself. Was the door to the roof locked? Could the woman have jumped, even with the safety precautions?

"Do you have a honeymoon suite?" Cliff asked the manager.

"Yes, we do, Detective. As well as a Presidential Suite. They are the finest suites in all of Chicago. And they rival rooms in Paris or London for that matter."

He sounded like a commercial.

"Does it have a balcony?" Cliff asked.

"Of course, it does. The Presidential Suite and the Honeymoon Suite both have balconies. The rooms are quite exquisite. All of our rooms are but the honeymoon and presidential suites are really quite luxurious."

"Is it occupied?"

"I believe so. Yes."

"I need to see it, Mr. Hildebrand."

"The guests are probably asleep at this time of night. Can't this wait until tomorrow morning? We really don't like to disturb our guests in the middle of the night."

"Absolutely not. I understand this is an inconvenience for every-one involved but there are no other options. I have a job to do. I ap-preciate your cooperation."

The manager hesitated.

"I need to see it. Right now," Cliff said more forcefully. When the manager hesitated again, he just started walking toward the hotel lobby.

The manager followed him.

Cliff quickened the pace. The lady had to be connected to the hotel.

He was determined to find out how.

4

The elevator door in the lobby of the hotel was already open and Cliff didn't wait for the manager. He entered and pushed the button for the top floor where he presumed the suites were located. It didn't light up. He realized immediately that the top floor required a key card to activate the elevator.

Confirmed when the manager said, "The suite area requires a passkey."

Cliff would prefer to look around on his own. That clearly wasn't going to happen.

"I assume you have one," Cliff said, pointing at the slot in the panel for a key card.

"I do, but I can't let you disturb our guests. They're on their honeymoon. I'm sure you understand the need to respect their privacy."

Cliff could feel the frustration rising inside of him. Not just because of the manager's words but his tone. He had a dismissive aloofness about him. Like he was better than some lowly detective.

"I have a dead woman, lying on a sidewalk wearing a nightgown fancy enough for her honeymoon," Cliff said slowly for effect. "Somebody didn't respect her privacy."

"You don't even know that she's a hotel guest," the manager said more tersely.

Cliff was getting more annoyed. He didn't feel like arguing with the man.

"Please try to understand. The woman was wearing lingerie. She was found dead right outside the hotel. In all likelihood, she is one of your guests. At any rate, the hotel is the obvious place to start."

The manager opened his mouth to say something, but Cliff cut him out."

"The kind of lingerie the woman was wearing is the kind she might wear on her wedding night. It's also expensive. It makes sense to check the honeymoon suite. She may have fallen off the balcony. Or been pushed."

"If the woman fell from the balcony of the honeymoon suite, I'm sure her husband would've reported it by now. That's not something you wait until morning to call down to the front desk. That's ridiculous."

"Not if he's the one who pushed her!"

"And why would he do that? He's on his wedding night. I'm sure he had other things on his mind. If you know what I mean."

The manager had a sly, almost lustful grin on his face which rubbed Cliff the wrong way considering they were dealing with a murder. Cliff took a deep breath to keep from going off on the man. He needed the manager's cooperation. He wasn't getting to the top floor without the manager's key.

"With all due respect, it doesn't matter what you think. It doesn't matter what I think either. I have to rule out all possibilities. So please enter your key into the slot and take me to the suite area."

"I'm sorry, Sir. I can't do that."

"You can and you will!"

The manager clenched his jaw like he was ready to dig in his heels. He stepped out of the elevator. Cliff stayed inside.

"Are you obstructing my investigation?" Cliff asked roughly, more than willing to meet his intensity.

"Our guests have rights!" the manager said in an angry tone, letting his emotions start to get the best of him as well.

Then the conversation turned confrontive. "I didn't fall off the turnip truck yesterday. I've been a hotel manager for more than twenty years. I know that you can't search a hotel room without a warrant. My guests have rights."

"I don't intend to search the room. I want to confirm that the bride is in the honeymoon suite. And you're wasting valuable time. Time is of the essence in a murder investigation. Unless you've already conveniently forgotten, a young woman was found murdered on your property. There may be a murderer on the loose in the Regency Hotel."

Cliff made a point to emphasize 'Regency Hotel,' hoping that would help him get through to the manager. This wasn't just any hotel. It had a long-standing, excellent reputation to protect.

The manager wasn't giving in. "You have no right to knock on the door of the honeymoon suite, or any of our rooms for that matter, in the middle of the night. There are protocols to follow."

"If I feel like someone's life is in danger, then I can do whatever I feel is necessary."

The conversation was heated but still civil. Cliff wasn't sure how long it would remain that way. The manager was getting on his nerves. Even though Cliff knew this was an argument he couldn't win. The manager was right. Cliff was limited in what he could do. The guests had a right to privacy. That didn't mean he couldn't push the limits of his authority. Including waking a guest from his sleep if necessary.

He had nothing else to go on. The honeymoon suite seemed like his only lead. He really wanted to make sure the bride was there. She probably was. His curiosity was amplified by the manager's obstruction. Like a kid told he couldn't have a piece of candy. It made him want it even more.

Clearly, the manager wasn't going to be bullied or scared into letting him on the floor. Cliff could search other parts of the hotel. He was perfectly within his rights to snoop around the public areas. Observing the lobby or a floor was reasonable. If he saw something suspicious, he could seal the area and go through the proper channels to secure a warrant.

But he didn't expect to find anything inside the hotel in the public areas. The woman wasn't killed in the lobby. She also wasn't killed inside the hotel and then taken outside and dumped on the sidewalk.

He had to rule out a fall from a balcony.

To do that he had to verify that the bride was in the honeymoon suite. While the couple might complain about the inconvenience, what was the actual harm? And who would they complain to? The manager of the hotel? That was his problem. Cliff's boss? He'd throw a complaint like that in the trash can. They had bigger fish to fry than a complaint from a hotel guest who'd been woken up in the middle of the night about a murder.

Thinking about all the possible scenarios, an idea popped into his mind.

"Can you show me the roof?" Cliff asked.

"Of course," the manager said. "I don't see how that can hurt anything."

He re-entered the elevator and put his hotel key card in the slot and pushed the button for the roof.

"I don't mean to be difficult," he said smugly. "But I know the law pretty well. I took a class in college."

"So, have you always wanted to be a hotel manager?" Cliff asked. Perhaps friendliness would work better. He could put on a pleasant demeanor if it helped get this murder solved sooner than later.

"Always. My father and grandfather were in hotel management. It's in our family's blood. My major in college was hotel and restaurant management."

"Seems like you're good at what you do."

The elevator sped to the roof. It stopped abruptly and opened to a hallway that led to a door.

Cliff exited the elevator and walked toward it.

"As I said, the bar closed at ten," the manager said. "No one is allowed up here after it's closed. For obvious reasons. Our guests' safety is our first and foremost concern."

"Let's confirm that the roof door is locked."

The manager tried the door, and it was locked. He inserted his keycard, and the green light came on. Cliff heard a click signifying the door was now unlocked. The manager motioned with his hand for Cliff to go first.

Once outside, Cliff felt the rush of the cooler air. It had to be at least five degrees cooler than it had been on the ground. And windier.

The notorious wind off of Lake Michigan and Chicago's humidity made it slightly uncomfortable. Cliff could see where this would be a good spot to come in the summertime.

The area was dimly lit, and the concrete floors were still wet. Like they'd been rinsed off with a garden hose. The chairs and tables had been washed off as well and were stacked in an area next to the bar. A hot tub was in the far corner and lights illuminated the blueish water.

Cliff walked with a purpose toward the side of the building where the body was found. The manager was right. A railing circled the entire roof area. Not as high as the manager had inferred, but high enough that someone would have to climb to get over it. A net extended several feet out from the building. The webbing was tightly wound and didn't have any holes in it. It looked strong enough to hold a body.

Clearly, the woman didn't jump from the roof. Cliff didn't bother looking for any more clues in the area. He might take a look again in the daylight.

"I've seen enough," Cliff said and walked back toward the elevator.

"Like I said, there's no way she jumped," the manager said in a 'I told you so' tone.

Cliff didn't respond.

The manager stuck his key card in the slot, and the elevator doors closed. Cliff reached over and hit the button for the lobby.

"Thanks," the manager said.

Before he could react, Cliff pushed the button for the twenty-third floor. Where he assumed the suites were.

"What are you doing?" the manager barked.

"I want to see the honeymoon suite."

"I told you that I will not allow you to disturb the guests! They pay thirty-five hundred dollars a night for those suites. I won't have them bothered."

It didn't take long for the door to open on the twenty-third floor. Cliff stepped out before the manager could say anything more. He walked into a large foyer area with a hallway off of it. The foyer was about thirty to forty feet wide. Gold and red. An opulent chandelier hung down in the middle. The carpet below it had a circle with a large R in the middle of it. The Regency Hotel logo.

The hallway went two directions and had two sets of double doors halfway down. A sign read honeymoon suite to the left, presidential suite to the right.

Cliff thought he knew the answer but asked anyway. "Which side of the hotel is the honeymoon suite facing?" he whispered. No reason to disturb the guests in the presidential suite.

"The east side," the manager answered. "They face the water."

"That's the side where the body was located?"

"That's correct. Detective, I must insist that we go back to the lobby!"

"I want to look around."

Cliff walked up and down the hall. He didn't know what he was looking for but would know it if he saw it.

He didn't see anything of note.

"Can we go now?" the manager asked roughly.

Cliff stood in the middle of the hallway. Thinking. A few seconds later, he walked right up to the door of the honeymoon suite and banged loudly.

"Hey!" the manager said. "You can't do that. I'm going to call your supervisor. You're violating our client's right to privacy. I won't have it!"

Undeterred, Cliff banged on the door a second time. This time even louder. He was on the floor to the suite and wouldn't let this opportunity to gather crucial information slip through his fingers.

No one answered right away.

"The bedroom is off the main living area," the manager said. "They might not hear you."

Cliff pushed the button next to the door and heard the doorbell ring inside. All he wanted was to confirm the woman was, or wasn't, in the honeymoon suite. Under the circumstances, he didn't feel like he was crossing a line, even if technically he was.

A few seconds later, he heard sounds coming from inside the suite. The door cracked open. A man stood there wearing boxer shorts and a white T-shirt. His hair was mussed, and his eyes were glossed over. He appeared to have been awakened from a deep sleep.

He didn't look happy.

Cliff didn't care, but he would be respectful.

"Hello, sir. I'm Detective Cliff Ford. Chicago P.D. I'm sorry to bother you. Is your wife in the suite with you?"

"Yes, she is," the man said in a curt voice. "She's sleeping."

Before Cliff could ask to speak to her, the man abruptly slammed the door in his face.

5

The manager glared at Cliff. He glared back.

The door had just been slammed in his face by the groom who said his wife was fast asleep. Cliff was so stunned that he didn't react right away which was unusual for him. It took a second to process what had just happened and even longer to consider his next move.

Why did the groom react in such an abrupt manner? It seemed strange. He wasn't the least bit curious as to why a detective was at his hotel room door asking about his wife.

Cliff decided to ask him. He raised his arm in the air to knock a second time.

The hotel manager stopped him.

He grabbed Cliff's arm by the wrist stopping it in midair. Cliff quickly broke the grip and applied a wrist lock of his own to the manager's wrist. Within seconds he had the man's arm behind his back. The manager winced and let out a yelp.

The adrenaline was flowing. Cliff pushed the manager against the wall and leaned in pressing the man's face against it. The manager let out a gasp along with another yelp. He probably couldn't believe Cliff would react that way.

Cliff was surprised as well. For some reason, the man had gotten under his skin.

"Don't ever touch me like that again!" Cliff growled a bit too loudly, nearly forgetting he was in the hallway of a hotel floor.

The frustration of the night was taking its toll. Cliff would rather be at home in bed with his wife. Since he couldn't, the last thing he felt like dealing with was an uncooperative, arrogant hotel manager and a rude groom.

"Let me go," the manager said. "I'll have your badge."

Cliff had to bite his lip to keep from laughing out loud. He tightened the arm lock.

The manager let out another moan. Cliff considered handcuffing the man and then knocking on the door.

Then he decided against it. He realized all this was likely on camera. To that point, he could justify his actions. The manager had grabbed him. Impeded his investigation. Laid his hands on a homicide detective in an aggressive manner. Cliff could even make the case that the manager was a suspect. Acting strangely. Trying to prevent him from doing his job.

He was fairly certain the manager had nothing to do with the woman's death, but it justified his actions. And he hadn't ruled out the manager. Hadn't ruled out anyone in the hotel. Stranger things had happened in a homicide investigation. Sometimes the suspect was the most unlikely person.

At any rate, calmer heads needed to prevail. Cliff took a deep breath and loosened his grip on the man's arm. The manager took several steps back. Probably a good idea. Cliff had gotten control of his anger, but it was boiling just below the surface.

He considered knocking on the door of the honeymoon suite but thought better of it. It could be considered harassment. The groom said his wife was asleep in the suite. He had no evidence to suggest otherwise. Perhaps he should talk to the groom when he was in a calmer state.

And... he couldn't make the groom wake his wife. If he did, and the woman was alive and well in the suite, that was the type of thing that could rile up Cliff's lieutenant. Banging on hotel room doors in the middle of the night with no reasonable cause to do so, was not standard police procedure.

It also defied common sense. Why would a husband kill his bride on their wedding night? If she fell off the balcony, the man would know that his wife was not sleeping in bed with him. The only reason he even knocked on the door, was because Julia had suggested it. Cliff couldn't run an investigation on hunches or his wife's intuition. He needed clues and he needed them fast if he were going to continue this thread.

To get clues, he needed more information.

He needed a name. Who was the dead woman? It shouldn't be that hard to find out if she was a guest at the hotel. It'd help if he knew the name of the couple in the suite. With that information, he could look them up on-line and see if the woman's picture matched the dead woman on the sidewalk.

He decided to play nice again with the manager. He softened his tone when he asked the question, "Do you know the name of the couple in the honeymoon suite?"

They were walking back toward the elevator. The manager rubbed his wrist like it was still in pain. Which it probably was. Cliff was proficient in martial arts and self-defense. He also worked out four or five times a week and was strong for a man with average build.

"You know I can't tell you that. There are strict privacy laws. So, no!" the manager said curtly.

"Can you look it up?" Cliff asked, not willing to give up that easily.

"Do you have a warrant?" the manager asked roughly.

The anger returned with a vengeance. It'd been a simple question. He wanted to put his hands on the hotel manager again and say, 'This is my warrant,' but decided against it. Once could be explained. Twice was bordering on police misconduct.

He needed to regroup and get control of his emotions. Find out why he was this upset. Maybe because it was his day off. Perhaps because it was hours past his bedtime. Frustration over the possibility that his wife's birthday could be ruined.

Mostly because he had no answers, and the manager wasn't cooperating.

Even though he didn't have to. Technically, Cliff did need a warrant to see the guest list. But only if the manager refused to show it

35

to him. He could get a warrant, but it'd take hours. A judge probably wouldn't be happy having to deal with something like a guest list that could be handled tomorrow morning, just as easily.

Nevertheless, Cliff decided to call the manager's bluff. The elevator had reached the first floor and they stepped off into the outer edges of the lobby.

"I can get a warrant if that's how you want to play it," Cliff said. "It'll take about an hour, and after that I'll be back here all up in your business. I can also take you down to the station for questioning. Your behavior is suspicious. Like you have something to hide. Maybe you killed the girl."

The manager laughed. In a way that further confirmed to Cliff that the manager had nothing to do with the murder.

"I doubt you can get a warrant this late at night," the manager said, "but more power to you if you can. As to questioning me, you and I both know I had nothing to do with that poor woman's demise. Besides. . . I won't be here when you get back with your warrant. I'm going home and going to bed. I suggest you do the same."

"You don't seem very concerned about a dead woman in front of your hotel. Why is that?"

"I'm very concerned. I'm just not going to let you take me and my guests on a wild goose chase because you don't know how to do your job."

Cliff could feel his fists ball. Being insulted wasn't new to his job when people were angry, scared or guilty, but it never settled well with him. He was more than willing to go toe to toe with the manager in a match of wills. The manager would regret it if they did.

Nevertheless, the manager kept up the vitriol.

"We're not going to solve the case for you," the manager said. "You're a detective. Do your job. Run fingerprints on the dead woman. See if there are reports of a missing woman."

"Don't tell me how to do my job!" Cliff said as he took a step toward the man. Not to touch him but to get in his face. There'd be cameras around the lobby as well.

"I'm not. I'm just saying it's not my job to help you solve the murder, if that's what it is."

"Look at your guest roll," Cliff said, raising the tone to its highest crescendo of the evening.

The manager looked around concerned there might be people in the lobby. Clearly not wanting to make a scene in front of guests. That'd work to Cliff's advantage.

Unfortunately, the lobby was empty.

"You can find the identity of the couple in less than a minute," Cliff continued to argue. "I need their names. It's for their benefits. I'd like to rule them out."

"You can already rule them out. The husband said his wife was asleep in the suite."

"I didn't see that for myself."

"Why would he lie?"

"If the dead woman is his wife and he killed her, then I can think of a hundred reasons."

"Don't be ridiculous. What groom kills his wife on their wedding night? I think your whole idea is preposterous. Why rent the most expensive suite to kill your wife? It just sounds to me like you're barking up the wrong tree. I don't get it."

"Are you going to tell me the name of the couple or not?"

"I'm not. If you're a good detective, you can find out that information without my help."

"Thanks for nothing."

Cliff stormed away muttering under his breath, "You worthless example of a human being."

Then began to mimic him. "I went to college. I took a class."

Like that took the place of Cliff's years of experience as a homicide detective.

Frustrated and knowing he had to look elsewhere to get an ID on his Jane Doe, his brain was scrambling for the fastest way to accomplish that without any cooperation from the manager on duty. He might have to go above the man's head. He wondered what that guy's boss would think of his lack of cooperation.

Cliff walked out the lobby door and back to the crime scene. After spending five or more minutes pacing around, he decided to get in his car and leave. He felt like there was nothing more he could do that night. This wasn't the first time an investigation got off to a slow start and wouldn't be the last.

He should be relieved that he could justify going home. Technically, he could start his day off and put the entire case on hold. The woman was in the morgue. The case would still be there in a couple of days. That wasn't his style. He took his job far too seriously to leave a new case sitting for a few days.

If tomorrow wasn't his wife's birthday, he would've headed back to the office and worked the case some more. He hoped to pull off something birthday worthy for her. She would understand if he needed to work, but he wasn't about to do that to her.

Time to go home.

Cliff pulled around the front entrance of the hotel. It took him past the huge digital marquis in front of the hotel along the main road. He glanced at the marquis and slammed on his brakes. He could hardly believe the words he read on the sign.

Congratulations Mr. & Mrs. Platt.

Next to the words were pictures of a wedding cake and wedding bells.

A bolt of excitement jolted him out of tiredness that had suddenly come upon him. He had the name of the couple in the honeymoon suite.

Probably.

"I guess I am a good detective after all, you pompous fool!" Cliff said to the manager. It felt good, even though the jerk wasn't around to hear him say it.

6

The cemetery smelled of freshly cut grass. Cliff and Julia walked through the other graves until they arrived at her sister, Rita's, head-stone.

Julia bent over and replaced the flowers in the vase on the grave marker. Then stood there silently for several minutes. Like she was praying. This was the first time Cliff had seen Julia visit her sister's grave without tears streaming down her cheeks.

Probably only a matter of time.

When Julia was done, she handed Cliff the flowers she had re-placed. He noticed they were like new and not more noticeably worn than the new ones she had put in their place. Julia must have sensed what Cliff thought because she said, "I wanted to put fresh flowers on the grave."

Then she twisted her lips to the side and frowned, obviously re-alizing what she'd just said.

The flowers were silk. She had picked lilies, sunflowers, several roses, and some greenery to fill out the bouquet. They were high quality which was probably why they had withstood the elements so well.

"I know it's silly," Julia said, as a tear slowly escaped from her eye and slid down her cheek, leaving a slight streak in her makeup.

After a five-mile run earlier that morning, Julia had showered and changed into a nicer outfit. Slacks and a blouse. Not dressy, but a rung above casual. Cliff was in a polo shirt with tan slacks.

"I know they aren't fresh," Julia explained. "But I wanted to change them anyway. Seems like the right thing to do for Rita on her birthday."

Cliff was standing next to Julia. He put his arm around her, and her head collapsed onto his chest. He could feel the pain in her heart and could see it on her face.

"It's not silly at all," Cliff said. "I understand. The flowers look good. I'm sure Rita appreciates the gesture."

Now Cliff was the one who could feel the frown on his face. An equally stupid thing to say.

"What I meant to say was that it's the right thing to do. To change out the flowers whenever you want. I appreciate the sentiment, and I'm happy to come along anytime you want me to."

It was a struggle for him to find the right words. So, he added, "Rita was an amazing woman. We should change out her flowers whenever you feel like it's a good idea."

The moment was awkward. What did you say in a circumstance like this? Visiting a grave.

Complicated by the fact that it was Julia's birthday.

Rita's as well.

He'd asked Julia that morning what she wanted to do for her birthday, knowing that visiting Rita's gravesite would be at the top of the list. Something Julia had to do today because they shared the same birthday.

That's why. Julia and Rita were twins.

Identical.

Triplets actually.

There was another sister. Anna.

The third sister, Anna, was identical as well. The three girls were mirrors of each other. At first, Cliff couldn't tell them apart. Still couldn't if they didn't say something. He'd gotten used to their voice inflections and tones along with their mannerisms. If they wanted to fool him, they likely could.

According to Julia, the odds of identical triplets were many millions to one. That gave the girls a certain bond. Cliff had read where twins could be separated at birth and be reunited years later and still have similar lives. The same health problems. Similar career paths.

Cliff squeezed Julia's shoulder a little tighter and then she pulled away. He saw her wipe another set of tears off her cheek.

Although going to the cemetery wasn't high on his list of things to do on a birthday, Cliff knew he'd better get used to it. Julia would probably always want to visit her sister's grave every year.

Didn't matter. Whatever she wanted. He'd be here for his wife. Anna would be there too, but she was in New York.

Another loss.

When Anna married a man of high finance, the couple moved to New York City. Julia was happy for her sister but missed her deeply. Cliff noticed a decided change in Julia's mood after Anna left. A void. He wanted to fill it, but it was impossible to do so. Anna had been a great comfort to Julia after Rita died.

Cliff didn't know Rita. The first time he saw her was in the city morgue. Rita was gunned down outside a coffee shop by a member of the Strikers gang. A notorious gang in south Chicago. Cliff solved the murder even though he hadn't technically been the one assigned to the case.

It's how he met Julia.

Ironic.

Rita's death was what brought them together. How could he be thankful for such a tragedy? He couldn't. He just had to accept it as fate and be grateful to have Julia in his life.

"It feels weird to me," Julia said as she knelt by the grave marker. "Seeing my birthday on a gravestone. Why am I alive, and Rita is dead? It's senseless."

Her voice cracked as she said it.

"These things never make sense," Cliff said, almost whispering. "I don't think you can explain it. Besides that, Rita knew the risks she was taking with her job. She was passionate about her work."

Rita had worked for the FBI in the sex trafficking division. She'd gone undercover in the Strikers gang and rescued several girls who were being held as sex slaves. Rita was a vigilante of sorts and had made some headway. She rescued several of the girls. Something that didn't sit well with the boss of the Strikers. They killed her in retaliation.

Rita earned a commendation posthumously for her actions.

"Rita was a brave woman. That's what got her killed. Maybe not so senseless if you look at how many lives she saved. It's no consolation. But she didn't die in vain."

The men responsible for Rita's death were behind bars and still awaiting trial. They would face the trial in the not-too-distant future. Cliff would have to testify. Julia might have to as well.

Julia ran a shelter for abused women. Rita had asked her to hide some of the girls in her shelter and one in her house. Cliff worried that the trial might put his wife at some risk again. The Striker gang had been dismantled with the incarceration of numerous gang members including the leader. A man named Shiv. That didn't mean the men behind bars didn't have connections.

Something he thought about almost every day.

Cliff was aware of the risks. He signed up for them. Julia didn't. He had to figure out a way to continue to protect her. He hadn't been able to with his first wife. She was killed in a drive-by shooting by the same man who killed Rita.

An odd and disturbing coincidence.

Strange how Cliff and Julia were connected. Now they were soulmates. Husband and wife. Cliff wasn't sure he could stand losing another wife.

He could feel the tears well up in his eyes. He tamped them down. This was not how he wanted them to spend his wife's birthday.

"Julia, are you ready to get something to eat?" Cliff asked after a couple more minutes of silence had passed.

She stood to her feet and nodded her head. Then brushed her tears aside. She crossed her arms in front of her and began walking back to the car.

Cliff followed.

The plan was to take Julia to her favorite breakfast restaurant. Plan B, actually.

He had intended on making Julia breakfast in bed. The dead woman at the hotel had put a kink in that plan.

Cliff didn't get home from the hotel until after three in the morning. It was almost four before he'd gotten into bed. He had to take a shower first. A habit. When Cliff left a crime scene, he felt dirty. Contaminated. Like he was covered in blood even though there was little to no blood at the crime scene.

When he got into bed, Julia had turned over and groggily said, "Did you solve your case?"

"Not yet."

"You will," she muttered and then fell back asleep.

It took him nearly an hour to fall asleep. He couldn't quit thinking about the case. The hotel manager. The groom and his strange behavior. The woman's dead body was etched in his brain, almost haunting him.

He might have a name. Mrs. Platt. The name on the marquis. He considered getting out of bed and looking it up on the computer but thought better of it. He had to get some sleep if he would be worth anything to his wife the next day on her birthday.

The last time he looked at the clock, it was after four in the morning. He must've fallen asleep around then because that's the last thing he remembered. When he woke up, it was after eight. Julia was already up.

He bolted out of bed and hurried downstairs to the kitchen where he found a note. She'd gone for a five-mile run. Something he usually did with her three to four times a week.

The message told him what he already knew.

Don't bother making me breakfast. I've already eaten.

Julia had had a quinoa bowl with bananas before the run. He deduced that fact from the dish in the sink and the banana peel in the trash.

So, he made plans to take her to brunch.

They arrived at one of her favorite restaurants about twenty minutes after leaving the cemetery. Neither of them barely said a word on the ride over.

They sat down at the table and ordered.

Cliff struggled to keep his mind on Julia and her birthday.

But. . . he couldn't stop thinking about the dead woman.

7

Breakfast brunch was better than the conversation Cliff and Julia were slogging through. A heavy cloud of depression hovered over their table like a San Francisco fog. The restaurant was one of Julia's favorites, but it hadn't brightened her spirits the way Cliff had hoped when he made the reservation earlier that morning.

The dark mood was out of character for the two of them. While they both were on the more serious side of the personality chart, they usually had a good time together and were able to make each other laugh. Julia with her witty remarks; Cliff with his propensity to say the strangest things entirely out of the blue.

None of that was working, although neither had made much of an effort. Julia was clearly still thinking about the visit to her sister's grave, and Cliff was having a hard time thinking about anything other than the dead woman on the sidewalk of the Regency Hotel.

He needed to snap out of it. It was his wife's birthday, and he felt like he was ruining it. Even though it wasn't his idea to go to the cemetery causing the sadness in Julia, he had an obligation to focus. Put his mind off the case. Get her out of it. His case would still be on his desk tomorrow morning.

He decided to take control of the conversation.

"Have you talked to Anna?" Cliff asked.

A risky question to ask. Julia was probably missing Anna as well. This was the first birthday they hadn't celebrated together. Although, if anyone could get Julia out of the malaise, it'd be talking to her sister.

"She sent me a message with a cute birthday meme," Julia said with a forced smile. "We're supposed to talk later."

Cliff took the last bite of his food and set his fork down and motioned for the waiter. He had ordered the cornflake fried chicken and buttermilk waffles with spicy maple syrup. While the food was delicious, Cliff felt like he had a pickup truck sitting in the pit of his stomach. It'd be a few hours before he could move with any sense of urgency.

"What do you want to do now?" Cliff asked.

The waiter was on his way to another table with a tray full of drinks and motioned that he needed to deliver them first.

"I don't know," Julia said. "What do you want to do?"

"We could go for a bike ride along the shore," Cliff said, although he was hoping she'd say no.

Julia sat back in her chair and rubbed her stomach. "We just ate. I don't think I could. Not for an hour or so."

"That's swimming."

"What?"

The conversation was as stilted as Cliff's bloated stomach.

He explained what he meant. "My mother said that you aren't supposed to go swimming for an hour after eating. I never heard anything about having to wait to go for a bike ride."

"I need to let my food digest. I never eat this much in the morning. Besides, I already did a five-mile run. I got my exercise in for the day."

"We could do a triathlon," Cliff said with a huge grin on his face even though she'd know he was kidding. "Running, biking, and swimming. You've already gotten the first leg out of the way."

"If you wanted to do a triathlon," Julia said with her own playful smile, "you should've said so before I ordered eggs benedict."

"I read where triathletes consume fifteen hundred calories during a race. We just got them all at the start of the race, not during."

That caused a bigger smile to form on Julia's face which warmed his heart. He'd hit on a conversation that might make her feel better.

"How do they eat that many calories while they're competing?"

"Triathletes eat those gels and spike their liquids with energy concoctions. It helps them perform better."

"I doubt that hollandaise sauce is in the liquids."

"Let's do it! You already ran five miles. We could bike twenty and jump in Lake Michigan and swim a few miles. A birthday triathlon. It'll burn off all those calories."

Julia let out a good laugh releasing more of the tension they both were feeling.

"I hope you're kidding."

"Consider our breakfast a form of carbohydrate loading."

"Saturated fat loading."

They both laughed again. Cliff loved it when Julia smiled, and her laugh sent a bolt of energy through him. Not enough to exercise any time soon, but enough to want him to find something fun for them to do today.

The waiter interrupted their banter. He began clearing the dishes from the table.

"Can I get you anything else?" he asked.

"Two double shot vanilla lattes," Cliff said.

An infusion of caffeine would add some fire to the momentum that the triathlon conversation had created.

"Would you like whipped cream on them?" the waiter asked.

"No!" Julia said emphatically.

"Yes!" Cliff said just as strongly. "We're running a triathlon this afternoon. We need carbohydrates."

The waiter twisted his lips and raised his eyebrows. Clearly confused.

"Just the lattes," Julia said to him. "Hold the whipped cream."

"It's her birthday," Cliff said. "Do you have any cake?"

"I can bring a dessert menu."

"No, thank you," Julia said. "Just the lattes and a check."

When the waiter walked away, Julia said to Cliff, "Are you trying to put me in a sugar fog?"

"I'm trying to cheer you up."

"You think putting ten pounds in one meal on me will do that?"

"I'm hoping the combination of sugar and caffeine will brighten your spirits."

This time Julia twisted her lips to the side and frowned.

"Hey! I'm not the only one who's a bit of a downer," she said. "Why have you been so quiet?"

The picture of the dead woman on the sidewalk flashed into Cliff's head. He summarily dismissed the corresponding urge to turn his mind back on the case.

"I don't mean to be quiet," Cliff said.

"What are you thinking about?" she asked. "The case from last night?"

How was he supposed to stop thinking about the case if she was going to bring it up?

"No!"

"First you try to put me in a sugar coma, start me on the path to diabetes, and now you lie to me!"

Before Cliff could respond, the waiter arrived with the two lattes and a piece of cake. Chocolate with chocolate icing and dripping with chocolate syrup. With whipped cream on top. One lit candle in the center.

The other wait staff gathered around the table and sang their own rendition of Happy Birthday.

Julia skulked back in her chair and put on a sheepish smile. Her cheeks turned slightly red. Clearly embarrassed at the attention. The entire restaurant applauded when the chorus was done.

"Thank you," Julia said, and gave the restaurant a slight wave of the hand.

"Why did you tell him it's my birthday?" Julia said after the staff were out of earshot.

"Because it is your birthday!"

Cliff picked up a fork and took a bite of the chocolate cake.

"Um," he moaned. "Dig in! You're going to need the energy for our triathlon."

"What I'm going to need is for you to carry me out of here?"

"That I will gladly do."

Julia picked up a fork and took a bite and then let out her own moan. "That's heavenly," she said.

"So are you, sweetheart. Happy birthday."

Cliff took another bite of cake and then washed it down with a swig of his hot latte. As good as it tasted, he still felt like his stomach was going to explode. He sat his fork down. Julia had already done so. She probably wouldn't take another bite. He was done as well although he hated to waste the delicious cake.

"Chocolate has a chemical called theobromine that has the same stimulating effect as caffeine," Cliff said.

Julia lifted her eyebrows in surprise.

"How do you know this?" she asked.

"I had a case once where the defendant used it as part of his defense. He claimed that he had eaten so much chocolate that it caused him to kill his wife."

"That's ridiculous."

"Yeah. The defense attorney brought in experts and everything. The jury didn't buy it. They convicted him anyway. But it was an interesting argument."

Julia took a deep sip of her coffee and then licked her lips which sent a chill down Cliff's spine. It also made him think of another trivial fact.

"Chocolate is an aphrodisiac. It will make you fall in love with me."

"I'm already in love with you."

"Eat the rest of that chocolate and you might fall head over heels in love with me. Instead of the triathlon, we can go home and make love. The chocolate will make you want to."

Julia's face turned red for the second time, and she looked around to see if anyone had heard his remark.

"If we did that, I think I'd throw up."

"Ow! That's a mean thing to say. You sure know how to hurt a guy's feelings."

"I didn't mean that. I'm sorry. I meant that if you laid on my stomach... Never mind. I'm not having this conversation with you."

The waiter returned and laid down the check inside a black check holder. Cliff picked it up, opened it, and reached in his pocket to get his wallet. He took out three twenty-dollar bills and a ten and put them in the sleeve. The waiter could keep the change.

Then he sat forward in his chair.

"Which is it? A triathlon or marathon sex?"

"It's my birthday! I should get to choose."

"You do get to choose. Pick one."

"If you wanted to do either of those, you shouldn't have fattened me up like a pig."

"So, no triathlon then?"

"No!"

"That's good. Sex it is," Cliff said.

"Later," Julia said. "After my food has digested. Much later."

"That's probably better. I'm tired. I didn't get to bed until after three. Let's do something that doesn't require a lot of physical exertion. A movie or something."

"I vaguely remember you coming in last night."

"I tried not to wake you. But I couldn't get to sleep. Too much on my mind."

All the thoughts of the previous night came rushing back to him like a flood in a canyon. The brief bantering had distracted him from thinking about it. Now he'd have to force the thoughts back out again.

Julia leaned forward on the table and took another sip of her latte. Then sat it down and rested her chin on her hands with her elbows propped up on the table. She looked directly at Cliff with a sweet smile, but with a serious look in her eyes.

"Tell me about the case," she said.

Cliff changed positions in his chair and broke eye contact. The statement made him uncomfortable. It didn't seem appropriate to talk about a murder on his wife's birthday. So, he said so.

"It's your birthday. I don't want to talk about it now. We should be celebrating."

"You're already thinking about it. What's the difference? At least when you're talking to me about it, you won't be off in your own world. Come on! Tell me what you found out. Did you find the groom?"

Cliff remembered the door of the honeymoon suite being rudely slammed in his face by the groom.

"I don't know. I mean... Yes and no. The hotel has a honeymoon suite. I knocked on the door."

Julia's mood had definitely changed. She was sitting on the edge of her seat. The caffeine from the latte and the one bite of chocolate might have given her a brief rush of energy. This was a good thing. Talking about his case might be the very thing to get her mind off of Rita.

"And?" Julia asked.

"The groom answered."

"And?"

Cliff didn't answer right away because he wasn't sure what to say.

Julia threw up her hands. "Geez! This must be what it feels like when you're interrogating an uncooperative suspect."

"I don't know what to say. I knocked on the door and the groom answered."

"What did he say?"

It almost felt like an interrogation.

"He said that his wife was in bed sleeping."

Cliff picked up his glass and took a big enough swig of coffee. Then tried to figure out why he suddenly felt so nervous.

"Did you talk to her?" Julia asked.

"I didn't get the chance."

"Why not?"

Cliff squirmed again in his chair. His lieutenant sometimes questioned his actions in the same way.

"He slammed the door in my face."

"Oh my!" Julia said. She threw her hands in the air a second time and sat back in her chair.

"There's your killer!" she said emphatically.

"We don't know that."

"It's him."

"It was past midnight. I woke the man up. He was probably mad about being disturbed from a deep sleep. I know I would be annoyed."

Julia stood to her feet and slipped her purse over her shoulder. It startled him. He quickly stood up as well.

"Let's go," Julia said.

"Where are we going?"

"To the hotel!"

"What hotel?" Cliff asked. Then he got confused. "Do you want to have sex at a hotel? That sounds like something we should do on my birthday."

Julia rolled her eyes.

"No silly! The Regency Hotel. We're going there."

"Why would we go to the Regency Hotel?"

"We're going to go to the honeymoon suite and talk to the groom again. This time demand to speak to his wife. And don't take no for an answer. We're not leaving until we get some answers."

Before Cliff could stop his mouth from gaping open, Julia was already headed for the door.

8

Cliff pulled into a parking space at the hotel near the sidewalk where the dead body was found. As was usually the case, the crime scene looked different in the daylight hours than it had at night.

A hotel employee had removed the yellow police tape and was cleaning the sidewalk. Usually, Cliff might take issue with that. Being a hotel, he understood why they would clean it up so fast. He was more lenient with places of business who wouldn't want to advertise to the world that something horrible had happened on their premises.

So, he wouldn't say anything to the poor guy given the responsibility of mopping up the crime scene.

Cliff and Julia exited his vehicle. He gave her a quick rundown of what he had seen the night before.

"Right there is where they found the body. Where the employee is cleaning up." He pointed toward the man and kept his tone barely above a whisper so the employee wouldn't hear their conversation.

"Which way was she facing?" Julia asked.

"Her head was facing the hotel. Her legs were facing toward us. She was on her stomach. Sprawled into a contorted position. Severe injuries to every part of her body. Her face was crushed almost beyond recognition on one side. Like she had been badly beaten or suffered from a fall from a high structure."

They both simultaneously looked up.

Cliff could clearly see the balcony off the suite on this side of the hotel, which he hadn't been able to see in the dark. He walked past the sidewalk and toward the hotel so that he was directly under the balcony and looked up again. He flashed his badge at the hotel worker as he walked by him, so he'd know who Cliff was and why he was there.

The maintenance worker's face went white.

Julia followed behind. "The angle is right," she said, after looking at the balcony, then the sidewalk, and back up at the balcony again.

The sidewalk was about ten to fifteen feet out from the balcony. Cliff lifted his arm in the air and tried to simulate the angle. Julia was right. The body could've fallen from that balcony and landed on the sidewalk.

Hard to say with certainty, considering the balcony was twenty-three stories high.

"Is that the balcony to the honeymoon suite?" Julia asked.

Cliff thought back to the night before. When he exited the elevator, the honeymoon suite was on the left. The balcony was now on his right. He turned around so he was facing away from the hotel. The balcony was now on his left.

"Yes. That's the balcony to the honeymoon suite."

Cliff felt a bolt of excitement pulse through him when he said the words. The type of feeling he got when he was near a breakthrough in a case. It didn't mean the woman was on that balcony. It did mean it was possible.

A clue. Something to go on. They called clues threads. He pursued threads until they were no longer possible. This one was promising. The woman was dressed in lingerie. Julia was convinced she was on her honeymoon. The injuries sustained were consistent with a fall. Maybe he had more than a thread. This might be a real breakthrough.

"I was right!" Julia said with the same excitement in her voice that he was feeling. "Yesterday was her wedding day. Her husband did kill her!"

"Can you keep it down?" Cliff said. The employee had stopped mopping and was looking their way.

He moved closer to his wife and whispered, "We don't know that. Not yet. But I agree that the woman could have fallen off that balcony."

"Not fallen. Pushed."

At least Julia had lowered her voice so only he could hear her.

"Maybe," he said, tamping down the enthusiasm in his voice. "But let's not advertise it to the world."

Cliff tried to remain emotionless in an investigation. Not that he didn't feel the highs and lows. He just didn't show them to anyone. Especially to witnesses and suspects.

And now, Julia was an added complication. He was walking a fine line. It was her birthday, and she was clearly out of her earlier funk. Acting like a kid at a circus. Cliff appreciated his wife's passionate approach to life, and oddly, the murder he was tasked to solve. But he didn't want her giddiness to interfere with the investigation.

"Let's go inside," Julia said barely above a whisper. "We need to see if the husband is alone in the honeymoon suite."

That was the next step. But Cliff hesitated.

He had mixed feelings about going back in. He didn't have a warrant. The manager would demand he have one. He might get lucky, and the manager was off. A new person in charge might be better, but also might be worse to deal with. He looked at his watch. It was shortly after noon. Time was of the essence. Check out time was probably one. Maybe the couple rented the suite for more than one night. More than likely, they would check out and leave for their honeymoon.

He had no choice but to figure out a way to get around the manager without a warrant.

He'd make his arguments.

It wasn't the middle of the night.

He wouldn't be disturbing the couple from their sleep.

He didn't need a warrant.

The case could be made that he had probable cause to search the room. Given the proximity of the body to the balcony. At least enough evidence that he wouldn't get any blowback from his boss. In fact, his lieutenant would be impressed that he returned to the crime scene on his day off. Even more impressed if Cliff could solve the case in the first twenty-four hours.

Julia could be a problem though. His lieutenant wouldn't understand why his wife was with him. The prudent thing to do was to tell her to wait in the car.

But he might be the one lying on the sidewalk if he did so.

That thought caused him to laugh out loud.

"What's so funny?" Julia asked, as she crinkled up her nose in confusion in the cute way she often did at one of his off-handed remarks.

"Nothing," Cliff said, as he purposefully made his face stone cold and detective-like again.

"I agree. We should go inside. Just let me do the talking," Cliff said. "The manager on duty last night wasn't very cooperative. I hope he's not the one working this morning."

"I'll sweet-talk him," Julia said, batting her naturally long and dark eyelashes. "We women can get men to do anything we want them to do."

Julia laughed as she sashayed away looking back at him with a grin on her face.

Cliff pointed his finger at her. "You keep quiet! This is a police investigation. You're not even supposed to be here. My boss would not be happy if he knew you were here."

"Not if I help you solve a murder case on my birthday," she giggled.

Julia grabbed Cliff's finger and twisted it playfully but with enough effort that it hurt. He let out a yelp. She then kissed him on the lips to let him know she was kidding.

"I'm serious. I could get in trouble."

"I'll be a good girl. I promise. You do all the talking."

"Thank you. Let's go."

They walked into the hotel lobby and Cliff's heart sank when he saw the manager from the night before standing behind the registration counter.

Cliff almost turned around and walked back outside. Before the man saw him. But Julia kept walking toward the counter giving Cliff no time to decide his next move. She got to the front desk well before Cliff did.

Thankfully, she didn't say anything. Instead, she stepped to the side and lifted the palm of her hand in the air in a sweeping motion for Cliff to take the lead.

"Welcome to the Regency Hotel," the perky clerk behind the counter said. "Are you checking in today?"

"Actually, I'm inquiring about one of your guests." Cliff flashed his badge at the woman. Her face turned as white as a sheet.

The manager looked up from what he was doing. Probably recognized Cliff's voice.

"Hello, Mr. Hildebrand," Cliff said, when they made eye contact. "I didn't expect to see you here today. Do you ever sleep?"

The manager was wearing a different suit. He'd likely gone home and slept a few hours.

Hildebrand immediately stopped whatever he was doing and walked over and stood next to the clerk. "Good morning, Detective," he said. "Do you have your warrant?"

Cliff had hoped to avoid a confrontation. The manager seemed to be itching for one. Clearly not in the mood for chitchat. Cliff wasn't either but was trying to be friendly. Hoping the manager was in a better mood. He wasn't.

"I would like to talk to the couple in the honeymoon suite again," Cliff said in a serious tone. He thought of it as his detective voice.

Hildebrand started to speak, but Cliff raised his hand in the air to stop him.

"I don't have a warrant. But I don't need one. It's the middle of the day. I'm sure I won't be waking them up. I just want to knock on the door and verify that the bride is okay. That's all."

"I'm sorry, but you can't talk to the couple," Hildebrand said.

"Are we going to play that game again?" Cliff asked more roughly. It didn't take long for his angst to return.

This time the manager was the one who raised his hand in the air to stop Cliff from saying anything further.

"The couple already checked out," he said in a smug voice, like he'd won the argument which didn't sit well with Cliff.

The words had more effect than the tone, though. Cliff could feel the air in his lungs and the excitement leave his body all at once.

"Okay. Thank you for your time," Cliff said, and turned to walk back outside the hotel to regroup. Not sure how to react to this frustrating turn of events.

He was halfway to the door when he noticed that Julia hadn't followed him. She was still at the front desk. Cliff hurried back when he heard her speak to the manager.

"Were you there when the couple checked out, Mr. Hildebrand?" Julia asked. "Did you see them?"

"I did not," he replied.

"I was there," the clerk piped up. "I checked them out."

Julia put her elbows on the counter and leaned in.

"Who did you check out, honey? Was it the husband or the wife or both?"

Cliff was back at the counter and was about to take Julia by the arm and usher her out of the hotel. But he heard the question, and it was a good one. He wanted to know the answer as well.

"The husband is the one who checked out," the clerk said.

"Was his wife with him?" Julia asked.

"No ma'am, I didn't see her," she said.

Cliff had heard enough.

"I'm going to need to see the honeymoon suite," Cliff said with authority.

Mr. Hildebrand started to say something. Clearly wanting to object. It wasn't going to do him any good to try and prevent them from heading up to the honeymoon suite. Not this time.

"Now!" Cliff said angrily. "Or I'll have this place crawling with cops within ten minutes. I'll seal off all the exits and no one will be allowed to enter or exit. So, Mr. Hildebrand, we can do this the easy way or the hard way. It's your choice."

"Follow me," Mr. Hildebrand said softly, as the blood suddenly left his face.

"Good choice," Cliff said.

The three of them began walking toward the elevator.

Thank you, Julia, Cliff thought to himself as he flashed her a smile.

9

Earlier that morning

Robert Platt had watched enough television crime dramas and read enough murder mysteries to know there was no such thing as the perfect crime.

That didn't stop him from trying to commit one.

Successfully getting away with killing his wife Sylvia, would test all of his skills. He needed ingenuity, creativity, intelligence, and a little bit of luck.

The first bit of luck came in the middle of the night when the police detective didn't knock on the door a second time to ask to speak to her. Had he done so, all the other preparations were out the window. He'd have to face the music and hope the authorities believed his story. The story was rock solid, but things would go much easier if he got away from the hotel before they discovered Sylvia's identity and tied her to the honeymoon suite.

He'd been sound asleep when the detective knocked on his door, although he went to sleep expecting it. Once Sylvia's body was found, even an amateur sleuth would deduce that it might've come from the balcony above.

In his planning, he'd thought about not answering it. That's not something that could be explained. So, he answered it and hoped for the best. His story would be that he was asleep. She must've fallen off the balcony or jumped.

How could anyone prove otherwise?

He hadn't planned on slamming the door in the detective's face, but it worked out. The man never returned.

Still hadn't.

Robert watched the imbecile from the Chicago P.D. drive away from the hotel from the shadows of his hotel room. He may have caught a break and gotten an incompetent buffoon handling the case.

After the man was gone, Robert wasn't able to go back to sleep, so he sat in the dark going over his plan again and again in his mind. It was excruciating waiting for the sun to come up.

Nerve-wracking expecting a second knock on the door.

When one didn't come, he prepared to move on to Plan B.

Plan A was getting out of the hotel undiscovered. Plan B was getting on the plane and going to his honeymoon destination. That'd hinder the investigation further. It'd be days before the police could question him.

He honestly never thought he'd get to Plan B.

When the sun came up, he went to work with a sense of urgency. He couldn't leave the hotel right away, though. He had to cover his tracks.

The first thing he did was double-check Sylvia's phone to make sure it was on silent. Then he called her phone from his cell phone and left her the first message.

"Hello, Babe. I just woke up, and you aren't here. You must've gone for a walk or something. I'm going to hop in the shower. Then we can order breakfast. I can't believe we're married! See you soon. Love you."

He hung up and analyzed the message. Did he set the right tone? Did it sound believable? Should he have said something about the plane reservation?

No! Stick to the plan.

Improvising was where he might make a mistake. They were scheduled to fly out to St. Thomas for their honeymoon that afternoon and then catch a boat to the British Virgin Islands. He intended to be on that flight. No reason to tip off a detective that they had plane reservations that afternoon.

CLIFF HANGERS: MR. AND MRS. PLATT

He had a million things to do between now and then. The most important thing was to avoid the police detective while leaving him a trail to follow. A trail that would prove his innocence.

A tough task to pull off. Everyone would be skeptical of him. Sylvia's parents would probably think he killed her. They never liked him.

He'd be a step ahead of everyone. How would a groom act if his wife was missing on the first day of their honeymoon? That's how he would act. He'd spent days planning and going over the plan until his head hurt.

Robert took a shower, got dressed, and left his second message on Sylvia's phone.

"Hi, Love. It's me. Where are you? I'm starving. I'll come find you. Bye."

Perfect.

A hint of annoyance.

With no concern in his voice at all.

The detective would eventually hear those messages. He might not believe them, but what could he do?

Robert left the room and got on the elevator. Time was of the essence. The detective could come back to the hotel at any time.

He'd gone over the interrogation a thousand times in his mind.

"Where did you think your wife was?"

"I didn't know."

"Why did you leave the hotel without her?"

"What else could I do? I went to her house to find her. I had no idea she was dead."

"Why did you get on the plane?"

"I was hurt."

It'd serve her right. He'd tell the detective he was devastated when she didn't show up at the airport. He almost got off the plane but went anyway. The honeymoon was no fun. He left angry. Jilted. Hurt that his wife had abandoned him.

"Why waste the plane tickets and the excellent hotel? Maybe she'd come to her senses and eventually join me later. I kept expecting her to call."

63

Robert had to wipe the smile off his face as he walked around the hotel. He wasn't out of the woods yet. He wouldn't be for months, actually. The plan was good, but he was a long way from pulling it off. Cockiness could be his downfall. He had to stay focused on the task at hand. He couldn't afford to get sloppy.

The route around the hotel was mapped out in his mind. He had walked the hotel grounds beforehand to ensure he knew where to go. Places that would catch his face on the security cameras.

He was looking for his wife. Something a groom would obviously do if he woke up and his wife wasn't in the room.

The first stop was the lobby. He walked into the restaurant off the lobby and looked around. He was approached and asked if he wanted to be seated.

"I'm looking for my wife. A pretty blond. Petite," he said to the hostess.

"I don't have anyone like that here right now, but feel free to walk through one more time in case you missed her."

After pretending to scan the restaurant one more time, he left and walked over to the large atrium with several sitting areas. He couldn't help but notice how lush it was. A small river ran through the impressive tropical foliage and ended with a waterfall that cascaded into a large pool with lily pads and goldfish in it.

Robert walked all around the area. Several times. Like he was pacing. His head on a swivel. Pretending to look for Sylvia. Actually, looking for the detective. No sign of him.

The fitness area was next. He got back on the elevator and went down one floor. It didn't take long to walk through the area. The room was less than a thousand square feet. Smaller than the bedroom in the honeymoon suite. It had six treadmills. A series of half a dozen weight machines and a rack with free weights. A large mat lay in front of a mirror that took up one wall.

A sexy redhead was stretching on the mat wearing tight-fitting workout attire. He managed to resist the temptation to ogle her. That wouldn't look good on surveillance tape.

Instead, he asked her, "Have you seen my wife? A pretty blond. Petite. She likes to run on the treadmill."

"I haven't seen her," the woman replied.

"Thank you."

Perfect. Another witness. The detective would definitely question her.

"What did the man ask you?"

"He asked if I'd seen his wife."

"What did you say?"

"I told him I hadn't."

"What was his demeanor?"

"He seemed concerned. Like he couldn't find her."

Robert was patting himself on the back. Even he was impressed by his ingenuity.

He went out of the fitness area and into the adjacent room with the indoor swimming pool. An employee was cleaning the pool and setting out towels. Robert asked him the same question.

A third witness. Things were going well.

He got back on the elevator and made another trip around the hotel lobby. Then went outside and looked around the back of the hotel. Not the front. He didn't want to go anywhere near where Sylvia's body was found. He assumed there'd be police tape up. The detective might even be there. He didn't want to be asked any questions about it.

He looked at his watch. The key was to search the right amount of time. Not too little and not too much. Satisfied, he went back to his room and left her a third message.

"Sylvia. Where are you? I looked everywhere. You aren't in the hotel. Call me. Is this like the stunt you pulled in Florida all over again? I don't understand why you would do this."

When considering his plan, one problem he came up with was how to explain Sylvia's behavior. Why would a new bride suddenly disappear on her honeymoon? Most normal grooms would call the police and file a missing person's report. Why hadn't he?

He'd thought about that for days. Almost canceled the plan over it.

Then he had an idea.

Create a pattern of behavior.

Sylvia had done this before. Disappeared for stretches at a time. Once in Florida on vacation. It took him several hours to find her.

Who was going to contradict his account? No one. The only person who could was dead. He would tell the detective that Sylvia had a mental disorder. She hid it from her family. Also suffered from an eating disorder. Another thing her family didn't know about for obvious reasons.

She had admitted it to him in Florida. The day she disappeared for more than eight hours.

"I thought she was better," he'd tell the detective.

"Why didn't you tell anyone about her condition?"

"She swore me to secrecy."

"Did she see a psychiatrist?"

"She wouldn't. I encouraged her to do so."

Robert left a fourth message. This one was trickier. Required acting skills. He had to be angry. He pulled out his phone but didn't dial right away. Went over the script again in his mind. He'd memorized it. Practiced it in his apartment several times already. Finally, he made the call.

"Sylvia! I can't believe you're doing this again. On our honeymoon! Are you at your house? I'm checking out of the hotel. I have all your stuff. I'm coming to your house to find you and we're going on our honeymoon. I don't know what's going on with you, but we'll get through it. Please call me."

Robert's heart was pounding out of his chest as he said the words. A good thing. It helped him sound anxious on the message. Leaving the message had actually gone better than when he practiced it. Probably because of the adrenaline flowing through his veins.

He packed up all the bags, including Sylvia's. He picked up the hotel phone and pressed the button and summoned a bellman. The help arrived promptly and gathered their luggage. They took the elevator down to the lobby in silence. Robert went to the front desk and checked out, careful to keep his demeanor somber.

Sylvia's dad's credit card was on file, so he didn't even bother reviewing the charges. He didn't care if they were right or not. The

Goldmans had more money than they knew what to do with. It was hardly fair.

The valet pulled Robert's car around right away. The bellman gingerly loaded the bags in the trunk. Robert gave him a big tip this time. Fifty bucks to the bellman and another fifty to the valet. He didn't want them to be angry with him. On the contrary, he wanted them to remember him being a pleasant but despondent guest at his departure. They'd eventually be witnesses. They could testify to his demeanor.

He could hear how the conversation would go with the detective.

"What was his mood?

"Did he seem agitated?"

"Did you ask him why his wife wasn't checking out with him?"

Their responses would be the same.

"He seemed upset."

"Distracted. A good guy."

"He left a generous tip."

"He didn't say why his wife wasn't with him and I didn't ask."

Robert drove away from the hotel. Once out of sight of any scrutinizing eyes, he broke out in a big smile and roared in laughter. He had done it! And although he was tempted to floor it, he made sure to stay under the speed limit just enough that there was no reason he could get pulled over.

He made his escape from the hotel without getting caught.

On to Plan B.

Plan A went better than expected.

10

Even though the honeymoon suite was empty, and the groom had already checked out, Cliff expected to find some clues. If the dead women really did fall from the balcony. If so, it wouldn't take long to learn her identity. They also might discover that the bride who stayed in the suite was alive and well. Either scenario would help move the investigation forward.

Cliff didn't care where the investigation led, only that it kept moving quickly toward a resolution, and he found the killer and got him behind bars. The worst part of the job wasn't dealing with murders. That's the career he chose. It was the unsolved murders that kept him up at night.

He could tell Julia was excited to be included in the investigation. He could see it in her eyes which were bright and gleaming. When they entered the elevator, and the hotel manager put his keycard into the slot and pushed the button for floor twenty-three, Julie touched Cliff's hand. Subtly, but reassuringly. She could probably sense as well that they might be on the verge of a breakthrough in the case.

He was impressed. She'd surmised that the woman was on her honeymoon. She also pegged the husband as the killer from the beginning. The investigation wouldn't be as far along without her input. That's why he let her come upstairs with them.

Cliff realized that he hadn't introduced Julia to the manager. Hildebrand was probably wondering who she was. He decided to keep him guessing. None of his business.

"I know the name of the couple who is staying in the honeymoon suite," Cliff said smugly to the manager.

"Who?" he answered without making eye contact.

"Do you remember what you said to me last night?" Cliff asked.

"I said a lot of things."

"You said that if I was a good detective, I'd be able to find out the couple's name on my own. That I wouldn't need your help. Well... I know the name of the couple."

"Good for you."

"Mr. and Mrs. Platt."

"Congratulations. You're a good detective. Your wife must be proud."

"I am," Julia said, taking care of the need for an introduction.

Then she rolled her eyes up and to the left and tilted her head like she thought the testosterone battle going on in the elevator was unnecessary. Childish. Cliff knew precisely what she was thinking. He'd seen that look before.

But Cliff couldn't help himself. The manager was a jerk. More importantly, the manager knew the name of the couple in the suite. He'd just confirmed Cliff was right.

Cliff was convinced that the manager didn't know the couple's name the night before. He was also one hundred percent certain that the first thing the manager did when Cliff left was look it up. While Cliff didn't know the couples' first names, he'd get that from the manager before leaving the hotel.

The elevator dinged, and Cliff was the first one off. He walked with a purpose through the foyer and made a left toward the honeymoon suite. What he saw set him in a panic.

"No! No! No!" Cliff said.

He practically ran down the hallway to the suite. The maid was outside the room with her cleaning cart in front of the door.

"Are you coming or going?" he said with a sense of urgency that startled the housekeeper.

She cowered back, keeping the cleaning cart between herself and Cliff. The woman was probably in her mid-twenties. Average looking.

Slightly overweight. Her hair was pulled back and under a maid's hat, and she wore a hotel uniform. The lapel tag said her name was Shay.

Cliff pulled out his badge and shoved it toward her face with a little too much exuberance. She let out a slight gasp.

At the same time, her eyes widened to the size of a 57 Chevy truck's hubcaps. She seemed so scared she couldn't talk. He hadn't phrased the question well, so he needed to tone it down a bit and ask it differently.

"Have you already cleaned this room?" Cliff asked a little more gently.

When the manager walked up and stood beside Cliff, the maid seemed relieved, and Cliff heard her exhale the breath she'd obviously been holding. Julia stood on the other side of Cliff and made eye contact with the girl and gave her a warm smile.

Hopefully, that would reassure her as well.

Cliff asked the question again. "Did you clean this room? Please tell me you haven't started on it yet."

Shay moved her eyes from Julia to the manager. As if she needed permission from him to talk.

"Did I do something wrong?" she asked.

"No, Ms. Richards," the manager said. "You didn't do anything wrong. You can answer Detective Ford's questions."

"I just finished cleaning the room," she said hesitantly.

"Shoot!" Cliff said. He then began pacing around in a circle with his hand on his forehead.

"Shoot!" he said a second time.

This was a disaster. If the maid was thorough, she had likely destroyed any potential evidence. Fingerprints. Bodily fluids. Blood. DNA fibers. At best, smudged by her cleaning rag. At worst, obliterated altogether. Certainly enough that a reasonable defense attorney might be able to get all the evidence found in the room thrown out.

Cliff wasn't angry with the woman. He was mad at himself. He should've pressed the issue the night before with the groom. Knocked on the door a second time and insisted on talking to the bride.

Well, it was too late now. He needed to get his focus back and make the best of a bad situation.

"What was the room like when you found it?" Cliff asked.

Shay shrugged her shoulders and replied, "Nothing unusual."

"Was Mr. Platt in the room?" Cliff asked.

"Did you see Mrs. Platt?" Julia chimed in.

"Were the guests still in the suite this morning when you began your shift," the manager asked.

The questions were coming rapid-fire and from several directions.

She shook her head no.

"She wouldn't clean the room until they checked out," the manager explained.

She might not have seen the couple, but she would have information.

"Were both sides of the bed messed up?" Cliff asked.

"I didn't notice," Shay said. "I mean. I just took the sheets and pillowcases off like I usually do."

Shay's hands were shaking, and her lips were quivering.

"Take your time, Shay," Cliff said in a softer tone. "And think about my questions. It's important. You aren't in trouble. You didn't do anything wrong. But you may have important information."

"Is this about the woman who was killed last night?" Shay asked.

"I don't know," Cliff said. "That's what I'm trying to find out. Did both sides of the bed look like they had been slept in?"

"I think so. Yes."

"Had the shower been used?" Cliff asked.

"Yes. There were two used towels."

"Did you see anything suspicious? Did you find any blood?"

"No, sir."

"Any sign of a struggle? Broken lamps? Furniture out of place?"

"No, sir. I didn't see anything out of the ordinary. The room wasn't even very dirty. Like it was hardly used."

The woman clearly didn't know anything. He'd question her further at a later time. After some time had passed and she had more time to think about it, she might remember something.

"Open the door," Cliff said to the manager. He didn't bother to say please. "I want to take a look around."

When the door was opened, Cliff pushed his way past the manager brushing him aside with his shoulder.

Once inside, he stopped to look around the suite and get his bearings. They'd entered into an open area. The living area was to the right. A massive dining room table was straight ahead under an opulent chandelier. The kitchen bar area was to the left of the dining room. Cliff presumed the kitchen was on the other side of the bar. To the right were two large double doors. He could see a large king-sized bed with a massive, decorative canvas on the wall behind it. The room was luxurious as Cliff expected.

Sliding glass doors were along the far wall. That's where the balcony would be. The curtains were pulled back, and Cliff could see the waves of Lake Michigan lapping at the shoreline off in the distance.

He decided not to go directly to the balcony. Time to pull back. Take his time. Slow down his questions. Give Shay time to think. The worst thing he could do was rattle a prospective witness's memory. It was hard enough for people to remember a fragment of a detail, let alone if they felt pressured.

He used his eagle eye to scan the room for clues. While he wanted to go to the balcony, he was more concerned about what Shay saw when she entered the suite. Something she might think was insignificant could be crucial to the investigation.

"What did you see when you first entered the room?" Cliff asked.

Shay took a noticeable deep breath and looked around. They were all four standing just inside the door, which had automatically closed behind them.

"There were two food trays on the dining room table," Shay said. "A bottle of champagne."

"Was it empty?" Cliff asked.

"Yes."

That might be important. The woman might've been drunk and fallen off the balcony. If so, why would the husband leave the hotel without her?

"What else did you see?" Cliff said. "You're doing good."

For the next ten minutes, Shay gave them a tour of the suite and was able to describe things in more detail as time went on.

They finally got to the sliding glass doors.

"Was the balcony door open or closed?" Cliff asked.

"It was closed."

Cliff took out a handkerchief, put it over his hand, and slid it open. Then stepped outside. He walked over to the railing and looked down. Careful not to touch the railing. He leaned over the side and looked down at the sidewalk where the woman was found. No question, the body could've fallen from the balcony. It didn't mean that she did. It just meant that it was possible.

The manager followed him outside. Cliff put his arm out to stop him before he could touch the railing. There might be evidence on it. This was one area the maid likely didn't clean.

"Don't touch anything," Cliff said. Julia and Shay were now on the balcony as well. Technically, they probably shouldn't even be walking on it.

After a minute or so, the four of them stepped back inside, and Cliff closed the sliding glass doors.

"You said the bottle of champagne was empty. Is that correct?" Julia asked the maid.

"Yes."

"Was there one glass or two next to the bottle of champagne?" she asked.

Shay's eyes suddenly widened again, and her mouth gaped open. She raised her hand in the air like a schoolgirl asking for permission to speak.

Julia walked over and stood next to her.

"What is it, honey? You don't need to raise your hand."

"There's one thing I remember," Shay said.

"What's that?" Cliff asked.

"There was broken glass on the balcony."

"What! Why didn't you say so before?" Cliff asked, immediately regretting his harsh tone.

He saw her eyes water.

"I'm so sorry," she said. "I forgot. I mean... I didn't remember. It just never occurred to me. This whole situation is terrifying. I was already nervous knowing a murderer might be somewhere in our hotel. And then to have to be the one that has to clean this room, of all things. I've never been questioned like this. It has really shaken me up. I just cleaned it up and put the broken glass in the trash. I was doing my job."

Cliff felt his heart pounding in his ears. A broken glass on the balcony was all the evidence he needed to call in forensics.

"It's understandable." Cliff said. "Just a few more questions. And relax. You've done nothing wrong, but something as simple as a broken glass could provide important information."

"What kind of glass was broken on the balcony?" he asked.

"It looked like a champagne glass. A flute. One of the very expensive ones used here at the Regency."

"Show me where you found it."

Cliff took out his handkerchief and opened the sliding glass door again. He told Julia and the manager to wait in the suite. The two of them went back on the balcony, and she showed him where she found the broken glass. The concrete didn't have a noticeable stain telling Cliff that the glass was empty when it hit the concrete.

They went back inside.

"I need to clear this room," Cliff said. "I now consider it a potential crime scene."

11

"Let's go back inside," Cliff had said to the maid.

They had stepped out on the balcony of the honeymoon suite, and she showed him where she found the broken glass. Unfortunately, she'd already cleaned it up, at the very least contaminating the scene. Possibly destroying the evidence altogether.

Once back inside, Cliff motioned for the manager to step to the side. Not really out of earshot of the two ladies, but far enough away to create the desired effect. He wanted Hildebrand to know that the situation was serious and that he expected his full cooperation from this point forward.

"I need to seal off this room and call in a forensics team," Cliff said.

As expected, the manager turned belligerent.

"You'll need a warrant for that," the manager said. "We also have another couple checking in today."

"I can get a warrant, and I will. Or you can give me permission."

"I'm not going to give you permission."

"Yes, you are. Because if you don't, you can forget about that couple checking in today. They won't be staying here. Which is a shame. This is a nice room. But it won't be available."

"Why is that?"

"If you give me permission, I can have the team out of here by four or five o'clock. Your next guests can check-in then."

"What if they get here earlier?"

"Not going to happen. The earliest the wedding would start is eleven o'clock in the morning. Then they have the reception. The couple won't get here until late this afternoon. If it's an afternoon wedding, they won't get here until tonight. It's best to get this over with before they arrive."

Cliff paused again hoping the argument won the day. He definitely didn't want to go get a warrant. He leaned in and whispered in a firm tone, "If you don't give me permission, I'll get that warrant. I should have it around four or five o'clock this afternoon. I will want the team to be thorough. They might not be through until ten o'clock tonight. Then I'm going to want to look at the room again. After I get done with it, I'll turn it back over to you. But. . . you'll have to clean the room again."

Hildebrand's jaw was clenched. His fist was balled like he was angry. Backed into a corner like a treed cougar.

"I think you should go ahead and cancel the reservation with your guests," Cliff said. "Put them in a standard room. I'm sure they'll understand."

The manager's eyes were on fire like embers of coal.

"Are you sure you can give me back the room by four o'clock?" the manager asked in an angry tone.

"No later than five."

"Okay. I give you my permission."

Cliff patted him on his lapel. "Good choice."

"I need everyone out of the room," Cliff said. "Don't touch anything. Shay, leave the cleaning cart where it is."

"I still need to clean the Presidential Suite," she said to her manager.

"We'll get you another cart," he responded. "Do what the detective says."

Cliff made some calls. It took ten minutes for a beat cop to arrive. Cliff gave him instructions to stand guard at the door. The forensics team arrived within the hour. He showed them what he wanted done, including searching the trash on the maid's cart. Focusing on the broken glass.

Julia stood off to the side, on her phone. Cliff suddenly remembered it was her birthday.

"I'm sorry," Cliff said to her. "I'm ruining your birthday."

"You do what you have to do. I don't mind. This is the most exciting birthday I've ever had."

Cliff laughed.

"This is my life," he said. "It feels like work to me. I can leave now. Let's go home and decide what to do."

"It's okay if you need to stay. I understand."

"I don't need to stay. There's nothing I can do. The forensics team will send me a report."

"Give me one second," Cliff said to Julia.

He gave the cop instructions to stay until the team left. After that, he was free to go as well.

"Before you leave, check in with the front desk and release the room to them," Cliff told him.

The cop said he would.

Cliff and Julia rode the elevator to the lobby, got in their car, and drove away.

They rode in silence for several minutes. Cliff could feel her gaze on him. He decided to break the silence.

"My dear birthday girl. What are you thinking about?" he asked.

"We need to find the killer," Julia said. "The husband."

Cliff let out a laugh and said, "Oh, we do, do we?"

"Don't you want to pursue the leads while the irons are hot on the fire? You don't want the case to grow cold."

"We don't have any leads. I don't even know who the dead woman is."

"Mrs. Platt."

"That's who was staying in the room. I don't know if she was the one lying on the sidewalk."

"What more do you need?" Julia said. "The body was found right below the balcony. The groom checked out by himself. There's a broken champagne glass on the balcony. How many smoking guns do you need?"

"The body could've been dumped there. She might've been a guest in a different room. They might've taken two cars to the hotel, and she left early and told her husband to handle the check out. There could be any number of explanations as to why the glass was broken. It was their wedding night. The couple might've been fooling around on the balcony and knocked over the champagne glass. Who knows?"

Cliff was making the arguments half-heartedly. He thought the evidence was starting to pile up as well but felt the need to push back. Things were not always what they seemed. More importantly, he was searching his thoughts to see if it was bothering him that his wife was telling him what to do in a murder investigation.

Julia let out a disconcerting sigh. He knew she didn't like having her feelings summarily dismissed. He needed to be careful. The day was not going as planned, but she didn't seem to mind. Julia was clearly enjoying herself. The last thing he wanted was to get in an argument with her or hurt her feelings.

They drove the rest of the way in silence.

When they got home, Cliff sat his keys down on the kitchen counter and said, "Look, I agree with you. The evidence seems to point to the Platts. That's why I called in the forensics team. I just wish I knew for sure the identity of the woman in the morgue. Then I'd know if she was or was not the bride in the suite. Anyway... today's your birthday. I'll work on it tomorrow. Let's try to have some fun with what's left of your special day. You deserve it."

Julia sidled up to him. She wrapped her arms around him and pressed her body against his, sending a chill down his spine.

"I like helping you," she said. "It's fun being part of your world. I hope you don't mind me making suggestions."

"I'm sorry," Cliff said. "I wasn't trying to sound like I didn't hear you. I appreciate all your help."

She kissed him on the lips. Cliff could feel his heart start to beat faster.

"I was impressed," she said.

"With what?"

"You're a good detective. The way you questioned that maid was masterful. How you pieced together the evidence was brilliant. I've never really seen you in action. It makes me want you."

She kissed him again. Harder this time. And deeper. When she finally pulled away, he was slightly out of breath.

"I need to take you on all my investigations," Cliff said.

"Meet me upstairs," Julia said, batting her eyelashes at him seductively.

They were still standing in the kitchen.

"Do you mean what I think you mean?"

"You'll find out."

"I have to take a shower first," Cliff said.

"You already took one this morning."

He wasn't sure how to explain it. Even though there hadn't been a dead body in the hotel room, it was still a crime scene. He always felt dirty after leaving a contaminated scene.

"I'll feel better if I take a hot shower."

"Okay," she acquiesced. "I'll meet you in bed. Don't dilly-dally." She was smiling broadly as she said it.

Apparently, today was the day for silly and obscure words and sayings.

When Cliff got out of the shower, Julia wasn't in bed. That was strange, considering having a romp had been her idea. She didn't often initiate their lovemaking, but this time, she'd been clear. He hadn't misinterpreted her signals.

He slipped on a pair of shorts and went to look for her.

She was downstairs. In the office. On their computer.

"What are you doing?" Cliff asked. "This clearly isn't our bedroom. Did you have a change of heart?"

"Is this the girl?" she asked in her most serious tone.

"What girl?"

"The dead girl! For goodness sakes! Who else would I be talking about?"

Cliff walked around the desk and looked over Julia's shoulder. On the screen was a wedding announcement. At the top was a picture of a man and a woman. The woman looked familiar. Cliff read the first line of the newspaper article.

PrattGoldman

Robert Platt and Sylvia Goldman, both of Vernon Hills, IL, announce their engagement. Ms. Goldman is the daughter of Josef and Emilia Goldman...

The article went on to describe Mr. Goldman. The parents were part of the high society social circles in the Jewish community. They annually hosted very lucrative fundraisers for a variety of charities. It said nothing about Robert's parents. Platt wasn't a name he was familiar with.

Cliff didn't bother reading the rest of the announcement and, instead, focused on the picture. He tapped into his imagination. Was it possible? The beaming bride-to-be in the newspaper article. Could she be the woman on the sidewalk with her beautiful face caved in?

It was definitely possible.

"Is that her?" Julia asked again. "The woman on the sidewalk."

"It could be. I'm not completely sure. But it looks like her."

"The dead woman had blonde hair, right? And it was in a fancy hairdo, like a bride on her wedding day. She was clearly rich."

"Yes. She was blonde and wearing what looked like very expensive lingerie."

"This lady has blonde hair. She's beautiful and looks to be the age you described to me when we talked while you were at the crime scene. Her family is Jewish. They are obviously rich."

"I just can't say for sure. The woman I saw had half of her face caved in. And lots of women have blonde hair."

"This is her," Julia said. "I just know it. Look at the date of the wedding."

Julia pointed to the bottom of the screen.

"Yesterday," she said. "That's the day the Platts checked into the Regency Hotel. It has to be them."

It made sense. He was convinced. The threads were starting to come together. That didn't mean he'd solved the case. It just meant he had a place to start the investigation in earnest.

Julia stood up and said, "Get dressed. Let's go."

"Where are we going?"

"To find Robert Platt."

"I thought we were going to... you know... the bedroom..."

"We'll have sex on your birthday," she said.

"That's six months from now!"

Julia left the room without responding.

12

Robert was running ahead of schedule. Probably due to his meticulous preparations. He left the hotel and went directly to Sylvia's parents' house in Vernon Hills. A suburb north of Chicago with a large Jewish population.

The house was a monstrosity even by a gated community's standards. More than 16,000 square feet. Eight bedrooms, with ten full baths, and two half baths. It had two stories with a floating staircase, elevator, game room, wine cellar, home theater, two three-car garages, a swimming pool, tennis court, and a putting green. It sat on twelve acres.

Sylvia's father, Josef Goldman, founded the Goldman Group before Sylvia and her brother Josef II were born. The conglomerate held interests in banking, construction, oil, and telecom. Seeded by a modest fortune Josef's father made by supplying men to contract to build the first subway in Chicago.

Robert and Josef didn't get along from the moment they met. Not just because Robert wasn't Jewish, although he converted prewedding, but because old man Josef considered Robert a slacker. A loser with no work ethic. A college dropout who would never amount to anything.

If Josef could see him now, he would know Robert was far more brilliant than Josef gave him credit for. Robert had put a lot of work into killing his daughter.

That thought made him smile broadly. He quickly wiped the smile off his face when he got within the view of the security cameras at the entrance of the estate.

He pulled up to the gate and entered the gate code. The heavy iron doors with a big G in the center opened and Robert drove in. Part of his plan. His face would now be plastered on those security cameras. And the one in the back of the house and the camera at the entrance of the guest house.

Robert wasn't concerned about running into anyone. Sylvia's parents left immediately after the reception on their private jet to a Greek Island for a month-long extended vacation and cruise. Josef said he wanted to get his wife Emilia some time off after the stress of the wedding. Robert surmised that Josef didn't want to be home when Robert and Sylvia returned from their honeymoon and took up residence in the guest house.

Fine by him.

A stroke of fortune Robert hadn't counted on. It'd take days, if not a week, to contact them. Even longer for them to return to Chicago.

He didn't see any signs of activity at the house. The housekeeper was off today, and the groundskeeper wouldn't come to work until after three. Robert intended to be long gone by then.

Sylvia's brother was at work.

The perfect scenario for Robert to continue to pretend to be searching for Sylvia while not worrying about running into anyone.

Robert entered the guest house calling out Sylvia's name, loud enough for the cameras to pick up his voice. He went into the bathroom and splashed water on his face. Then looked at himself in the mirror. He was surprisingly calm. Confident.

Then the anger returned. He tolerated Sylvia but hated her father. Josef Goldman might be one of the wealthiest men in Chicago, but as smart as he was, he wasn't as smart as Robert. He'd just taken from him the one thing Josef's money couldn't buy. His only daughter. And he'd get away with it.

Hopefully, he'd take some of the man's fortune as well.

The thought made him smile but also brought him back to reality. The days ahead would be difficult. Things were going good now, but he had no idea how long that would last. Eventually, the idiot detective would figure out Sylvia's identity. The spotlight would be on Robert. He'd be the prime suspect. No one would believe that his new bride committed suicide. He just had to make sure they couldn't pin her death on him.

So far, so good.

But he needed to get out of town. He looked at his watch. Three hours before his flight. He wouldn't allow himself to fully relax until he was on that plane. He needed to get away from the house.

He couldn't yet.

He picked up his phone and left Sylvia another message. The fifth one. Overkill maybe. He'd studied other killers. The ones who got caught were the ones who left one or two messages. By text or phone. Too obvious they were trying to cover it up. Robert was striking the perfect tone.

"Sylvia! I'm at your parent's house. I really thought you'd be here."

He let his voice crack. Made it sound like he was crying.

"Call me and let's talk about things."

Long pause.

"I know you're feeling anxious. With all the stress of the wedding. I get it. We're married now. We have our whole life ahead of us. We're going to have a great life. Three kids like we talked about. It's what you wanted. Call me. Please. I need to know that you're okay."

He hung up and brushed away actual tears that had built up in his eyes. Robert didn't know he had such good acting skills. He'd practiced that. He could cry on demand. A skill he'd need when he met with the detective.

He looked at his watch again. It was too early to leave for the airport. He couldn't stay at the house though. Too risky. The groundskeeper could come into work early. A neighbor might stop by. He couldn't afford to be seen by anyone who would ask questions. Between now and the time he boarded the plane, he had to make sure he didn't run into anyone he knew.

Especially the detective.

Then he laughed. There's no way the detective knew Sylvia's identity as of yet. He was a bozo. No match for Robert. The detective had missed his chance at the hotel.

Still, he felt himself starting to get nervous. He'd feel safer at the airport. The detective would never find him there. It'd take him days to find out that Robert was in the British Virgin Islands.

He waited a little longer, then got in the car, and made the drive to the airport. He parked in long term parking. Near a security camera. He found a luggage cart and loaded his and Sylvia's bags onto the cart.

The biggest pain of his entire plan was having to haul her luggage all the way to the British Virgin Islands and back.

It couldn't be helped.

It'd make his story more believable.

"Why did you take her luggage on your honeymoon?" the detective would ask.

"Why wouldn't I? I truly believed that she was going to show up at the airport. She would need her personal belongings. Sylvia spent weeks packing and repacking to make sure she had exactly what she needed. I wanted her to have her luggage."

He could see the detective's face. It was etched in his mind from the night before. He couldn't wait to see the frustration on the man's face when he tried to poke holes in Robert's story.

Something he'd never be able to do.

He couldn't stop thinking about the interrogation. It'd been on his mind for weeks. Playing like a movie. He could even picture the room. One table, two chairs. Moldy. Cold. For the first time, he had a face to put with the interrogator.

"Why would I go to the trouble of hauling her luggage to the airport if I knew she was dead?" Robert would argue.

The luggage was piled high on the cart. Robert strained to push the cart with the bags through the parking lot, and into the terminal. He checked the bags at the counter. More security cameras would capture his every move. He had both tickets in his hand on purpose but checked the bags with his ticket. Airplanes didn't depart if they had luggage in the cargo hold for a passenger who hadn't checked in.

Once free of the bags, he quickly made his way through security. Made easier by the fact that they were traveling in first class. That allowed him to breeze through.

He arrived at his gate two hours early.

Robert went to the bar and ordered a scotch neat. He put on an appropriately sad face. Kept his head on a swivel, like he was looking for Sylvia. Needing all surveillance video to point to a sad, jilted groom. He ordered another scotch still scanning the crowds looking for his new bride with an unhappy look on his face.

He paid his bill and left a good tip. Like when he left the hotel, he wanted to be remembered favorably. And in this case, forlorn, since he was just dumped by his new bride. Not that he shared that information with the bartender. The bartender thanked him and wished him a good flight. Robert met the bartender's eyes, dropped his chin, shook his head side to side, and went and sat at the gate.

Boarding the flight couldn't come soon enough. He felt like he was sitting on pins and needles. He was so close.

He still had work to do, though. He had come this far and couldn't afford to get sloppy.

Robert needed to send a few more messages. It was unnerving but necessary. He had to focus. Keep his eye on the ball.

"Sylvia. I'm at the airport. I have your luggage. I'm at the gate. I hope you're on your way. I waited at the house as long as I could. You need to be here. I'm at Terminal C, Gate 23."

Short and terse.

The intensity increased with the next message.

"Sylvia. This is not funny! We're boarding soon. I'm leaving without you. You're not here. I can't believe you're doing this to me on our honeymoon!"

The big finale.

"You are so selfish! All you think about is yourself. How do you think I feel? Sitting here at the airport all by myself. I'm so mad at you. I'm leaving without you. I swear. You think I won't? You're wrong. I'm going. I hope you're happy. I don't even care anymore.

Ruin our honeymoon if you want. It's on you. I will never forgive you for this. If you were going to jilt me, why didn't you just leave at the altar. Then you could have added the horrific embarrassment I would have felt to the list."

He hung up angrily for the camera's benefit. He'd botched that last message. What did the last sentence mean? That was supposed to be the last message.

A few minutes later, he decided to leave one more.

"I'm sorry, Sylvia. I didn't mean it. I do forgive you. Please come. We're boarding soon. I want you to be with me. Please! We're supposed to spend the rest of our lives together. You're my wife. I love you. You know that. I'm going on our honeymoon. You have to come. Please come to paradise with me so we can start our marriage in a perfect, loving way. I love you so very much. I'll be waiting for you."

Robert hung up the phone. Satisfied.

Much better.

He hung his head in dismay so any camera footage would record a despondent man on the verge of tears. He was satisfied with the way he had handled the voicemails he left for Sylvia. He didn't need to send any more messages. Too many would look suspicious. He'd done all he could.

A sense of euphoria came over him. He was almost out of the woods, or in a tropical paradise as the case may be, where he could sip umbrella drinks to his heart's content.

Plan B was going well. He was seconds away from boarding the plane. Once the doors were closed and he was in the air, then he could relax for a few days.

The idiot detective was probably twiddling his thumbs. Without a clue. He certainly wouldn't know that Robert was at the airport. It was no wonder people got away with murder with buffoons like that one in law enforcement.

The gate agent began preboarding. Then called for first class.

Robert was second in line.

A voice came over the intercom.

"Mr. Robert Platt please pick up the nearest white courtesy phone. Mr. Robert Platt. Please pick up the nearest white courtesy phone."

Robert's heart skipped a beat.

13

Earlier

The opportunity for intimacy had passed. Neither of them was in the mood. They were still talking about the case. Cliff hadn't gotten dressed yet, and they hadn't left the house. Finding Robert Platt was a good idea. But he didn't know where to look. So, he voiced his concerns.

"How are we going to find him?" Cliff asked Julia.

"You're the detective," she said. "I got you a name. The dead woman is Sylvia Platt. Her parents live in Vernon Hills. That's up north. We can start there."

"I know where Vernon Hills is," Cliff said, slightly irritated. He was the detective. He wasn't even sure why he was discussing it with her. Probably because she was enjoying it and had helped move the investigation forward.

"Why would Robert kill his wife and then go to her parent's house?" Cliff asked.

"That's a good point. At least you can talk to the parents. They need to know their daughter is dead."

"Wait a minute!" Cliff said. "I don't know that Sylvia is dead. I can't go traipsing in there and tell them their daughter is dead when I'm not a hundred percent sure."

"You can't go what?" Julia interrupted.

"What?"

"You said traipsing."

"Yeah. It means walking around willy-nilly."

"You're cracking me up. I've never heard you use these words. Traipsing. Willy-nilly. Are these detective words that you only use at work?"

"I don't know. I've used these words before."

"Never around me."

"Can we focus? We've got a whacker on the loose."

"A whacker?"

"A whacker. A sandman. An Icer."

Cliff was trying to keep a straight face but couldn't control the wide grin he could feel on his face. Those were real code words detectives used behind the scenes.

"You're making fun of me," Julia said.

"Those are the words we use for a killer."

"Whatever."

Julia forced back a smile as well.

The banter was funny, considering the seriousness of the topic.

Cliff tried to make his tone more serious. "Anyway... As I was saying. I don't want to go *traipsing* up to Vernon Hills and knock on the Platt's door and tell them she's dead if she's very much alive and on her honeymoon."

"I agree that you will need to use some discretion."

"It can be delicate. I don't want to alarm them for no reason. Especially when I don't have verification that it's even their daughter."

"It is."

"Nevertheless... we need to tread lightly."

"And carry a big stick."

"Right. That goes without saying. If Robert Platt murdered his wife, I'm going to find him and put him away for life. My stick is very big."

Julia twisted her lips to the side and Cliff warned her not to take the bait and make an off-color joke.

Instead, she said, "I like it when you're angry. It's sexy. I don't usually see this side of you. I'm also impressed by your expanded vocabulary."

"Shut up," he said.

"I don't like that part of your vocabulary."

"I'm just kidding."

"What would a detective do in this situation?" she asked.

"I am a detective."

"Then what's the next move, Mr. Detective?"

He had to think. He wasn't really sure. This whole case had been thrown into his lap in the middle of the night. It sounded like Julia thought he should solve it right away. Some cases were never solved. He wondered if Julia knew that.

After thinking another few seconds, he said, "What I would do is what you did. Try to find a name and then a picture. I don't know if I would've thought about the engagement announcement. That was a smart move. Good job."

Julia beamed from the compliment.

"Thanks," she said. Then added, "So you have a name. Sylvia Platt."

"That's a good start. It helps to know who we are looking for. Keep up the good work."

"Okey-Dokey, smokey."

"Are you going to start with the strange words?" Cliff asked.

"Yes."

"For how long."

"Until I get tired of it."

"Good to know."

"Besides, you started it. Anyway. . . let's recap what we know. The woman's name is Sylvia Platt. Her husband is Robert Platt. She kind of looks like the dead girl on the sidewalk. What's next?"

"I'd try and find an address."

"How would you do that?"

"I'd pull her driver's license."

"What's holding you up?"

"You are! Talking about my vocabulary."

"Hop to it. Time is wasting. Shouldn't you also find the parent's address?"

Cliff was sitting in a side chair in the home office. Julia was still behind the desk in front of the computer. He was still in his shorts with no shirt on.

"It's my day off. It's also your birthday. I thought we'd go to a movie or something."

"Why go watch a detective solve a murder on the big screen when I can watch you do it in real life? I love this. I've never helped you on a case before."

"It might be dangerous."

"I hope so."

"I'm serious, Julia. I'm looking for a potential killer. If he'd kill his wife, he might not hesitate to kill my wife."

"I'm not worried about it. I have you to protect me. Call your office and find an address. I'll keep surfing the net to see what I can find. And get dressed. We're going to go find the Platts. Robert anyway. We know where Sylvia is."

The plan sounded sensible. Cliff left the room and called his office. Then he went upstairs and put on his suit and tie. If we were going to meet the parents, he wanted to look the part of a detective.

Within fifteen minutes, his office sent Sylvia's driver's license and her parent's address to his phone. He studied it closely.

Five ft. 2" and 103 pounds.

Blonde hair.

Brown eyes.

Cliff did a quick calculation of her age from her birthday.

She was thirty-two years old.

The picture on the license sure looked like the woman on the sidewalk. She was about that size. Same color hair. Height and weight matched the description.

The excitement rose up inside of him. He got that feeling when he was on the right thread. A lot of questions remained but knowing the woman's identity was the most important question to answer. After that, what happened to her.

Her address matched her parents, which made sense. She probably lived at home until her marriage.

Cliff walked back into the home office, where Julia was still on the computer.

"I got the woman's address. She still lives at home. Or at least did until she married Robert."

"I found something, too," Julia said.

"What did you find?"

"First thing I did was look up obituaries. I found one for Eli Goldman. Vernon Hills. Eighty-nine years old at the time of death. He is survived by a son, Josef, and his wife, Emilia Goldman. That's the same name on the engagement announcement. Julia's parents."

"Can't be a coincidence."

"I agree. Josef and Emilia have two children. Sylvia and Josef II. Sylvia has a brother."

"Good to know."

"Is that all?"

"No. There's more. I found a wedding announcement. In a local Jewish newspaper."

"Okay."

"Listen to this. Following the reception, the couple will be leaving for Virgin Gorda."

"The British Virgin Islands."

"Yes. I looked up flights. To get to Virgin Gorda, you have to fly into Saint Thomas. There are four flights from O'Hare going to St. Thomas. Three of them left this morning. One leaves this afternoon at 4:13 pm."

Cliff looked at his watch. It was nearly three o'clock.

"We have a little over an hour."

"Call the airlines and see if they checked in for the flight," Julia said. "If they both did, then we know the woman is alive. If they canceled the reservation, that'd let us know we're on the right track."

Cliff shook his head no.

"The airlines won't give me that information. Not without a warrant. Privacy issue."

"Then we'll have to go to the airport and see for ourselves."

"I don't know if we have time."

"We have to try. We can go to the gate. If Sylvia is there, then that'll clear up a lot of questions. I bet Robert canceled the plane reservations. Or he's there trying to make a quick getaway. You should catch him before he leaves the country."

He couldn't argue with that logic.

"Let's go," Cliff said.

They made it to the airport faster than Cliff thought. He put the blue lights on and raced there, helping them make better time.

Cliff parked the cruiser at the curb outside ticketing and kept the blue lights going. He showed his badge to a cop outside working traffic who said he'd watch it.

Once inside, they looked at the flight information display for departures. The flight was on time. They were cutting it close. Cliff wasn't sure they were going to make it.

So, he went directly to the information desk. An older man was sitting behind the counter. He looked bored.

Cliff flashed his badge and the man sat up in his chair.

"Can you page someone for me?" Cliff asked.

"What's the name, sir?"

"Mr. Robert Platt."

"I'll have him call the courtesy phone."

"Thank you. If he does, then call me at this number."

Cliff pulled a card out of his wallet and handed it to the man. "That's my cell phone."

He looked it over and then said, "I will, sir."

"Thanks."

"We've got to run," Cliff said to Julia. "The plane's leaving soon. I'm sure they're already boarding."

They rushed to security. Cliff took Julia by the arm and led her into the employee line where he showed them his badge. He was glad he put a suit on. He lifted his suit and let the TSA agents see the gun on his hip.

That complicated things. Security was more thorough when a gun was involved. It took several minutes before they were cleared.

While they were waiting, he heard the announcement.

"Mr. Robert Platt, please pick up the nearest white courtesy phone. Mr. Robert Platt. Please pick up the nearest white courtesy phone."

They ran to the train. The ride took nearly ten minutes. The train came to a stop, and they prepared for the doors to open.

"We're not going to make it," Cliff said. It had already taken thirty minutes for them to get through security and get to the gates of Terminal C. "We'll have to high-tail it."

"What's that word?"

"High-tail. You've never heard of it?"

"I've heard of it. I've just never heard you say it."

The train opened and they emptied into the terminal. They raced up the stairs and sprinted down to Gate 23.

The door was closed.

Cliff could see the plane backing up from the gate.

"Dang it!" he said. "We were so close."

The jetway door opened and the gate agent appeared.

"I'm going to ask her if the Platt's were on the flight," Cliff said.

"I thought you said you needed a warrant."

"Sometimes I get lucky."

He walked up to the counter and showed his badge.

"How can I help you, officer?" the woman said with a tired smile.

Technically, he was a detective. "I'm looking for two passengers. Mr. and Mrs. Robert Platt. Can you tell me if they're on this flight?"

"I'm sorry, sir. I can't without a warrant. Company policy."

Cliff rubbed his hair. Roughly.

He'd expected that response. It wasn't worth arguing with the gate agent. She couldn't do anything about it. Asking for a supervisor would make things worse.

"Thank you," Cliff said.

He walked over to where Julia was standing and put his arm around her. He gave her a gentle hug. They were both still breathing hard.

"Back to square one," Julia said. "What do we do now?"

"Go to Vernon Hills. To the parent's house."

14

"What do we do now?" Julia asked Cliff.

"I'm not sure," he answered.

They were in front of Josef and Emilia Goldman's house in Vernon Hills. They'd pushed the intercom button at the gate several times, and no one answered. It didn't look like anyone was home. They saw no signs of activity.

Julia was noticeably frustrated. Cliff was used to it. Investigations had these kinds of ebbs and flows. People weren't home. Witnesses didn't return phone calls. Suspects went into hiding.

"We're always a step behind Robert Platt," Julia said with disdain in her voice. She was clearly convinced he killed his wife.

Cliff wasn't sure. He'd been a detective long enough to resist the urge to jump to conclusions. One of the biggest mistakes an investigator could make was becoming too focused on one suspect. Tunnel vision could cause you to miss the other clues that weren't as obvious. While all the evidence pointed to Sylvia being the dead woman, he had no actual proof.

He also had zero evidence that Robert killed her. Other than the fact that he hadn't reported his wife missing. Cliff didn't even know that. He'd forgotten to check the missing person's reports when he called the office.

"It's frustrating. I know," Cliff said.

"If only we'd gotten to the airport ten minutes earlier."

"Or the hotel an hour earlier this morning. Before he checked out."

"Water under the bridge, so to speak," Julia said. "What do you always say? Worry about the things you can control. Not the things you can't. Good advice. I guess we should just wait. Someone will show up soon. Most people are just getting off work."

While Julia's words were meant to be supportive, they caused a bolt of anger to shoot through his heart. Not at her. At himself. Two things were nagging him. One was that he didn't knock the second time on the door of the honeymoon suite the night before. He should've. The husband's behavior had been unusual, to say the least. Criminal, if his wife wasn't in the suite.

The second thing bothering him was that today was his wife's birthday. The last thing he wanted to do was to have her sit on a stakeout. He'd done it many times and knew it could be a waste of time. They could sit there for hours for nothing.

If Robert killed his wife, he wouldn't show up at her parent's house. That much was for sure.

Who knew if and when the parents would get home?

They should leave, and he should take his beautiful wife to a nice dinner. Give her the ring he had hidden in his closet at home along with the sappy birthday card. They could finish what they started earlier that afternoon.

What Julia said next floored him.

"I say we go to the morgue," she said.

"What are you talking about?"

"I want to see the woman. I can tell you if she's Sylvia Platt."

Cliff was wrong. A few minutes ago, he thought the last thing he wanted to do was sit with Julia for hours on a stakeout. No. Taking her to the morgue was the last thing he wanted to do with her. By far.

***

City morgue

"I can't believe you talked me into this," Cliff said.

"It's a good idea. We have to know if she's Sylvia."

That's the only reason Cliff agreed to it. It was a good idea. He'd already planned on doing it himself. Take another look at the dead woman. Compare her to the picture on the internet. Study the features more closely. The coroner could tell him the dead woman's height and weight. Her eye color. He could compare the information to the driver's license.

His hesitancy was because Julia had no idea what she was getting into.

Cliff had been to the morgue dozens of times and still hadn't gotten used to it. Talk about needing to take a shower. After going to the morgue, he felt like he needed to be stripped naked and power washed. Even that wouldn't work. Unless he could somehow wash the images out of his mind.

On the drive over, he tried to prepare her for what it was like, knowing he couldn't possibly paint the entire picture. The morgue was something you had to experience to really know what you were in for.

As soon as they walked inside the newly remodeled building, Julia's demeanor completely changed. Walking up the steps to the entrance, she was rushing. Excited. Like she was about to go to a museum or an amusement park.

Once inside, she almost stopped in her tracks. The smile left her face. She looked up at the ceiling and then in every direction.

She felt it.

He could tell.

The ominous cloud of death. The coldness. The floors were marble, and the entryway was void of furniture. A couple of paintings lined the walls. Former city coroners. A portrait of the mayor of the city. Their steps echoed through the high ceilings. Bouncing off the walls and back in their faces.

"This place is creepy," Julia said barely above a whisper.

It had the feeling of a funeral home. Cliff had never been in an embalmment room, but imagined this building had that feel, times ten. He could smell chemicals. It wasn't actually burning his eyes and nose, but it felt like it.

"We don't have to do this," Cliff said.

"I'm okay," Julia said.

Cliff hesitated. He suddenly had a very strong feeling that this wasn't a good idea. He'd felt it on the drive over. Now the feeling was overwhelming. Something was tugging at him, telling him to get out of there as fast as possible.

Julia grabbed his hand and began pulling him forward.

"Don't worry about me. I can do this. Where do we go?"

"To the elevator. We go down to the basement."

Once they exited the elevator, they were hit by a rush of cold air. Julia shivered.

He started to take his jacket off and put it over her shoulders but wanted to maintain his professionalism. The employees of the morgue didn't need to know who Julia was or that they had a personal relationship.

The assistant coroner, Patel, was sitting in his office. Cliff had called and given him a heads up that he was coming, so he was expecting them. He waved, set down the file in his hand and walked out of his office toward them.

"Hello, detective," Patel said.

"How are you doing? I hear business is booming."

Cliff had gotten an alert that Chicago had twenty-five murders the night before. Eight of them in one incidence of gang violence. The coroner's office was stretched as it was. The morgue was likely overflowing.

"Never a dull moment," Patel said.

"This is Julia," Cliff said.

Patel nodded. He didn't extend his hand. Patel had once told him that he never did because people were freaked out touching hands that were constantly inside dead bodies. He understood it even though it flowed from ignorance. Coroners always wore gloves and meticulously washed their hands dozens of times a day.

"Pleasure to meet you," Julia said.

"You're here to see the Jane Doe from the hotel," Patel said. A mix of a statement and a question.

"Do you have any information for me?" Cliff asked.

Patel laughed sarcastically. "Not hardly. We just got her yesterday. We're backed up. We picked up eight gang members last night. All gunned down. I shouldn't even be here this late."

"I appreciate you staying to help us."

Patel nodded. "Ms. Julia. Do you know why the morgue is so busy?"

"No. Why?"

"People are dying to get in here."

Julia gave him the obligatory laugh as did Cliff. He'd heard the joke several times before. Patel probably told it to most new visitors.

"Patel, did you hear about the layoffs at the county morgue?" Cliff asked.

"They're really cutting coroners," he responded.

He'd probably heard all the jokes. It did seem to ease the tension somewhat. Julia's shoulders lowered slightly. She still had a terrified look on her face. Her eyes were wider than he'd ever seen them.

"Everyone needs to put on masks," Patel said.

On the wall were several. Patel's was around his neck. Cliff handed Julia one and slipped one on himself. Then they walked into the room. More of an oversized ice box than anything else. Where the bodies were held was kept at a temperature slightly above freezing. Thirty-six to thirty-nine degrees. Rows of tables filled the room. White sheets covered what were the obvious forms of bodies.

Patel walked halfway down the left row. He checked the clipboard attached to the portable cold steel slabs. Along both sides of the walls were steel, drawer-like slots that held bodies that could be pulled out of the wall.

Several bodies were piled up in body bags in a corner. Probably from the gang shooting.

Patel checked the clipboard and then pulled back the sheet, so the toe was showing. He compared the tag on the toe with his clipboard.

"This is her. She was brought in yesterday morning. From the Regency Hotel. Female. Approximate age thirty to thirty-five. Blonde hair."

"That's her," Cliff said. "We want to try and make an identification from a picture. Maybe we can put a name on that clipboard."

Patel walked to the front and lifted the sheet.

Julia gasped.

The woman looked worse than Cliff remembered. He knew the side of her face was caved in. But the other side of her face was so swollen and purple, it would make identifying her from her facial features next to impossible.

Julia moved in closer and held her phone out and next to the body to compare the picture that was on her screen. Her hand was shaking.

"What do you think?" Cliff asked her.

"The hair is the same color, but not the same length. Or the same style."

"Let me see."

He took the phone from her hand and stared at the engagement photo. The head size seemed similar, although Jane Doe's head was more prominent. Probably from swelling and fluid build-up in the brain.

The hair in the picture was noticeably different. Longer. Not as blonde. It didn't flip up on the sides.

"Do you think it's her?" Julia asked. Her face was as white as the sheet on the body.

"I'm not sure," Cliff replied.

"Me either," Julia said. "I thought I would be. Now I'm fifty-fifty. Maybe sixty-forty."

"Which direction?"

"Sixty-forty that it's her. The hair is different, but the features are similar. But it's hard to say in her condition."

Patel stood perfectly still, holding the sheet. He'd probably done this many times before, although the morgue had a viewing room for next of kin to identify a body. The normal populace wouldn't be allowed inside this room.

"We're done," Cliff said to Patel.

He carefully placed the sheet back over her head.

"Let me know when you get more information," Cliff said. "I'd like to know her height and weight. And the color of her eyes."

Cliff wanted to compare that to the driver's license. The information wouldn't confirm beyond a shadow of a doubt that it was the same girl, but it could exclude her. If the measurements were significantly off, that'd make it impossible for it to be the same woman. Identical would be nearly conclusive, even though Cliff as a detective, always had to consider the possibility of coincidences.

"Thank you, Patel," Cliff said.

"Yes. Thank you," Julia said.

They began to walk back to the exit.

Julia suddenly stopped in her tracks.

Her mouth gaped open. Then she burst into tears.

"What is it?" Cliff asked.

Julia buried her head in her hands.

Then Cliff remembered.

Rita.

The first time he saw Rita was in this room. She was lying on the table. The last one on the right.

Julia struggled to regain her composure. Tears streamed down her face. "This was where they brought Rita. Wasn't it?"

Cliff nodded.

He now knew what the nagging voice in his head was all about. That voice was now screaming at him. Why hadn't he listened and not brought Julia to the morgue?

They hadn't been able to positively identify the woman, and he'd just opened a horrible wound inside his wife.

And on her birthday, no less.

15

Based on the gloomy mood and painfully slow-moving conversation, an observer would never guess that Cliff and Julia were celebrating her birthday.

Both of them were mostly pushing the fancy, high-priced Italian food around their plates between bites. They'd split a dish. Not because of the price but because neither of them had an appetite.

What did he expect?

Most people would have a hard time enjoying a fifty-dollar-a-plate dinner immediately after visiting the morgue. Even if they didn't have the personal connection like Cliff and Julia had with Rita.

Cliff was kicking himself for taking his wife there. He'd always tried to shelter her from his work. She never seemed that interested. Supportive, but they had their independent work lives, and they never really intersected.

When they first started dating, Cliff didn't think it would last. He was afraid that he'd always remind Julia of her sister. They'd somehow gotten past it. Now he had screwed it up by reminding her of the connection. When Julia brought up going to the morgue, Cliff hadn't even thought about the fact that Rita had been there. It never occurred to him.

Stupid.

He had to make the best of a bad situation. Try and salvage his wife's birthday. So, he raised his glass of water and made a toast.

"To the most beautiful woman in the room," he said.

Julia lifted her glass of red wine in the air and smiled faintly.

Cliff added, "To the prettiest woman in all of Chicago. No! The World. No! The universe." He thrust his glass high in the air as he said it.

They clinked glasses, and each took a drink.

"I'm not sure I should drink to a lie," Julia said, twisting her lips into a frown.

"It's not a lie."

"Have you seen all the women in the universe?" Julia asked.

"Not all of them."

"Then how do you know I'm the prettiest?" She had a sly smirk when she said it.

"I've seen *Star Trek* and *Lost in Space*," Cliff retorted. "Do you remember Wioslea from Star Wars?"

"No!" she answered with emphasis like of course she hadn't. "I don't remember that character."

Cliff was a bit of a *Star Wars* junkie growing up. He liked everything about Sci-Fi.

"She's the woman... if you could call her that, who bought Luke's land speeder so he could afford to buy the Millennium Falcon. Do you remember her now? She had an oval head, a long neck, and twelve eyes on the antennae. You're definitely prettier than her."

"Sounds like I might be prettier than... what was her name?"

"Wioslea."

"How do you spell that?"

He spelled it out for her. Then added, "She's a Vuvrian."

Julia smiled. "Aren't you embarrassed to know all of that?"

He'd told Julia about his obsession when they were dating. She'd even given him a *Star Wars* action figure for his birthday earlier in the year. It sat on his desk at work. Not because he liked it. The figurine wasn't a collectible. A cheap knock-off. But it was there because his wife had given it to him. A thoughtful gift that he cherished.

He wouldn't trade it for the most expensive *Star Wars* collectible. Not that he collected them.

"I like knowing things other people don't know," Cliff answered.

Julia shrugged her shoulders. Neither of them said anything for nearly a minute. The diversion had helped ease the tension somewhat as they both took substantial bites of their food.

"Vuvrians are an insectoid people," Cliff blurted out.

This time Julia laughed out loud. She'd just taken a drink of wine, and a few drops escaped her mouth and slid down her chin. She embarrassingly grabbed her napkin and dabbed at it.

"I was hoping we'd get through the evening without you throwing out one of your strange words," Julia said.

"I assume you're referring to the whole willy-nilly, okey-dokey smokey conversation we had earlier today. Do I need to remind you that you started it?"

"I did not. You started it by saying traipsing."

"Oh yeah. That's right. I forgot."

"Like I said, I'd hoped we would get through the evening without you throwing out words like Vuvrians and discussing people who look like insects."

"What were the odds that that would happen?" Cliff quipped.

"Not good," Julia admitted. "That'd be too much to ask of you."

She raised her glass and made a toast to mock him. "To my extremely weird husband."

"I'll drink to that," Cliff said in a fake drunken voice. Which caused them both to laugh heartily again.

After that came another minute of awkward silence, as the conversation lost momentum and ground to a halt.

"I'm sorry I ruined your birthday," Cliff blurted out, not thinking through where the conversation might lead.

Julia immediately perked up.

"You didn't ruin my birthday! I'm having a wonderful time. This food is delicious. So is the company."

"I could've made it better."

"By not talking about Vuvrians!" Julia smiled widely so he'd know she was kidding.

"We've been married for a year now," Cliff said. "We've run out of things to talk about."

Julia roughly rubbed her eyes.

"Tell me about it. It's my birthday. I can't believe I'm a year older. We're old fuddy-duddies!"

Julia had a playful grin on her face now. It warmed his heart. Maybe his attempt to get them both out of the funk again worked.

"Now look who is using strange words."

"You're rubbing off on me."

"You're never allowed to use that word again!" Cliff said.

"I tell you what word should be banned."

"What's that?"

"Whatever?"

"Yes! I hate it when people say that."

"Me too. It's so dismissive. Like the person isn't even willing to make an effort to refute what you said."

"I agree. But... It is what it is!"

"That's another one!" Julia giggled. The wine was kicking in. "There should be a law banning that phrase from the English language."

"I agree! I have another saying that should be banned."

"Let's hear it."

Julia started to take another sip but stopped herself. Probably in case he said something else that was funny.

"No worries," Cliff said. He could feel the wide smile on his face.

"Yes! Does anyone speak in complete sentences anymore?"

"I blame it on text messages. Everything's abbreviated. In code. It's carried over to our conversations."

"What are they teaching kids in school?" Julia said with emphasis.

"The only word they're teaching them is the word like."

"I know! Tell me about it. Like, like, like. Every other word out of a teenager's mouth is like."

"Not just teenagers. Adults are just as bad."

Julia got a silly grin on her face as she clearly had something she wanted to say. Something funny. "I read that a couple had a baby.

The toddler's first word was like. Not mommy or daddy. Like. Can you believe that?"

"I don't believe that because you made it up," Cliff said.

He was trained to tell when someone was lying. Julia was kidding. Not lying. But she wasn't good at telling fibs. She should never play poker.

"You're right. I was kidding. How did you know?"

"I always know when you're lying. It's written all over your face. I can see it in your eyes."

"Remind me to never lie to you?"

"Why do I need to remind you?"

"Maybe if I had a face like a Vuvrian, you wouldn't know I was lying. If I had twelve eyes, you wouldn't know which one to look into."

Julia put two fingers on her head and moved them back and forth like they were insect antennae.

Cliff had just taken a drink and had to press his lips shut to keep from spewing out his drink.

That cracked Julia up as well and she struggled with laughing so hard she'd make a scene. People at nearby tables were looking at them.

Cliff felt a lot of the tension leave his shoulders and neck. The sudden burst of energy from the stimulating conversation made him realize how tired he was. He'd barely slept the night before. Today had been an extremely emotional day. This evening was finally transitioning to what it was meant to be. Fun and relaxing.

They both began to eat in earnest. Taking bigger bites. Julia ordered a second glass of wine. Cliff rarely drank and only at home. A detective was always on call. Even on his day off. Cliff always carried his badge and gun. He was required to. He never knew when a dangerous situation might present itself. If he ever had to discharge a gun, he didn't want alcohol to be in his system.

The conversation stalled because they were eating. Not because they had sunk back into a depression. Cliff couldn't wait to get home and give Julia her ring. That'd hopefully salvage what had been an eventful, if not horrendous, day. He made a mental note not to put a visit to a graveyard and morgue on a birthday things-to-do list.

Julia suddenly sat down on her fork, and the look on her face turned serious. Her entire face tightened, and her shoulders stiffened.

"I was thinking about the lady at the morgue," she said. Not soberly, but in a steady voice.

"Julia. I don't think we should talk about it."

She ignored him. "Sylvia Platt was just married. Yesterday. What do women do on their wedding day? Or the day before?"

"What?" Cliff asked after realizing there was no way to change the subject.

"They get their hair done."

"I suppose."

"They do. I did. My hair looked different at our wedding than it did on our engagement announcement."

He saw an opening to change the subject.

"We had an engagement announcement?"

"Of course. Don't you remember?"

He did, but he had successfully changed the subject, so he decided to run with it. As a detective, he was very skillful at lying. He never lied to Julia unless it was harmless and for a purpose. Which this was.

"Was it in the paper?" Cliff asked in an inquisitive voice.

"Yes. I can't believe you don't remember. Do you remember taking our engagement pictures? At Lurie Garden."

"I remember that. I didn't know you put our picture in the paper."

Julia let out a sigh.

"I'll show you when we get home."

"I have something to show you at home as well," Cliff said.

"What?"

"It's a surprise. I got you a present."

"You shouldn't have! I thought this dinner was my present."

"No. It's just the appetizer."

"An expensive appetizer."

Cliff got the attention of the waiter and asked for the check. The bill was nearly a hundred dollars after tip. They'd been charged $50.00 plus fifteen for a shared meal. Salad was extra and they were charged for the two glasses of wine.

It didn't matter. Julia was worth it.

***

They got home, and Cliff excused himself for a minute while Julia looked for their engagement announcement. Coming back downstairs, Julia was standing there with the newspaper clipping and proved to Cliff that she was right. He knew she was. He was surprised at how quickly she found it. Impressive.

"That didn't take you long to find," Cliff said.

He had a small box in his hand, and he gave it to Julia.

"You found that, and I found this," he said.

She opened it. Then let out a loud gasp.

"You remembered!" she said exuberantly. Then she threw her arms around his neck and squeezed tightly and gave him a big kiss.

They'd been walking downtown back when they were dating. They'd gone into a jewelry store just for fun. Julia tried on rings showing Cliff what she liked. She gravitated toward one particular ring. Had gushed over it. Cliff put the picture of her and the ring in his memory vault. He decided then and there that he was going to buy her that ring someday. He was just waiting for the right occasion.

He was relieved when he went back to the store, and they still had it. Or one like it.

Julia put the ring on her finger.

It fit perfectly.

Seeing her wearing the ring felt good to Cliff. He'd somehow been able to redeem the day and made it special. Hopefully, she'd remember it for the ring she was enamored with and not the other gruesome parts of the day. Things he should've sheltered her from. He always had until today. He wouldn't make that mistake again.

"Let's go upstairs," Julia said seductively. "In case you've forgotten, we have unfinished business. I'm going to ravage you."

She didn't have to ask twice.

Cliff went upstairs and took his third shower of the day. To wash the morgue off of him.

After the shower, they got into bed and snuggled. Didn't get to things right away. They both needed to relax. Julia laid her head on his chest. He could feel her breathing.

After a couple of minutes, Cliff felt a slight dampness on his shoulder and realized Julia was crying. He was afraid to ask why. Better to just try and comfort her than to talk about it.

"I love my ring," she said softly.

"I'm glad. I love you, honey," he said.

"I love you too."

"Happy birthday."

"Thank you."

Julia sat up and looked deep into Cliff's eyes. He could see her stained cheeks and her still watery eyes. Behind it all, he could see her love for him.

She kissed him. Gently at first. Then harder. Deeper.

The emotion of the day engulfed them. Like an avalanche on a mountain overwhelms everything in its path.

Their lovemaking was intense. Emotional. Passionate. Unlike anything they'd ever experienced before.

Unexpected.

Somehow, surprisingly, and against all odds the events of the day had brought them closer together.

16

White Sands Resort
The British Virgin Islands
Virgin Gorda

When Robert Platt arrived at *White Sands Resort*, he knew it would be a luxurious five-star resort in the incredibly gorgeous Virgin Gorda. He had no idea how fancy it would actually be. The couple were booked into the Diamond Suite. A four thousand dollar a night villa right on the beach.

He checked into the hotel suite reserved for Mr. and Mrs. Platt. The hotel clerk said nothing about him arriving alone, nor were any questions asked. He followed the bellman who handled their bags and carried the key card to open the door. The uniformed man deposited the luggage inside the suite. Robert was feeling good and tipped him generously and went to unpack his bags. He stowed Sylvia's bags in the closet.

Then allowed himself to take a deep breath. He made it. The flight had been stressful. He'd heard his name announced over the intercom at the airport right before boarding. The gate agent didn't hear the announcement or didn't remember his name on the reservation. When he took his seat on the plane, he prepared himself for the inevitability that he was going to be hauled out of the plane and dragged off to jail. When it didn't happen, and the doors were closed and the flight departed, he was certain law enforcement would be at his arrival gate to meet him in St. Thomas.

To his shock, no one was there. He had escaped Chicago and was safely several thousand miles away. Eventually, he'd get a phone call and be told to return to Chicago immediately. In the meantime, he intended to enjoy the luxurious suite for as long as he could. Courtesy of Sylvia's father, Mr. Josef Goldman. The biggest jerk on the planet.

After he landed in St. Thomas, the trip to the hotel had been laborious. He was met by a driver in the airport with a placard reading, Mr. & Mrs. Platt. The driver made no mention of him being by himself as he took him to the marina, where he caught a boat to the resort.

Fortunately, he had someone handling the bags from the moment he got off the plane until they were unloaded in his suite.

Robert plopped down on the bed and considered stripping off his clothes and going right to sleep. But he needed a drink. He had three on the plane, but they'd worn off.

He changed into shorts, a t-shirt, and flip-flops. He felt more relaxed already and knew a few cocktails would be just what he needed to help him relax further. Once dressed, he set out to find the outdoor bar that the front desk said was on the beach area off the pool.

The bar was still open even though it was nearing midnight. He was a bit surprised but then remembered that he was in paradise. A resort this extraordinary would make sure its guests could access nearly anything they desired at most any hour.

He sat down on a stool at the bar, ordered a whiskey sour, and took in his surroundings. The moon shimmered over the water, and a local reggae band blasted out tunes to a dance floor of drunk patrons having a good time. Usually, he'd be out there in the middle of them, but he was too tired.

Killing his wife and getting out of town had been downright exhausting.

He quickly downed his drink and ordered another.

"Long day?" he heard a woman's voice say.

Robert looked up and to his left toward the sound of the sexy voice. An above-average-looking woman was the source of the words.

He hadn't noticed her because another guy had been sitting in between them. The man had left. She appeared to be alone.

"You don't know the half of it," Robert said.

The thought of his wife flying off the balcony came to mind. He quickly tamped it down.

The image reminded him of something though.

His ring.

He lowered his hand under the bar and slipped the wedding ring off his finger and stuffed it in his pocket. Then turned slightly to the side to get a better look at the girl.

Blonde hair. Like Sylvia. More sandy blonde, though. Shoulder length. A little longer than Sylvia's. Freckles. Hot body. Slim. Medium height. Surgically enhanced breasts that bulged out of her tight fitting shirt.

"Can I buy you a drink?" Robert asked.

As he said it, the bartender set a drink down in front of her.

"I've got one," she said, pointing to it.

"Can I pay for your drink?" he asked.

He suddenly didn't feel tired at all.

"Maybe the next one," she said.

"Why maybe?"

"I have to see if I like you."

"I think I'll be buying you a drink in no time."

Robert stood up and moved down to the stool next to her.

He held out his hand. "I'm Bob."

Better not to use his real name. But one he would answer to.

"I'm Angel."

"Yes, you are," Robert said, grinning slyly.

The conversation went well. Angel nursed her drink while they made idle small talk. By the time she finished it, Robert was burning with desire.

She took the last sip and set it down on the counter.

"Would you like another one?" Robert asked.

"I'd better not," she said.

She motioned for the waiter to bring her a check.

"Let me pay for it," Robert said.

He pulled out his wallet. He had small bills but pulled out a wad of hundreds. And flipped through them. For Angel's benefit. Impressing her with a wad of cash could work in his favor. Then he decided to charge it to his room. Let Sylvia's dad pay for it.

The thought brought a smile to his face, which he could see in the mirror behind the bar. It was all he could do to hold back his laughter. Sylvia's dad was helping him pick up a girl. More irony.

"Put these charges on my room," he told the waiter. "I'm in the Diamond Suite."

"Ooh," Angel moaned seductively. "I'm impressed. That's the nicest villa in the resort."

"Would you like to see it?"

"Do I look like the kind of girl who'd go back to the hotel room of a guy she just met?"

"I'm hoping you are."

She stood up from the stool and said, "You're right. I am. Let's go."

They walked along the beach then took the trail to the Diamond Suite. The gentle lapping waves serenaded them along the way.

He took her hand and led her up to the back door and entered the code.

She hesitated.

"How do I know you're not a killer or someone who is going to take advantage of me?" she said.

Robert laughed nervously.

"I'm not a killer. But I do intend to take advantage of you."

And he did. Twice.

***

When Robert woke up the next morning, Angel wasn't there. At first, he panicked. Did she rob him? Did she take all the money out of his wallet? He jumped out of bed and started to take inventory of the small number of things he brought with him on the trip.

He breathed a huge sigh of relief when he found nothing was missing. Then was chastising himself for his carelessness. Last night was terrific but reckless. He was supposed to be the jilted, depressed

CLIFF HANGERS: MR. AND MRS. PLATT

husband on his honeymoon without his wife. Picking up a woman at a bar and bringing her back to his room didn't fit the persona he was trying to portray.

He came up with an excuse. If surveillance tapes were ever checked, he would claim he was so despondent he took solace in another woman's arms. Who could fault him for that when his wife didn't show up for their honeymoon? A momentary weakness on his part. Certainly not the actions of a murderer.

Robert was glad Angel was gone. A complication out of his life. Fun while it lasted.

He pulled out his phone and got back to following his plan. He dialed Sylvia's cell phone number which was still in one of her bags in the closet of the suite.

"Sylvia, it's Robert," he said sternly. "I'm at the hotel on the island. It's beautiful. Obviously, you're not coming. Does that mean things are over between us? I don't understand what I did to deserve this. You're ripping my heart out. And you don't even care. Is there someone else?"

Robert held the phone out from his mouth and forced back a smile. Another bit of irony considering what happened the night before in the bed where he was sitting.

He let his voice crack and resumed leaving the message. "That's all I can think of. You met someone else. I hope you're happy!"

A knock on the door startled him. He heard his name. Bob. Robert quickly hung up the phone.

He went to the door. Angel was standing there holding two cups of coffee and a bag.

"Good morning, sleepyhead," she said. "I got us coffee and some Danishes."

She kissed him on the cheek as she entered the suite.

They sat in bed and Robert inhaled his decadent sweet roll. Then they started up where they'd left off the night before.

When they finished Angel asked, "What do you want to do today?"

The itinerary called for Robert and Sylvia to go on a boat and do some snorkeling on an island. Robert hadn't even thought through what he was going to do.

She must've sensed his confusion.

"I'm sorry. That's presumptive of me," she said. "I was hoping I wasn't just a one-night stand."

Robert hesitated again. Then he decided it was worth the risk. He was more than two thousand miles from Chicago. No detective was ever going to travel to Virgin Gorda to investigate him. Even if they did, who would remember him? This wasn't some quaint, overpriced bed and breakfast. This was a vast audacious five-star hotel. The number of rooms had to be in the hundreds. He was just one guest. The hotel thought he was there with his wife on their honeymoon.

As long as Angel didn't find out he was married, he'd be fine.

Angel stood up to leave. Clearly hurt.

Robert held out his hand to stop her. "I hadn't thought beyond last night. We were having fun. I didn't know you were expecting more."

"I'm not. I'll go."

"I don't want you to go. Stay. How would you like to go on an excursion? On a boat? Do you snorkel?"

"Of course. That would be unbelievable."

She'd said the night before that she was staying at the hotel for seven nights. She'd been there for two. Angel was a fitness instructor at a gym in New Mexico. She was single. Vacationing by herself. As a treat. She'd won the lottery.

Dollar signs flashed into Robert's head when she said she'd won the lottery.

Then she clarified. "I won ten thousand dollars on a scratch-off ticket. Just enough to pay for a mind-blowing vacation. I couldn't believe my luck. I'm not usually the luckiest person but when I saw the numbers come up, I knew exactly what I wanted to do with the money. I've never been on a trip like this in my entire life. Everything about this place feels like a forbidden garden. So luxurious. I mean, my room isn't nearly as nice as yours but it's the nicest hotel I've ever stayed at in my entire life."

"So, it's settled," Robert said. "You'll spend the day with me?"

"I'd love to," Angel beamed with a smile that went from ear-to-ear.

"I'm going to jump in the shower," Robert said. "Then we'll go by the concierge and get all the details for our excursion. We'll find out the time. Where to go. Those kinds of things."

The water had barely gotten hot when Angel got in the shower with him. Robert was ecstatic. Sylvia would've never done anything like that. Even on their honeymoon. She was cold and unaffectionate. Manipulative and condescending. Like she thought she was better than Robert. He could imagine her getting even colder after they were married. After she had him hooked, he imagined they would never have sex again other than to try to conceive a kid.

Not Angel. Her sexual openness was the opposite of Sylvia in every way. Robert had done his fair share of exploration with a lot of girls. Angel was one of the best he'd ever been with.

This was going to be the best honeymoon ever!

17

Chicago

Julia didn't sleep well the night before. She couldn't get the dead woman in the morgue's image out of her head. Even if the woman's body hadn't been in such horrible shape, Julia would've had a hard time scrubbing that horrible place out of her brain. Add that her sister had been lying there on that cold hard slab only two years ago. They say twins have a special bond that normal brothers and sisters don't have. Intuitively. Rita wasn't just a twin. She was an identical triplet. Julia felt the close bond with Anna as well.

Part of the reason Julia couldn't get the woman in the morgue's image out of her mind was because she kept comparing her to the picture in the newspaper. Trying to find some resemblance. After hours of thinking about it she had come to a conclusion.

It was Sylvia Platt.

It had to be.

She was sure of it.

As the minutes and hours ticked by in the dead of night, Julia became convinced that the woman in the morgue was indeed the bride staying in the honeymoon suite. Who else could she be? Julia wasn't an accomplished detective like her husband, but all evidence pointed to it being Sylvia. After a while, she could almost see Sylvia's face in the battered woman. She was hoping her mind wasn't playing tricks on her.

The features matched. The size of the head was the same. The shape of the chin. What was left of it anyway. The woman's nose had been crushed and was hanging limp to the side, but it seemed to fit the pretty little nose of the young woman in the picture. The eyebrow and eye on the right side were pretty much intact. They were distinctly similar to the girl in the engagement announcement. If it weren't so swollen and purple, they would've been able to tell for sure.

But she knew it was Sylvia.

Julia had a gut feeling about it. Her instincts weren't always right, but she relied on them in her line of work every day. She ran a women's shelter for girls and women of all ages who had been abused. She dealt with violence on a daily basis. The young girls and women that came to her for safety and care had been in horrible situations. Many were lucky to get out at all. And when some showed up on the doorstep of her shelter, she often wondered how they made it that far, how they were still alive.

This wasn't the first time she'd seen a battered and bruised face. Not even the first time she'd seen a dead body.

She didn't know how Cliff did it. He saw dead bodies every day. If not every day, at least once or twice a week. She had a new appreciation for what he did for a living. In the back of her mind, she knew he investigated murders. Frequently visited the morgue. But she had no idea the effect those things could have on a person's psyche. She thought her job was bad. Cliff's job was way worse. She'd be a lot more considerate of him in the future.

When he came home and said he'd had a bad day, she'd have a better idea what that meant. He didn't complain often. He had the fortitude of a Viking. When he did, she'd know it had to have been really bad for him to say something. If and when that time came, and it would, she'd do everything she could to comfort him.

That new resolve started that morning. Julia made him breakfast consisting of coffee, scrambled eggs with bacon, and toast with grape jelly. His favorite. She even packed him a lunch with a mid-morning snack and a piece of fruit. Along with a note.

When she kissed him goodbye, and he left for work, she went into the office and logged onto their computer. Careful to do it in privacy mode so Cliff wouldn't know she had done so.

She didn't like to go behind his back, but this had been nagging her, and she wanted more information. With a bit of amateur sleuthing, she might find something that could help track down Robert Platt, and if she got lucky, his wife. She might even come across a clue that would help her husband solve the case. Make his job easier. He already had enough pressure.

First, she checked her work emails and found nothing noteworthy. Since it was her birthday, she'd taken a few personal days. She hadn't expected to be spending them this way. Actually, this was exactly what she wanted to do. The task was daunting. She was discovering firsthand how difficult it could be to solve a case. And how invigorating it was to search for clues.

After logging out of her emails, she searched Virgin Gorda. She started with the time zone. The island was two hours ahead of them. That meant it was 10:29 in the morning on the island.

A map gave her the lay of the land. The island was bigger than the other islands in the British Island chain and close to St. John in the US Virgin Islands. She hadn't realized they were so close or that there were so many islands in the Caribbean.

Julia did a search for hotels through a popular website. There were only nine. Two that seemed high-end enough for the taste of a couple who had spent their wedding night in the honeymoon suite of the *Regency Hotel* in downtown Chicago.

She opened the desk drawer and pulled out a writing pad. Then wrote the two numbers down on the pad. That's where she would start.

Anxiety began to rise up inside of her when she took her cell phone out of her pocket.

Her palms were sweaty.

I can't believe I'm going to do this.

Without asking Cliff. He'd be furious if he knew what she was planning. But her curiosity was getting the best of her. She had to know. Did the Platts have reservations in Virgin Gorda? Did anyone check-in? Would the hotel give her that information?

If her planned work, they would.

Julia dialed the first number.

"I'd like Mr. & Mrs. Platt's room, please," she said nervously to the perky voice on the other end of the line.

"One moment, please."

Her heart started pounding in her chest to the point she could hear it in her ears. Did she find the couple already?

The lady came back on the line. "We don't have anyone by that name staying in our resort."

Julia's heart sank a notch, but she suddenly felt a sense of relief. Like she'd dodged a bullet somehow. This might not be such a good idea. What if Robert had answered the phone? Or Sylvia?

"Okay. Thank you. I'm sorry to bother you."

Julia hung up and dialed the second number right away. Without thinking. If she hadn't, she probably would've backed out.

Another perky voice answered on the first ring. This lady had a British accent.

"Mr. Robert Platt's room," Julia said.

"One moment, please."

Music began playing as she went on hold.

A few seconds later, she heard ringing. The urge to hang up was overwhelming. She fought it off.

It kept ringing. At the other hotel, it rang a few times then went back to the front desk. After about ten rings, the lady at the front desk did come back on the line.

"I'm sorry. There's no answer in their room. Would you like to leave a message?"

Julia's heart skipped a beat. She had confirmation. Someone checked into their room. Robert? Both of them? She had to know.

"Miss, are you there?" the lady asked Julia. "Would you like to leave a message?"

She had forgotten to answer the first time.

"No, thank you."

Before the lady could hang up, Julia said, "I'd like to send Mr. and Mrs. Platt a gift. They're friends of mine and are on their honeymoon. How would I do that?"

"I can connect you to the concierge. One moment, please."

Julia had to steady her nerves to keep her hands from shaking. She stood up from the desk and started pacing.

The phone was ringing.

"Concierge. How may I be of service?"

The point of no return.

"I'm calling about one of your guests. Mr. and Mrs. Platt. I'd like to surprise them with a gift. They're on their honeymoon. The front desk said you would tell me how to do that."

"Yes. Mr. and Mrs. Platt. A wonderful couple. They were just here at the desk."

Julia almost dropped the phone.

"Were both of them there? Mrs. Platt too?"

"Why yes. Pretty blonde lady."

Julia couldn't believe the words she was hearing.

"Did she seem okay?"

Did she look dead?

Julia forced back the second question that had popped in her head.

"Why yes. She was fine," the woman said. "They were cute together. Couldn't keep their hands off each other. I arranged their itinerary this morning. A private boat is taking them to an island for a day of snorkeling. They were both quite thrilled with the idea of a day of sun, fun, boating, and snorkeling. And of course, they will have a lovely variety of food and drinks. Why do you ask if the young lady was there?"

Julia had to think of something. An idea came to her.

"When they left the states, she was feeling under the weather. I'm glad to hear she's feeling better. I had hoped she wasn't holed up in her room for her entire honeymoon. That would be a shame."

"Some people do find the effort to travel here quite taxing, but she looked fine to me and ready for one of our lovely excursions. They will have a wonderful time."

"I'm glad to hear she's feeling better. It sounds like they will have a wonderful time," Julia said. It took everything she had to keep her voice from cracking and what little mental energy she had left after her nearly sleepless night to keep from saying the wrong thing.

"Could I send a gift to their room?" she asked.

"That sounds wonderful. What did you have in mind?"

"Can I do it anonymously?"

"Of course," the concierge replied.

"I'd like to send them a bottle of champagne. Is that possible?"

"I think that would be simply marvelous."

The woman had a charming demeanor. Julia could see why she got a job as a concierge.

"Thank you so much. I appreciate your help."

"I can arrange it, madam. It's no problem," the concierge said. "Along with a note. Oh, my apologies. No note. I understand that you wish to remain anonymous. How would you like to pay for it?"

"Let me call you back. I don't have my credit card on me. But thank you so much for your help."

"It's a brilliant idea. Champagne is always a wonderful choice for newlyweds. And who doesn't like that kind of surprise? Call me, and I'll take care of it for you. I'm here until five."

"I will."

Julia hung up the phone. Stunned. How was that possible? She had been sure the woman in the morgue was Sylvia Platt.

But she had just heard from the concierge that Mrs. Platt was in the Virgin Gorda.

Pretty blonde lady, the concierge had said.

Julia stared at the phone in disbelief.

How could she have been so wrong?

18

Cliff woke up surprisingly refreshed. Considering he tossed and turned all night worrying about Julia after the nearly unbelievable way her birthday turned out. Not that it had all been bad. After they got home and he gave her the ring, things turned around and they forgot about the horrendous events of the day. Or at least had a short respite from them.

Better than he could've hoped considering the circumstances. A criminal investigation, a tearful visit to the cemetery, and a trip to the morgue to view a dead body were not the things birthdays were made of.

Cliff was relieved when Julia got up an hour or so after him and came downstairs in good spirits. Better than good. It seemed like the events of the previous day were no longer bothering her. That was a relief

He'd gotten up early to formulate a plan. The identity of Jane Doe in the morgue would become his laser-focus. Once he knew who she was, then he'd figure out what happened to her. If she was murdered, he'd find the murderer and put him behind bars. He was anxious to get this case solved.

He thought he already had it figured out in his mind. The woman was Sylvia Platt. Her husband, Robert, threw her off the balcony of the honeymoon suite. The motive was one thing that continued to bother him. Discover the why and the case was usually easier to solve. This one was complicated by the fact that she died on her wedding night. That almost never happened. Cliff tried to find a similar case on the internet but hadn't found one.

His lieutenant, not to mention the district attorney, would be all on his case to find a motive.

First things first.

At least he had a plan formulated in his mind now. He'd go to the office and start a murder book. Then meet with his lieutenant to fill him in on the details. He'd spent more than an hour that morning making notes. Remembering all the pertinent events, including the interaction with the man in the honeymoon suite. He would leave Julia's involvement out of the murder book for obvious reasons.

Cliff printed out a copy of the Platt's engagement announcement and put it in a file folder along with his notes. Julia was in the kitchen busy preparing something that smelled good. He went in there to see what it was.

"What are you making?" he asked.

"Breakfast for you."

"Aren't you a good wife."

"I even packed you a lunch."

"Keep this up, and I'm going to get spoiled."

"You're already spoiled."

He kissed her when she put the plate in front of him. His breakfast was delicious, and he dug in. He was a lucky man to have such an amazing wife and told her so again.

"Don't worry about the dishes," she said, taking them from him and putting them in the sink.

"Sorry to run off."

He grabbed his keys and left after more kisses and more goodbyes.

"Thank you for such a wonderful breakfast, sweetheart. I love you."

"I love you too. Have a good day."

He left with her in good spirits, and he was in a good mood too. As he drove to his office, he made more plans. After meeting with the lieutenant, he'd go back to Sylvia Platt's parent's house in Vernon Hills. Maybe he'd get lucky, and someone would be home.

After that, his next stop would be the morgue. If the parents or brother were home, he'd ask them to come to the morgue and see if they could identify the woman as their daughter or sister.

If not, he'd ask a deputy coroner technician to weigh the body and measure the height and check the color of the woman's eyes. From that, he could compare it with the driver's license. If it was a match, then he'd assume the woman in the morgue was Sylvia Platt. If not, he could leave the Goldmans and Platts alone and move on to something else.

If he was able to determine that the woman in the morgue was Sylvia, then he'd start a full-court press to find Robert.

Cliff didn't have a chance to work on the murder book when he arrived at the precinct. A note on his desk said to see the lieutenant right away. The lieutenant's door was open, so Cliff headed that way.

John Louth was someone Cliff liked. The lieutenant had only been on the job for six months but had earned Cliff's respect. He was from Detroit and was old school when it came to work ethic. But he was also willing to try new things and accept new ideas and ways of doing police work. Louth was a self-starter and expected the same from his detectives, which was fine by Cliff.

Meetings were few and far between. The lieutenant would rather his detectives were on the streets finding killers than meeting with him for the sake of having meetings. Chicago's crime rate didn't leave room for idle chit-chat or anyone wasting anyone else's time.

Cliff appreciated that and mirrored the lieutenant's approach. He didn't meet with the lieutenant unless he had something to talk to him about.

Today he did have. He needed to bring up the Jane Doe case with the lieutenant, only later in the morning, when he had more information. Since he was meeting with him anyway, Cliff decided he'd better mention it. Especially with the events of the previous evening. The manager at the Regency Hotel hadn't been happy about Cliff waking up the groom. There might be some fallback on him. He wanted Louth to be prepared.

This also could end up being a high-profile case. Especially if the victim was a Jewish girl from a very wealthy family. She was killed at a high-end luxury hotel, wearing very expensive lingerie. Not that Louth cared that the girl's family was rich. He approached every murder with the same off-the-charts tenacity. Louth treated every victim the same regardless of race, sex, or social status. That was another thing Cliff appreciated and respected about Louth.

The lieutenant motioned for him to come in.

Cliff sat down in the chair, so the lieutenant would know he had something important to talk to him about as well.

"What are you working on?" Louth asked.

Cliff pulled out his little black book with the notes, even though he didn't need them. He knew the details by heart.

"A dead woman at the Regency Hotel. Female. Jane Doe. Thirty to thirty-five years of age. Wearing a very expensive nightgown. No suspects at this time."

"Any leads?"

"One thread. It's in the early stages."

"So, you don't even know if she was murdered."

"No sir. She may have fallen or been pushed from a balcony. That's still unconfirmed. But I'm going to presume she was until I know"

The lieutenant cut him off.

"Put that one on the back burner."

"Lieutenant. I need to find out the woman's identity. I have a potential lead. I was going to go by her parents' house."

"It can wait."

"I don't want it to wait. The case is fresh. I want to work on it."

Louth didn't mind his detectives speaking their minds. To a point. But he was still the boss and delegating the cases he felt were more important was up to him.

"It'll still be there tomorrow. I've got something more pressing."

"Okay."

Arguing the point wasn't going to get him anywhere.

"There was a gang related shooting. Eight people are dead."

"I heard about it."

"We have ID'd the suspect. Here's his file."

The lieutenant picked up a file off his desk and handed it to Cliff. He opened it and quickly scanned it.

"Here's the Cliff's notes version." The lieutenant laughed. "No pun intended. You know. Your name is Cliff."

Louth wasn't known for his humor.

The lieutenant continued after Cliff gave him an obligatory laugh. "Anyway. Lavay Lee Hall. Seventeen. No priors."

"A seventeen-year-old kid killed eight gang members? Are you sure you've pegged the right person?"

"He confessed to it. To his girlfriend anyway. She called the police. It's a sad deal. The gang members killed his mother. Accidentally. A drive-by shooting gone bad. They targeted the wrong house. Shot it up with the mother inside. Lavay was there as well. In the back room. His younger brother was killed too. Five years old. Died right next to his mother. Lavay found the bodies. He went berserk. Got a gun from a friend and blasted the eight gang members."

Louth paused.

"Sounds like he did the city of Chicago a favor," Cliff commented casually.

"I don't disagree. But we still have laws to uphold. The judge and jury will decide what to do with him."

"What do you want me to do?"

"The girlfriend told us where he's hiding out. She's worried about him. Says he's armed and not thinking right. I want you to bring him in. The address is in the file."

"Do you want me to take a small army with me?"

"No. That's why I'm giving it to you. Let's take this kid alive. Take backup for sure. Just low-key it."

"Will do."

Cliff stood to leave. Before he was out the door, the lieutenant said, "Go check the missing person's reports. See if anyone reported your Jane Doe missing. That might save you some trouble."

"I will, sir."

He'd already done that. First thing when he got into work. Nothing had come in. He didn't tell the lieutenant, so he'd feel like he was giving Cliff some good advice.

Cliff asked another detective to go to the house with him. Big Al Rollins. A teddy bear who was also tough as nails. He would have sympathy for the young kid but was like the lieutenant. He had to be brought in. If they got in a situation where they needed to talk the kid off the ledge, Big Al could be disarming. The kid might trust him. Not just because he was of the same race, but because Big Al came from the streets. From the same type of neighborhood.

Cliff filled him in on the drive over.

"The kid's supposedly armed and dangerous. He killed eight gang members so we can assume he's proficient with his gun."

"Man. This stinks out the wazoo," Big Al said.

The word, wazoo, caused Cliff to smile. It reminded him of the banter with Julia the day before. He was tempted to start the same conversation with Big Al, but thought better of it, given the solemnity of the task in front of them. They never knew how these things were going to end.

Big Al was deep in thought anyway and was looking through Lavay's file. "This kid had his whole life ahead of him. He's an honors student. He plays football. He holds down a job at a pharmacy delivering drugs. He's been at the job for two years. Nobody gives a kid that much responsibility unless they trust him. And now this has to happen. Makes me wish I could wave a wand and make his problems go away. But we both know that's not the way it's gonna go down."

"I know," Cliff said. "I hate it. They killed his mom and his little brother. I don't know what I would do, but I don't imagine I'd take it sitting down. Especially as a teenager. Anyone could snap."

"When I was his age, I'd have done the same thing. Before I got religion. Jesus changed my life. That got me off the streets. I was a lot more messed up than this kid. I'm lucky I got on the force with my record. A lot of people vouched for me. That's the only reason."

"Let's not give this kid a chance to screw up his life any more than it already has."

"How we gonna play this?"

"I'll go in the front," Cliff said. "You watch the back in case he tries to run. I'll knock on the door. If he answers, I'll try to talk some sense into him."

"Let me go to the front door," Big Al said. "You watch the back. He's more likely to answer if he sees me."

Cliff thought about it and saw the wisdom in it. Big Al had the slightly more dangerous job in that instance. If the kid didn't answer, then Big Al would put his foot through the door and go in with his gun drawn. Cliff would come in from the kid's blind side. Hopefully, things would go well, and the kid would surrender peacefully.

But you never knew. The kid could come running out the back door with his gun blazing and Cliff could be in the crosshairs.

No matter how things shook out, the kid was going to jail. The law says you can't go on a killing spree even if family members were gunned down in your own home. While Cliff didn't blame the kid, the law would probably see it differently. Someone else would decide the kid's fate.

They parked a block away from the house and got in position.

Cliff took up his location by the backdoor. He could see signs of activity inside. It appeared the kid was there, and his girlfriend's intel was good. Hopefully Lavay was alone.

He heard Big Al knock on the front door.

"Lavay. Open up. Chicago P.D."

A shot rang out.

"Dang it," Cliff muttered under his breath.

Then smashed his foot through the locked rear door and entered the back with his gun drawn.

19

Shots fired when Cliff couldn't see what was happening was his worst nightmare. Had he been alone, he would've retreated and called for backup and a negotiating team.

With Big Al inside the house taking the brunt of the fire, Cliff had no choice but to enter, ready to fire his weapon.

He stepped back and threw his weight into a sharp kick that shattered the back door lock. Once inside, he moved stealthily toward the sound of the gunfire and Big Al shouting.

"Chicago P.D. Drop your weapon," Big Al said for a second time, reassuring Cliff that his partner hadn't been hit.

When another shot rang out, and Big Al let out a loud shout, it was clear the situation was escalating, and the kid wasn't surrendering. It'd been a good idea for the two of them to split up. Otherwise, they'd both been the target of the gunshots. As it were, Cliff could sneak up on the kid from his blind side.

Hopefully in the commotion, the seventeen-year-old didn't hear the sound of Cliff breaking in the backdoor. Or if he heard it, he'd be confused and be forced to turn his full attention away from the front door to watch his back.

Cliff was in the kitchen. Off the kitchen was a hallway that Cliff presumed led to the living area where the sounds were coming from. He moved furtively down the narrow corridor with both hands on his gun.

More shots rang out.

Cliff's ears were ringing from the concussions reverberating through the house.

The shots weren't coming from Big Al.

Cliff knew the sound of the standard issued Glock 17, carried by most detectives. It sounded like the kid had a 9 mm semi-automatic handgun. Where did an honor student get a gun that powerful?

An unimportant question at the moment. All Cliff needed to know was that he'd already killed eight gang members with that gun.

Cliff winced when another shot rang out, and he heard more shouting. He wasn't sure exactly how to play it. He had a frightened but dangerous kid who was backed into a corner. Out of his mind in fear and anger over the loss of his mother and brother. Blinded by rage. Capable of anything.

Including killing an officer of the law.

Cliff didn't want to kill the kid, and his lieutenant had warned him not to. It didn't matter what Cliff, or the lieutenant wanted. His partner was under fire. He might not have a choice.

There was a second complication which was why Cliff hadn't acted right away. While it had been a good idea to split up, now Cliff and Big Al were at opposite ends of the house with the gunman between them. Cliff had to be careful about crossfire. He didn't want to spray shots at the kid and have them whiz past the boy and hit Big Al. Since he didn't exactly know where Big Al was, he'd have to hesitate before firing his weapon.

Hesitation could be deadly in a gunfight.

A split-second decision increased the odds of making a bad one.

Cliff hadn't yet identified himself to the kid. He didn't want to give away his position. He was behind the wall that led into the living room. He peered around it. Quickly.

The kid was in the hallway that appeared to lead to the bedrooms. He was crouched down and holding his weapon in his right hand. Cliff was directly behind him. With a clear shot. The kid didn't know he was there. Big Al was somewhere in the living room. Shouting at the kid to surrender.

"You'll never take me alive," the kid shouted back and fired a shot for emphasis.

"Drop your gun," Big Al shouted. "You don't need to die today."

Cliff saw the kid hesitate. Like he didn't know what to do. Tears were running down the boy's cheeks. That's how close Cliff was to him.

Rather than act, Cliff decided to wait. Let things play out.

The boy suddenly stood and pushed his head up and shoulders back. Like he was about to force the situation. When the kid lifted his gun into a firing position, Cliff had no choice. He stepped out of the cover of his hallway and was directly behind the kid.

The boy raised his gun toward Big Al in the living room. Cliff saw the boy take in a deep breath. Then he screamed at the top of his lungs.

He stepped to the right. Into the living room. Unloading his weapon. Firing crazily. Cliff came up from behind him.

The boy was shouting hysterically now. The words were unintelligible.

Cliff reacted. He fired six shots into the boy's back. The kid collapsed to the ground, and the gun fell to the side.

"Gunman down," Cliff shouted, so Big Al would know it was him.

Cliff rushed to the kid who was face down on the floor. He checked for a pulse. It was shallow. The boy's breathing was labored, but he was awake.

Cliff holstered his weapon and knelt beside the young man, and gently turned him over.

The kid looked up at him. His eyes were glazed. Frozen in fear. Maybe regret. His cheeks were stained with tears.

Big Al was standing over them now. He called it in.

"OIS. One suspect down. Situation under control. Need ambulance. Fast."

Cliff held the boy's head in his hands. His heart was breaking.

"Stay with us, kid," Cliff pleaded. "Don't die on me."

The boy tried to whisper something. Cliff leaned forward so he could hear what he was saying.

It sounded like, "I'm sorry."

Then he died.

Right in Cliff's arms.

Cliff tried CPR for several seconds, but it was no use. Big Al put his hand on Cliff's shoulder and lifted him to his feet.

Cliff's eyes were the ones watering now.

"It was righteous," Big Al said.

Cliff nodded. He knew it. Righteous meant that he did the right thing. It didn't make it any easier.

"You had no choice," Big Al said sympathetically. "I'm going to search the house. Make sure we're alone."

Cliff was pacing the room when he returned. The rush of adrenaline propelled him to keep moving.

"All clear," Big Al said when he returned.

The ambulance arrived within ten minutes. The kid was pronounced dead, and the coroner was called.

Lieutenant Louth came twenty minutes later. As did an investigator and forensics team.

The lieutenant pulled Big Al and Cliff to the side. "What happened?" he asked.

Big Al did the talking at first. "Detective Ford took up position in the back. I was in the front. I knocked on the door and identified myself. The kid fired a shot. I broke down the door and entered the premises. I got pinned down behind the sofa. Cliff was somewhere in the back. More shots were fired in my direction."

"Did you fire a shot?" Louth asked Big Al.

He shook his head no. Then explained. "I didn't have a good angle. I also wanted to let it play out. I tried to talk him down."

"Did the kid say anything?" Louth asked.

"He said we'd never take him alive," Cliff interjected.

"I counted six bullet wounds in the kid's back," Louth said. "Those must've come from you," he said, pointing at Cliff.

Cliff nodded. "Like Al said, I approached from the rear. I was behind him. The kid stood up. Like he was about to take extreme action."

"He was coming after me," Big Al said. "The kid was going Rambo on us. I lost count. I don't remember how many shots he fired. A lot."

Cliff continued. "I determined that Al was in danger. I came up from behind the boy."

"You came up behind the gunman," Louth said, correcting Cliff. "Anybody who kills eight men and fires at my detectives is not a boy."

"The gunman fired several shots at Al," Cliff said. "I determined that I had to take him down. That's what I did."

Louth began to pace around. Clearly disturbed by the events. They were still out of earshot of the investigator who was walking around the crime scene. Taking notes in a little black book.

"Cliff did the right thing," Al said. "He had no choice."

"That's what I think too," Louth said. "But it doesn't matter what I think. It matters what the investigator thinks."

Cliff knew that to be true. There were procedures in place for an OIS. Officer-involved shooting. The detectives knew what to expect.

"Give me your firearm," Louth said.

Cliff pulled his gun out of his holster and handed it to the lieutenant. Standard operating procedure on an OIS. Cliff's gun was now evidence and would be taken to the crime lab to be examined.

Louth advised Cliff of his rights even though Cliff knew them by heart.

"Go directly to headquarters," Louth said. "You too, Al. The investigator will take your statements there. Don't talk to him here. It's too fresh. Make sure you have all your ducks in a row and your stories straight. You can actually wait forty-eight hours up to seventy hours to talk to the investigator."

They both nodded.

"Cliff, you have the right to an attorney."

"I don't need one. I did the right thing."

"That's up to you. I'm just telling you that you have the right to have an attorney present when you give your statement. Later today, you'll need to go by the hospital and have your blood drawn."

The blood was drawn to see if Cliff was impaired at the time of the shooting by drugs or alcohol.

The lieutenant continued. "If you refuse to be interviewed or refuse to submit to the toxicology screening, you'll be terminated immediately."

"I'm not going to refuse anything. I have nothing to hide. I'm not under the influence of anything."

"I know. I'm just telling you the drill."

"Such a waste," Cliff said. "The kid should've surrendered."

"I'm not going to lie," the lieutenant said. "You could get some blowback on this."

Cliff already knew that. Tensions in Chicago were running high. Officer-involved shootings were drawing a lot of attention nationwide.

"Cliff may have saved my life," Al said. "If Cliff hadn't killed the kid, I would've. That's if he didn't kill me first. We had no choice."

"Be sure and tell the investigator that. But you've got a seventeen-year-old kid, shot in the back six times. Some people might see it differently."

"I feel bad for the kid," Al said, "But he made his bed. You can't fire on an officer of the law."

"The kid died in my arms," Cliff said, fighting back the emotion.

"You're suspended indefinitely," the Lieutenant said to him. "With pay. If the investigator clears you, you'll still need to see the psychologist. They'll make a determination if you're in the mental condition to return to work."

"I'll be fine."

"It's required. You have to see the shrink before you'll be reinstated."

"What about my cases?" Cliff asked. "Are you going to assign them to someone?"

The lieutenant shook his head no. "Everybody's plates are full. Don't worry about your cases. They'll be there when you get back."

Louth held out his hand, and Cliff shook it. The lieutenant leaned in and put his arm on Cliff's shoulder and whispered in his ear. "I'll support you all the way on this. You did the right thing in my book. I know it'll be tough. Hang in there. You'll get through it. It's part of the job. The worst part."

"How long before I'll be reinstated?" Cliff asked.

"Depends on the investigation. The best-case scenario is two weeks."

The weirdest image popped into Cliff's mind.

The dead woman lying in the morgue.

Two weeks was a long time for her to wait to get justice.

20

Virgin Gorda
Ten days later

Robert was seriously considering killing Angel.

The last ten days with her had been amazing, but a conversation a couple of days ago had gotten him thinking about it.

When he first met Angel ten days before in the bar, he thought he was pursuing a one-night stand. A slam bam thank you ma'am, no strings attached fun-filled night.

Since then, they'd been inseparable.

When they weren't acting like rabbits, they were following the honeymoon itinerary the concierge had set out for Robert and Sylvia and were having a blast.

Angel wasn't the problem. He wanted her around. Her body was as hot as a firecracker, and she was fun, passionate, and willing to explore new things. Her job as a fitness instructor gave her stamina and flexibility. Both in and out of the bedroom. Robert had done things over the last ten days he didn't even know were possible to do. He'd read somewhere that a bull had sex three thousand times a year. He might match that record if they were to continue on their present course.

Why would he want to kill someone giving him that much pleasure?

Angel was supposed to check out of the hotel and go home two days ago. She decided to stay over until Robert left, which was tomorrow. That wasn't the problem. She was already spending all her time in his room. She only went back to her hotel room to change clothes. Even her toothbrush was in the bathroom of his suite.

The problem came when she brought her bags to the room and opened the closet door. Robert forgot that Sylvia's bags were in the closet. In fact, that was about the only time he even thought about the shrew back in Chicago. He'd completely put her out of his mind. Occasionally he wondered why the detective hadn't tracked him down but chalked that up to the man's incompetence.

He never believed he would've been able to stay in Virgin Gorda for this long. So, he decided to enjoy it while he could, and deal with Chicago when the time came. Not that hard to do. Angel was such a fireball, he had little time to think about anything else other than keeping up with her.

This morning was different. He was thinking about Chicago a lot. What would be the consequences of killing two women in a little over ten days?

When Angel saw the expensive Louis Vuitton bags in the closet, her mouth gaped open, and everything changed.

"What are those?" she had asked.

Robert stammered for words.

"Luggage."

"I know that. I'm not stupid. Whose bags are they?"

"My wife's."

He couldn't come up with a better answer on the spot.

"You're married!"

Angel threw her hands in the air, plopped down on the edge of the bed, and fell backward. A few seconds later, she sat up.

"I wanted to tell you," Robert said. "I swear."

"How long have you been married?" she demanded to know.

"It's complicated."

Angel glared at Robert, which made him angry. It really was none of her business. They hadn't made any commitments to each other to be exclusive.

"Do you have an open marriage?" she asked. "Does your wife know you're with me?"

"Not exactly."

"I think you owe me an explanation. Why are her bags in this room, but she isn't? Where is she?"

In the morgue, probably.

That thought almost caused him to burst out laughing. He tamped it down and somehow managed to force his demeanor to match the seriousness of the conversation.

"My wife left me," Robert blurted. "At the altar."

He suddenly felt the weight he'd been carrying lifted off his shoulders. It felt good to talk to someone about it. Of course, he wouldn't mention the incident on the balcony.

Angel's mouth gaped open a second time, and her eyes widened to seemingly double their size. Robert wondered if he'd just made a serious blunder.

"She left you at the altar. So, you're not actually married."

"That's why I said it was complicated. She left me after we were pronounced husband and wife. On our wedding night. I woke up in the middle of the night, and she was gone."

"That's strange. Why are her bags here?"

Angel had just identified a flaw in Robert's plan. He hadn't thought about that. If he thought Sylvia left in the middle of the night, did he ever ask himself why she didn't take her stuff? He made a mental note to think of a good answer if the detective should happen to ask him that question.

"My wife left her bags at the hotel."

"Why?"

"I don't know why. We're supposed to be on our honeymoon. I brought them with me thinking she would eventually come to her senses and show up in Virgin Gorda. She never did. And I'm glad she didn't. I never would've met you."

Robert sat down next to Angel and took her hands.

"I'm sorry I didn't tell you sooner. I was embarrassed. Still am."

"I guess I understand. It's not like you owe me an explanation."

Angel's brow was still furrowed. He could tell she wasn't entirely comfortable with things.

They talked for several more minutes. Angel stayed. After a few hours, things got back to normal, and the topic never came up again. Robert, however, hadn't been able to get the conversation out of his head. Angel was now a complication that had to be dealt with.

Had he made a mistake getting involved with her?

Of course, he had.

He knew that all along but had ignored the angst. He was having too much fun. He had intended on coming to Virgin Gorda and playing the part of the jilted and depressed husband. Instead, he was on dozens of security cameras cavorting around with a hot fitness instructor. That wouldn't play well with a jury.

Although, he was determined to keep this away from a jury. Hopefully, the imbecile in Chicago, the detective, wouldn't go to all the trouble to come down to Virgin Gorda and start asking questions. He was counting on no one ever knowing about Angel.

Was he naïve?

If the investigation did come to Virgin Gorda, they'd find out about Angel. They'd question her. She'd tell them everything including finding the luggage in the closet.

The safest thing to do was make the problem disappear. Angel had checked out of her room. As far as the hotel was concerned, she had left the island. If he could get rid of her and they couldn't find her body, then the investigation might not ever lead back to him.

Overnight, while Angel was sleeping, he figured out how to make her disappear. The next day, he acted like things were normal between them.

"What do you want to do tonight?" Angel asked him.

"I want to go for a hike," Robert said. "Up to Gorda Peak. To watch the sunset."

"Great idea. I'm up for that."

Gorda Peak was the highest point on the island. The trail ran along a ridge. Robert was counting on finding a cliff-like area. It wouldn't be hard to get Angel to stand close to the edge so he could take a picture. When she did, he'd approach her like he was showing her the picture and then push her off.

Hopefully, in a wooded area dense enough that they wouldn't find the body for days or even months. That's why he wanted to go at night. So no one could identify him. The trail would not have people on it that time of night.

They found the trail and easily hiked to the top. They were both in good physical condition and it only took forty-five minutes. They watched the sunset and made out on a rock at the top of the ridge.

Robert saw several good spots along the trail where he could get her close to the edge and then push her off.

The sunset was incredible although Robert barely noticed it. He was feeling the anxiety. Same thing he felt right before he threw Sylvia off the balcony. It made him nervous. He struggled to keep his hands from shaking and his lips from quivering while he kissed her.

Robert finally got up the nerve to follow through with his plan.

"Are you ready to go?" he asked.

"One more minute," Angel said. "I have something I need to tell you."

Her tone was serious.

The moon reflected off her eyes. He wanted to kiss her again.

"Okay. What is it?"

"I have a confession to make. I'm married, too."

Robert stood to his feet.

"You're married?" he asked, shocked.

"Are you mad at me?"

He wasn't. He was relieved. He'd been concerned that Angel was falling for him. Getting married again was not in his future. Not soon anyway. If ever. He wanted to live the life of a bachelor. One woman for a lifetime seemed barbaric.

Robert sat back down next to her, and they faced each other. It seemed like she had more to say so he didn't say anything.

"My name's not Angel. It's Dotty. People call me Dot."

"What's your last name?"

"I don't want to say. I'm not really from Nebraska. I live in New York. My husband runs a hedge fund. We're very rich."

"So you made up that story about winning the lottery."

"I know. I'm sorry. I'm a horrible person."

"What are you doing in Virgin Gorda?"

"Looking for someone to hook up with."

"I guess you found the sucker," Robert said, with disdain in his voice.

"No! It's not like that. I had a good time. Really."

"Yeah, right."

Robert was too stunned for words.

"You're mad at me."

"Your husband doesn't care that you sleep with other guys?" Robert asked.

"He doesn't know. I do this once a year. I tell my husband that I'm meeting a group of girls that I went to college with. Girls only trip. He'd be furious if he knew what I really did."

"Why are you telling me all this?"

"Do you hate me?"

"No, I don't hate you. I actually respect you more. I'm impressed by your ability to lie and get away with it."

A truthful statement. It also uncomplicated things. He didn't need to kill her. An investigator would never be able to find out her identity. She'd never be questioned.

"I told you because you've been so honest with me. I'm the one who's been lying. I don't even travel under my real name. A guy in New York made me a fake passport."

Robert was impressed with her ingenuity.

"I have been honest with you," Robert said. "Believe me when I say that this has been one of the best weeks of my life."

"Mine too. Out of all the guys I've done this with, you're one of the best."

He ignored the comment and had no desire to explore it further.

Instead, they kissed passionately. It led to more kissing and eventually moved to the ground even though it was hard and uncomfortable.

Robert didn't care.

He was relieved that he didn't have to kill two women in less than ten days.

21

Robert Platt was as confused as a flock of geese flying north in a winter snowstorm. It'd been more than four weeks since his wife died, and he hadn't heard anything from anyone.

Not Sylvia's parents.

Not the detective.

Not even a cricket had made any noise.

He could barely sleep at night.

He expected the cops to break down his door at any time and haul him off to jail. He had intended to hire an attorney only if he got arrested. It might be a good idea to get some advice before he squared off with an investigator to make sure his story held up under the scrutiny of an interrogation.

So, he looked up criminal defense attorneys on the internet and called around until he could get an immediate appointment.

The man sitting across from him was slick. Thad Caldwell wore a shiny suit with a thin tie and a Rolex watch. Several impressive law degrees hung prominently on the wall behind him. The chair was fancy deep crimson leather, and Caldwell leaned back in it casually.

His office was immaculate and free from any files except one. There was a thin file folder sitting on his desk with Robert's name on it.

"What brings you in today?" he asked.

"I anticipate that I may have a legal problem sometime in the near future that might require your services."

"A criminal problem?"

"Perhaps."

"Let me stop you there. If you've committed a crime, I don't want to know about it."

"I thought whatever I said to an attorney was privileged."

Caldwell sat forward in his chair and placed his elbows on his desk.

"It is. But I can't represent you properly if I know that you're not telling the truth to law enforcement or the court. So, tell me your problem, but leave out any information that might be a confession of guilt."

"I'm not guilty of anything. But it might look like I am."

"I'm intrigued."

Robert took a deep breath and began telling his rehearsed story.

"I got married a little over four weeks ago."

"Congratulations."

"Not so fast."

"Go on."

"Everything was going well. We got married. We spent our honeymoon night at the Regency Hotel. In the honeymoon suite."

Caldwell's eyes widened. His interest clearly piqued further in Robert and his story. Mentioning the honeymoon suite let Caldwell know that Robert had money. What Robert probably saw in Caldwell's increased interest was dollar signs in his eyes. He couldn't blame him.

"When I woke up the next morning, my wife was gone."

Caldwell's eyes widened further.

"I haven't heard from her since," Robert added.

"Any idea where she went?"

"None whatsoever. I've left her dozens of messages on her phone. She hasn't responded."

"Sounds to me like you need a divorce attorney."

"I'm beginning to think that she might not be alive."

"Why would you think that?"

Before Robert could speak, Caldwell put his hand in the air motioning for Robert not to say anything.

"Remember what I said earlier. Please don't say anything to me that would implicate you in her disappearance. If you know for a fact that she's dead and you're responsible, I don't want to hear it."

Robert chose his words carefully. "I don't know, but... I'm afraid she might've killed herself."

"Why do you say that?"

"Sylvia... my wife has a history of mental illness. I should rephrase that. She's never gone to a shrink or anything that I know of, but her behavior has been strange, to say the least."

"In what way?"

"One time in Florida, she disappeared for several hours. Like she did now. That happened several times while we were dating and engaged. But she always came back. It's been four weeks since she went missing, and I still haven't heard from her."

"Does she have any relatives in the area?"

"Her parents. They live in Vernon Hills. She comes from Jewish money. Her dad owns the Goldman Group."

"I've heard of it."

"We were supposed to move into their guest house."

"Have her parents heard from her?"

"They aren't home. They went to Greece on a month-long Mediterranean cruise. They're not back yet. They should be back any day now."

"Any chance she ran off with another guy?"

"To be honest, I hope she did. That would mean she's alive. As weird as that sounds. I'm worried about her. I still love her. Even after what she's done to me."

Robert couldn't muster up a tear, though he tried. He actually never loved Sylvia. He was concerned he hadn't sounded believable.

"She'll probably turn up," Caldwell said. "Give it a little more time."

"I don't think so."

Caldwell gave Robert a stern look.

"What I mean is, what if she doesn't? What if she's dead? They might think I did it."

"Why is that?"

Caldwell immediately held up his hand. "Don't answer that," he said firmly.

After pausing deep in thought for several seconds, Caldwell finally said, "Let me see if I can articulate your concern. You get married. Book a suite at a fancy hotel. Paid for by papa. I presume. You have your wedding night. Things are going great. You do what couples do on their wedding night. The next morning your wife is gone. But you don't report her missing. You wait four weeks to say anything. If she shows up dead, even if she did kill herself, the police are going to wonder why you didn't report her missing. I'm starting to get the picture."

Robert nodded nervously.

"What did you do after you discovered your wife was missing? Did you go to the police? Did you hunt for her?"

"I went to Virgin Gorda. That's where we were supposed to go on our honeymoon."

"That's a problem," he said.

Caldwell's entire demeanor changed. His shoulders slumped, and his head went down like he was disappointed in Robert. Like he couldn't believe he'd do something that stupid.

Robert felt the urge to defend himself. "I was angry. I felt jilted. Part of me thought she'd come to her senses and join me."

"Did you make *any* effort to find her? Oh, that's right. You left messages on her phone."

"I also went by her house, but no one was home. The security cameras will verify that."

Caldwell raised one eyebrow. Clearly skeptical of Robert's story. A cause for concern. If Robert couldn't fool his attorney, how would he snooker an investigator?

He became even more defensive. "When I got back from Virgin Gorda, I went back to Sylvia's parent's house and dropped off her luggage in the guest house. What was I supposed to do? Sit in my apartment moping? Pining away for her?"

Caldwell showed no sympathy. "You said you dropped her luggage off at the guest house. When she left the honeymoon suite, she didn't take any of her things?"

"No, sir. That's what got me thinking that she might be dead. She'd want her things. I took them with me to Virgin Gorda."

"Why?"

"I was hoping she'd eventually join me there. She never did. If I killed my wife, why would I take her luggage with me on our honeymoon?"

"To make it look like you didn't kill your wife. A word of advice. If a detective ever questions you, and trust me, one will if she turns up dead, don't act defensively like that. It makes it look like you have something to hide."

Robert nodded.

Caldwell leaned back again in his chair and put his head to his chin. "I can see why you're concerned," he said. "I think you have a reason to be. Hopefully, Mrs. Platt is alive and will surface, and this will all turn out okay for you."

"I hope so."

"But you're wise to plan for the worst-case scenario. If she's dead, God forbid, then the cops will focus on you and come after you hard."

"That's why I came to you. Will you represent me?"

"Twenty-thousand-dollar retainer. I bill seven hundred dollars an hour. My clerk's bill out at two-fifty an hour."

"No problem."

"My assistant will give you wiring instructions. It'll go in my escrow account. The money will be taken out as we perform the work. If we don't use all of it, it'll be returned to you."

Sylvia had deposited more than a hundred thousand dollars in a joint account for them. She also had a couple million dollars in her own investments and a large trust fund that she shared with her brother. Sylvia had never worked a day in her life except for her father at his company, so the money obviously came from her sugar daddy.

Robert found it ironic that Sylvia's dad was going to pay for his defense.

"Fine."

"Now that we have the finances squared away, let's talk about your situation in more detail. We need to go through your story again," Caldwell said. "I want to make sure you have everything straight and that there are no inconsistencies in it."

For more than two hours, they went through everything again. This time in meticulous detail. At a cost of about fifteen hundred dollars. Well worth it. Caldwell kept interrupting Robert. Poking holes in his story. Thought of things Robert hadn't thought of. Caldwell didn't say, but Robert got the impression he knew Robert had killed Sylvia. But it didn't seem to matter to him. The only thing that mattered was winning. That's what Robert wanted in a defense attorney.

The man was good. Robert had lucked out when he found him. By the end of two hours, Robert had things cemented in his mind. He told his attorney everything except what happened on the balcony. Even told him about Angel.

The attorney seemed concerned but said they'd deal with it if and when the time came.

"Are we done?" Robert asked. He got the feeling Caldwell would keep him there as long as Robert wanted to talk. The meter was running. Caldwell was padding his billable hours and seemed extremely pleased with his new client.

"One more thing I want you to do for me," Caldwell said.

"What's that?"

"Go down to the police station and file a missing person's report."

A panic suddenly engulfed Robert.

"Why would I do that?" he asked. "Right now, the police aren't involved. They aren't looking for me. I'd like to put that off as long as possible."

"Sylvia's parents will be home soon from their cruise. When they do, they're going to notice that the happy couple is not in the guest house. In fact, they'll know their precious daughter never made it back home. They'll call her phone. When they don't get her, they'll go right to the police. I'd rather it be you than them who files that report. That'll support your story further."

Robert nodded in agreement. The attorney's argument made sense. While he dreaded it, it seemed like the right thing to do. He should've thought of it.

"When they find out Sylvia's dead... I mean, if we find out she's dead," Robert corrected himself, "What do you want me to do?"

Caldwell handed Robert a card.

"Call me. Twenty-four hours a day. My cell phone number is on the card."

"I will."

This was suddenly becoming very real.

He was ready.

No longer as worried.

His story was strong.

He'd file the police report.

Then wait.

22

It took more than four weeks for Cliff to be cleared of the killing of seventeen-year-old Lavay Lee Hall. Lavay was an honor student, starter on the football team, and came from the South Side. He had a lot of sympathy from a number of different sources.

There'd been concern that the killing might spark riots in the city, but none ever materialized. Thankfully, the national news didn't pick it up. For days everyone was on pins and needles waiting for the riots to take over the streets. Fortunately, the streets remained calm. At least to the extent that Chicago streets were calm.

Lieutenant Louth believed Cliff acted appropriately, as did Big Al. The investigator was skeptical the day he interviewed Cliff.

"Did you identify yourself as Chicago P.D.?" the investigator asked Cliff.

"No, sir. Detective Al Rollins had already done so. The kid knew we were police."

"Maybe Lavay didn't hear detective Rollins."

"He fired his gun at him. He heard him."

"How do you know? Maybe he thought you were gang members coming back to kill him."

Cliff wished the man would quit saying maybe.

"I couldn't possibly know what the kid was thinking. All I know is that we followed the book. I heard Detective Rollins identify himself, and I was outside by the backdoor. If I heard him, the kid heard him."

Cliff wasn't required to identify himself once Big Al had. The point was moot. That issue wouldn't get him fired.

The investigator got to the part that could get him fired. Excessive force.

"You shot the young man six times. Why did you shoot him in the back? He wasn't a threat to your safety."

"I shot him in the back because he was facing away from me."

"My point exactly. He wasn't a threat to your safety. The handbook allows deadly force if your life is in immediate danger. If the young man was facing away from you, your life couldn't have been in immediate danger."

The investigator had misstated the handbook. Maybe, on purpose.

"The handbook allows me to use deadly force if my, or someone else's, life is in danger. Lavay had his gun raised and fired several shots at Detective Rollins. The kid was clearly a threat to him."

"Did you consider tackling him from behind?"

"I did not. I thought taking him down with my weapon was a better course of action."

"What about tasing him? That would've disabled him."

"The thought never crossed my mind."

Cliff felt like a suspect. In a way, he was. The investigator was law enforcement, who could recommend Cliff be dismissed from the force or be suspended for several months. Even face criminal charges, ranging from manslaughter to negligent homicide to first-degree murder. The investigator's report could also be used to bolster a wrongful death civil suit, which was likely coming regardless. That's the day and age they lived in. Although Cliff wasn't sure which family member would bring it. All of Lavay's immediate family were dead.

A horrible tragedy.

Cliff had to remember that as he answered the questions. The investigator was only doing his job. He was supposed to be tough. Cliff had roughly interrogated suspects before who turned up innocent. They probably felt the same way he was feeling at that moment. He made a mental note to remember that the next time he interrogated someone.

"Why didn't you shoot him in the leg?" the investigator asked. "That would've taken him down."

"Maybe. Maybe not. The gun was in his hand. Not his leg. He could still shoot even if I happened to hit him."

The questioning went on for several more hours. It had been exhausting but necessary, and Cliff was more than happy when it was finished.

A few days later, Cliff met the psychologist. Standard protocol when an officer shot a suspect or killed one. The job of the psychologist was to evaluate the officer who fired the deadly shots. The psychologist's opinion would weigh heavily on whether or not Cliff was reinstated as a detective.

In a way, the questions asked were harder to answer. More personal and Cliff needed to keep his head about him remembering he did the right thing, regardless of how painful it had been.

"Have you ever killed anyone before?" the psychologist asked.

"Yes," Cliff replied.

"How did that make you feel?"

"Not good."

"Your first wife was killed in a drive-by shooting. Have you ever gotten over that?"

"No. And I don't think I ever will. But I've learned to live with it."

"Do you have trouble sleeping?"

"Sometimes."

"Irritable?"

"You should ask Julia, my wife. She might be better suited to answer that question."

The psychologist didn't smile or find any humor in Cliff's effort to lighten the mood. In fact, her expression was ice cold the entire interview.

"Do you feel responsible for Lavay's death?" she asked.

"I am responsible."

"So, you feel guilty about it?"

"That's not what I said. I'm responsible. I pulled the trigger. But no, I don't feel guilty."

"Any regrets?"

"Of course."

"Would you hesitate if put in the same situation again?"

"No. I'd do the exact same thing."

The psychologist's report took one week, and Cliff was given a clean bill of health. He was still capable of carrying out his duties.

Good to know.

The investigator's report took another two weeks. Cliff was dreading it. When it came back, he was surprised and relieved to learn that he'd been cleared. He expected the investigator to find fault in Cliff's actions. Louth made it clear that if he did, he and his supervisor would overrule the findings. They were behind Cliff one hundred percent. Cliff was a good detective that they were not going to lose.

As terrible as the whole situation had been, it made him feel good that his peers had his back.

The investigator recommended further training for Cliff on procedures, but that was nothing. It was also standard in this type of situation.

It could've been worse.

The day Cliff walked back into his office, he was given a standing ovation by the other detectives in the facility. They knew the shooting was righteous. They also knew that Cliff might've saved Big Al's life. At least that's what Big Al was telling them. And Big Al was right. No one knew how things might've turned out, but the kid turned his gun on Big Al and was prepared to unload his weapon.

After a few atta boys and slaps on the back, Cliff returned to work, and it felt good. He'd missed it. His desk was just like he left it. The Lavay Hall file was on the top of the stack. That one could be filed away. A closed case. A ping of regret knifed through Cliff's heart when he saw the file. Shooting the boy had been the right thing, but that didn't mean he didn't wish it had turned out differently.

Although perhaps Lavay was better off. Cliff thought about the night of the shooting a lot over the last four weeks. Had the kid surrendered, he would've spent the rest of his adult life behind bars. Maybe gotten out when he was an old man.

The file said Lavay and his family were churchgoers. Hopefully, the boy was in heaven with his mother and brother—a better alternative than a maximum-security prison. Hard time would've been horrific on a kid like Lavay. He would've been sharing a prison cell with the worst of the worst. The dregs and most violent men in our society. So violent that they had to be locked up like dogs and separated from the rest of the population, or they'd kill again.

Lavay didn't deserve that. Anyone would lose it if their mother and little brother were gunned down in their own home because the gang members targeted the wrong house. Cliff didn't approve of Lavay's actions, but he really couldn't fault him either.

It helped Cliff feel better and gave him the rationalization to put the whole terrible incident behind him.

The Jane Doe case was under the Hall file. The murder book was next to it. Cliff decided to check his voicemails before he dug into it.

One of the messages was from Patel. The assistant to the coroner. Calling about the Jane Doe.

"Are you ever going to get this case off my plate? I need the room," Patel said.

The man was probably wondering why nothing was being done with the case. Not Cliff's fault. He was forbidden to do anything about any of his cases. He would've been fired if he'd done so.

Julia and Cliff talked about the dead woman a couple of times over the past four weeks, but that was it. He'd thought about it a lot more than that, but his hands were tied as far as investigating it.

During that time, he didn't even log into his computer. Didn't listen to his voicemails or read his emails. The last thing he wanted was to breach protocol and get on Louth's bad side. Especially when he'd been so supportive of Cliff when it came to the shooting.

Patel left a couple more messages. "I sent the autopsy report two weeks ago," Patel said roughly. "Check your email."

Cliff scrolled down through his numerous emails until he found it. He opened it and began to scan the information on his desktop computer.

Jane Doe: Case No. J145773

Cause of death: Severe trauma likely caused from a fall from a high building.

It had to be the balcony of the honeymoon suite of the Regency Hotel.

Height: Approximately five-two.

Weight: 103

Blonde hair.

Brown eyes.

Cliff opened the murder book and found Sylvia Platt's driver's license. It said she was five-two and weighed 102 pounds and had brown eyes.

Close enough.

He could barely contain his excitement. While not conclusive, the evidence was compelling. The woman in the morgue was likely Sylvia.

He needed more proof.

Cliff pulled up his emails again. Looking for the forensics report from the hotel.

He found it and began to devour it like a hungry man with a candy bar. Fingerprints were recovered from the scene. As was DNA. Cliff was particularly interested in the facts regarding fingerprints on the railing of the balcony of the honeymoon suite. None were found, which he found very interesting. The cleaning lady specifically said that she didn't clean the railing. Only cleaned up the broken glass on the floor.

They did find some prints on the door handle leading out to the balcony. Three sets. Cliff guessed they belonged to the maid, Robert, and to Sylvia. Perhaps previous guests.

Cliff composed an email to the crime lab. He sent them the fingerprints of the Jane Doe that were lifted from the dead body by the coroner. With a note to compare them to the prints found in the hotel room.

He sat back in his chair contemplating his next move. That became obvious to him almost immediately.

Cliff logged out of his emails and logged into the missing persons reports website.

He conducted a search for Sylvia Platt.

He got a hit!

His heart flipped over several times in his chest.

A missing person's report had been filed for Sylvia Platt. Complete with a description and a picture of her. Finally, he could start putting pieces of this puzzle together.

He read through the details.

Last seen. Regency Hotel. It had a date she went missing. Cliff confirmed with the murder book that it was the day after her wedding. The day after he'd been called in to investigate.

Sylvia Platt was missing.

That's all the proof he needed. He was nearly through with the details of the report.

Cliff finally flipped to the last page. He wanted to see who filed the missing person report.

Robert Platt!

What?

"Holy cow!" he said aloud to himself.

Relationship to missing person. Husband.

One more thing he had to check. Date reported missing.

Two days ago.

What the heck?

23

Cliff asked Big Al to escort Robert Platt to an interrogation room once he arrived. An intimidation play. Nothing like a nearly three-hundred-pound monstrosity of a man to have a suspect shaking in his boots before the first question was asked.

Then Cliff would give Robert several minutes to wait. For Robert, the ten minutes would probably feel like an hour. That was the point. To get the suspect more agitated or terrified. Both could work well in favor of the detectives during the interrogation process. Cliff certainly didn't want Robert Platt to feel any level of comfort. He didn't make assumptions, but he had a feeling Robert Platt knew far more than he would let on.

Robert had put his cell phone number on the missing person's report. Cliff immediately called it and he answered on the first ring.

"Robert, this is detective Cliff Ford of the Chicago P.D. I'm calling about the missing person's report you filed two days ago."

"Yes, sir."

"Can you come down to the precinct so I can ask you a few questions?"

"Of course. Did you find my wife?"

"I was hoping you might have information to help us find her."

"I don't. But I'll do everything I can. When do you want to meet?"

"Today, if possible," Cliff replied.

"How about this afternoon?"

"One o'clock?"

"Perfect. I'll see you then."

Cliff gave him directions and instructions for when he arrived and then hung up. He was anxious to look the man in the eye and hear his story.

Things were in motion. He'd gone by the parent's house before lunch and spoken to a housekeeper and gotten some useful information. The parents were on a cruise in Europe. They were returning tomorrow. She didn't know where the newly married Mr. and Mrs. Platt were. They were supposed to be back from their honeymoon. They were to move into the guest house in the back.

The housekeeper told Cliff that Sylvia's luggage was in the guest house, but it had otherwise not been used since before the wedding.

"Did you touch or move the luggage?" Cliff asked.

"Oh, no, sir. I haven't touched it. Mrs. Platt is extremely particular about her things."

Cliff asked her a few more questions. She confirmed she hadn't seen Robert. The housekeeper also didn't know how to reach the parents, but she had a way to reach Sylvia's brother who'd know how to contact them.

She said she'd get a message to him and have him call Cliff.

Cliff didn't mention that Sylvia was dead. He now had definitive proof. Turns out Sylvia's fingerprints were actually in a database. Not for having committed a crime. She applied for a teaching position out of college. The school required a background check and fingerprinting. The crime lab had matched the fingerprints of the woman in the morgue with Sylvia Goldman's prints in the database.

Those fingerprints also matched those lifted in the honeymoon suite of the Regency Hotel. Clear prints were found on the broken champagne glass, the door leading out onto the balcony, and were all over the bathroom.

There was no doubt in Cliff's mind that the woman in the morgue was Sylvia and had been in the suite. She'd somehow fallen or been pushed off the balcony to her tragic death.

The most pressing question was why did Robert say she was in bed sleeping? An answer he'd soon have. The clock had just struck one.

Big Al suddenly appeared. Funny how a man this big could appear out of the blue without making a noise. A skill that made him effective in the field. He could be as intimidating as a grizzly bear and as stealth as a panther when he needed to be.

"Your man is in Room C," Big Al said.

"Thanks."

"Guess who he has with him?" Big Al asked, with a sly smile, suppressing a chuckle.

"Who?"

"Oh, come on guess," Big Al said smiling, tossing the question back in Cliff's court.

"Come on Big Al, just tell me who's in room C. I'm not in the mood for games."

Cliff was always nervous right before he interrogated a suspect he believed committed the crime.

"Thad Caldwell," Big Al said.

"The defense attorney?"

"Bingo," he said, pointing his finger toward Cliff. "You win a prize!"

Thad Caldwell was a prominent attorney with an impressive, well deserved reputation in Chicago. Cliff had dealt with Caldwell several times. The man was good. Above average as were his fees. He was quite surprised Robert Platt had already lawyered up. Interesting. That wasn't typical behavior for someone coming in to answer questions about a missing loved one.

"Why would he bring in a defense attorney?" Robert asked Big Al.

"You know why."

"Do you want to join me for the interview?" Cliff asked.

"Yeah, I do. I want to watch this man squirm. This could be fun." He said it with a wide grin on his face.

Big Al would provide the intimidation. Caldwell wouldn't be fazed but Robert might. Any advantage might help.

"Alright, let's go," Cliff said.

They both walked in together. Big Al's grin had been replaced by a near grimace, and Cliff's facial expression was neutral until he was about a half a step into the room. Also used for effect.

When Cliff saw Caldwell, he feigned surprise.

"Thad," Cliff said. "I'm surprised to see you here."

"Detective Ford. It's a pleasure to see you again," Caldwell said while he stood and held out his hand. "Although, I'd prefer it if we met under different circumstances."

Cliff shook the attorney's hand but purposefully ignored Robert Platt. Not even acknowledging his presence until Caldwell introduced them.

"This is my client, Robert Platt," Caldwell said.

Robert held out his hand and Cliff shook it. Robert's handshake was firm but sweaty. He was obviously as nervous as a turkey the week of Thanksgiving. That didn't necessarily mean he was guilty. Everyone except the most skilled sociopath was nervous in a police interrogation.

"Why would Mr. Platt need a defense attorney?" Cliff asked Caldwell. "Does your client have information that a crime has been committed?"

"Not at all. But as you're aware, my client is entitled to have an attorney present when questioned by police."

"I *am aware* of that. I'm just wondering why he feels the need for a defense attorney of your considerable skill. I thought this was a missing person's case."

"Precisely. Since my client doesn't know where Mrs. Platt is at the present moment, he came to me out of an abundance of caution. To tell you the truth, we don't really know what he might need in the way of counsel. Perhaps a divorce attorney. Seems his wife has up and abandoned my client on his wedding night. Regardless of the type of counsel, he has retained me to assist in finding his wife. Although criminal law is my forte, my firm represents clients in other areas as well."

Interesting.

They'd already telegraphed where they were going with the interrogation. Sylvia left on her own volition. Robert didn't know where she was. Cliff was prepared to blow holes in that story, if it wasn't true. Which Cliff suspected it wasn't.

Cliff motioned for them to sit. Big Al stood in the corner, arms crossed over his chest, tight lipped and expressionless while keeping his eyes directly on Platt. Another very effective intimidation tactic.

"We've met before," Cliff said to Robert, looking him square in the eye. Robert looked away and didn't match his gaze.

"Have we?" Robert said as his lips contorted to the side in what Cliff considered fake confusion.

"You don't remember?" Cliff asked.

Caldwell seemed genuinely surprised by the question although he got control of his face right away.

"I honestly don't," Robert said.

Cliff knew when suspects used words like honestly and to tell you the truth, it usually meant they were lying.

"At the *Regency Hotel*," Cliff explained.

He decided to come out swinging from the get-go. Not hold anything back. Not give Robert a chance to get his footing. If Robert killed Sylvia, filing the missing person's report was a ruse. A deflection. Meant to make Robert look innocent. Probably Caldwell's idea.

Their plan was to come in and feign ignorance. That they had no idea where Sylvia was. Pretend Robert didn't think she was even dead. He had to land a knockout punch at the very beginning to throw him off the story. Knowing Caldwell, Robert would be very well prepared.

"I knocked on your door in the middle of the night," Cliff said. "You answered it."

Robert shrugged his shoulders. He'd obviously been instructed by his capable attorney to only speak when asked a question.

"Do you remember what I asked you?"

"I don't," Robert stammered.

Robert squirmed in his seat. Looked over at Caldwell and then back at Cliff.

Caldwell didn't look particularly pleased. Like Robert hadn't shared this information with him.

"I asked you if your wife was in the suite with you," Cliff continued. "You were quite indignant. You said she was asleep in bed. And then you slammed the door in my face. Why did you lie to me?"

Robert was sweating profusely. He looked like he had just left the gym. Cliff was trained to look for signs of deception. Most people were nervous in this situation. Excess nervousness could be a tell-tale sign of deception.

"I don't remember that," Robert said. "I was probably out of it. We had a lot to drink the day before. You know it was my wedding day. I got a little plastered at the reception. Sylvia and I drank a bottle of champagne when we got back to the hotel. Honestly, I drank most of it. I must've still been drunk."

Caldwell jumped in and asked the obvious question Cliff wondered why Robert didn't ask. Then realized it was because he already knew the answer.

"Why were you at Mr. Platt's room on his wedding night?" Caldwell asked.

"The body of Sylvia Platt was found on the sidewalk of the hotel. She was directly underneath the balcony of the honeymoon suite. She was dead wearing very expensive lingerie."

Not even Caldwell could hide his shock at that revelation.

Robert buried his head in his hands and began to sob.

Cliff looked over at Big Al.

Neither of them were buying it for a second.

24

Robert had melted down. Caldwell asked if he could have a minute with his client. Big Al and Cliff stepped out.

"What do you think?" Cliff asked.

Big Al shook his head from side to side. "I think the man is lying through his teeth."

"I agree with you. I don't trust him further than I can throw him."

"He doesn't remember you knocking on his door in the middle of the night? Give me a break!"

"That's going to be his story," Cliff said. "He's going to feign ignorance. He was asleep. He doesn't know what happened to his wife."

"Yep. It's going to be hard to get him off it. You got anything in your back pocket."

"No. That's the problem. I don't have a smoking gun. It's all circumstantial. I wish I had something, but I don't."

"You just have to go after him hard and see if he breaks."

Cliff winced. "I don't think he will. Not with Caldwell there. If I get close, Caldwell will shut it down."

"Keep pushing. At least get his story on the record."

Ten minutes passed, and Caldwell still hadn't summoned them in.

"I'm going to the restroom," Big Al said.

While he was gone, Cliff's phone vibrated. He pulled it out of his pocket and looked at the caller I.D.

Julia.

He looked over at Room C, and the door was still closed, so he decided to answer it.

"Hi, honey."

"Hey, babe. I was calling to see if you got that really dirty note I left for you in your lunch sack. About all the things I'm going to do to you tonight."

Cliff felt his face blush from the words and the sultry tone in his wife's voice.

"Oh no!" Cliff said.

"What? What did you do?"

"I gave my lunch to Big Al. I didn't have time to eat it." Cliff could feel the wide smile on his face as he said it. He actually hadn't had time to eat it.

"Cliff! How could you? Oh my gosh! I'm so embarrassed."

"I hope you didn't put a picture in it."

"You know I don't do pictures."

"I bet Big Al got a kick out of that note."

"You're kidding! Tell me you're kidding."

"I'm kidding."

"Oh, man! I can't believe you did that to me! If you were here right now, I'd hit you!"

"I'm glad I'm not there then. Although, I can't wait to see what you're going to do to me tonight."

"Good luck with that. That's not going to happen now."

"Don't be mad at me."

"You're terrible. Good one. You had me going."

She sounded genuinely relieved.

"I actually haven't eaten my lunch," Cliff said. "I've been too busy. I bet you can't guess what I'm doing."

"What?

"Interrogating Robert Platt!"

"Get out of town!"

One of the things he loved about his wife was her passion.

"I am. He filed a missing person report. I called him, and he's here. With a lawyer."

"Oh... my... goodness. This is huge. I'd love to be a fly on the wall."

Cliff's tone turned sober. "Sylvia is dead."

"He told you that?"

"No. The autopsy came back. We verified her identity by finger-prints. The woman on the sidewalk really was Sylvia."

"You've had a busy morning. First day back and all."

"Tell me about it. I stepped out of the interrogation room for a few minutes. Platt is conferring with his attorney."

Big Al came back from the restroom and saw Cliff on the phone and motioned that he was going to make a call of his own.

Still no sign of Caldwell, so Cliff continued his conversation with Julia.

"I knew it all along," Julia said.

"I know you did. You were right from the very beginning."

"What's his story?" Julia asked.

Cliff lowered his voice. Technically, he wasn't supposed to discuss a case with anyone outside of the Chicago P.D. Even his wife. In this instance, it seemed unavoidable. She was invested almost as much as he was.

"We just started the questioning, but it seems like he's going to act all innocent. Like he has no idea what happened to his wife. He claims he was asleep at the time."

"Did he say why he lied to you and told you she was in bed sleeping when she wasn't?"

Julia's instincts were good. She went to the same question Cliff had asked.

"He said he doesn't remember! Can you believe that? That he was hungover."

"He's lying!"

"Yeah. I can't prove it, though. Not yet anyway. We're just getting started."

"If he's lying about not remembering talking to you, he'll lie about everything else."

"Yeah, well. I don't have much to go on."

177

Julia suddenly gasped. So loud Cliff wondered if others nearby could hear it over the phone. It startled him.

Then the phone went dead silent.

"Honey, are you all right!" Cliff finally asked.

More silence. He could hear her breathing.

"I may have done a thing," she said sheepishly.

"What are you talking about?"

Caldwell came out about that time and motioned to Cliff that they were ready. Cliff put his hand over the phone and said to Caldwell, "Give me a second."

He turned his back to the attorney and began whispering into the phone.

"What do you mean? You may have done a thing. Are you talking about the Platts?"

"Don't be mad at me."

"Julia, you're concerning me. What did you do?"

"I called Virgin Gorda."

"Okay," he said slowly and with a sound of confusion. Because he really was. He wasn't sure what she meant.

"I called the hotel where the Platt's were staying on their honeymoon."

Then it hit Cliff all at once. All the ramifications came flooding into his mind. Along with anger.

"Why would you do that?" Cliff asked roughly.

"I wanted to know if the Platts checked in."

"You didn't!"

"I did. I'm sorry. I was curious. We missed him at the airport. I knew from the wedding announcement that they were honeymooning in Virgin Gorda. So, I called around all the hotels. I know I shouldn't have. I feel bad."

"Why didn't you tell me?"

"I thought you'd be mad at me."

"I am. You can't just go off investigating my case on your own without even asking me first."

"I know. It was wrong. It won't happen again."

He wanted to yell at her, but now wasn't the time or the place. He wasn't that far from the bullpen where the other detectives worked. He'd have to deal with it later.

Once he got past the anger, he asked the obvious question he should've asked the moment she said what she did.

"What did you find out?"

"They did check into the hotel. They stayed at the *White Sands Resort* in Virgin Gorda."

"They?"

"Uh, huh. They. The two of them. Mr. and Mrs. Platt."

Cliff's curiosity was now off the charts. His heart was suddenly racing a mile a minute.

"What are you talking about?" he asked.

Her voice suddenly turned as excited as he felt. Her cadence sped up to a fast pace, only making his body give him another dose of adrenaline. He felt like he'd just taken a B12 shot.

"I called the hotel," Julia said.

"You said that already. Slow down and tell me everything. From the beginning. How do you know the Platts were staying there?"

"I'm trying to tell you."

"Go on."

"The lady at the front desk said they checked in. So, I asked to speak to the concierge. She verified that they were there."

"The Platts?"

Cliff couldn't believe what he was hearing. He was already past Julia making the call to begin with. This might be the break he needed. The smoking gun. Was Cliff in the Virgin Gorda with another woman? Was he having an affair? Did the two of them conspire to kill his wife? The questions were coming so fast he couldn't stop them.

"As in Sylvia and Robert," Julia said. "They were both there."

"Sylvia couldn't be there. She was dead."

"I didn't know that at the time. I figured the dead woman on the sidewalk wasn't Sylvia."

"Tell me exactly what the concierge said. Did she say that Robert was there with another woman?"

"I asked her if Mrs. Platt was there, too."

"What did she say?"

"She said she was. Even described her to me. That she had blonde hair."

Cliff couldn't believe what he was hearing.

"This is huge. Robert was on his honeymoon with another woman!"

"That's what I'm sayin'."

"Honey, you are the most incredible person in the world! I love you."

The fact that she'd called the hotel without his permission, no longer mattered to him.

"You're not mad at me?" she asked.

"No. You've given me an idea. I've gotta go. I love you. Thanks. You've been more helpful than you'll ever know."

"Love you."

Cliff hung up the phone and stood there stunned for several seconds. He got Big Al's attention. He was sitting at his desk in the bullpen and was off his phone.

"I may have something," Cliff said after he approached.

"What's that?"

"You'll see as soon as we go back in."

Big Al took up position in the corner. Cliff sat down in the chair across from Caldwell and Robert.

Caldwell spoke first. "Thank you for giving us a minute. As you can imagine, my client is traumatized. He just learned his wife is dead."

"I'm sure he's all broken up over it," Cliff said sarcastically.

Caldwell glared at Cliff but didn't take the bait. Robert seemed to have recovered fully from his fake meltdown.

"Detective Ford, before you begin again, I have a question," Caldwell said.

Cliff changed positions in his chair and put his elbows on the table and leaned forward. In an aggressive position.

"What's that?"

"Why did you wait four weeks to notify my client that his wife was dead?"

Cliff wasn't about to get into the suspension.

"I could ask you the same question," Cliff said. "Why did your client wait four weeks to file a missing person's report?"

"That's obvious. Because he didn't know what happened to his wife. He certainly didn't know she was dead. When he woke up that morning, she was gone. He thought she left him."

"How did that make you feel, Robert?" Cliff asked.

He needed to take control of the interrogation away from Caldwell. He also didn't want Caldwell testifying on Robert's behalf.

"I was devastated," Robert said. "My whole world was falling apart."

"I bet you were all shook up." Cliff's words were dripping with sarcasm.

Caldwell interjected himself again. "Detective, I want to remind you that Robert is here voluntarily."

Cliff leaned forward even further, causing Robert to sit back in his chair.

"Mr. Platt, do you know the difference between right and wrong. Truth and a lie."

"I do."

"If I told you that you were wearing a red shirt today, would that be true or a lie?"

"That'd be a lie. I'm wearing a blue shirt."

Defense attorneys often had their guilty clients wear blue. For interrogations, grand juries, and in the courtroom. Blue was the color of trust and responsibility. It had a certain calm quality. Cliff would've been wearing red if he'd known he was interrogating Robert that morning. Red signified passion. Anger. Intensity.

"Are you prepared to tell the truth today?" Cliff asked.

"Of course," Robert said. His eyes nervously flitted back and forth between Caldwell and Cliff.

"Then why aren't you?"

"I am. I swear."

"Do you have a question for my client?" Caldwell asked angrily.

"I do. Mr. Platt, tell me about the woman in Virgin Gorda."

Robert's mouth gaped open so wide Cliff could have driven a truck through it.

25

Robert had clearly underestimated Detective Cliff Ford. He wasn't an imbecile after all.

His attorney, Thad Caldwell, had warned him about that very thing. Detective Ford wasn't someone to be taken lightly. Caldwell had had several run-ins with Ford in the past and was impressed by his skills. He was a worthy adversary. A competent detective who was relentless in his search for the truth.

That's why Caldwell recommended Robert be upfront and honest about Angel and the fling in Virgin Gorda. It could be explained. But not if it was hidden. Robert was instructed not to bring it up but not to lie about it when the detective asked him what he did in Virgin Gorda. Which a thorough detective like Cliff Ford obviously would do.

Robert hadn't expected it to come up so soon or for Ford to even know about Angel. How could he? Had he been investigating Robert over the last four weeks? Following him? Were his car and house bugged? What else did Detective Ford know?

He could feel it. His face said it all. The guilt. He was on his honeymoon with another woman. Hard to explain. That wouldn't go over well in court, even claiming his wife jilted him right after their wedding. With Sylvia dead, it really looked terrible. But besides being with Angel, or Dot, or whatever her real name was, Robert was even more worried about what other surprises Ford might have.

Did he have evidence that Robert killed Sylvia?

What could he have? A security camera? A witness? If so, why did he wait so long to contact Robert? Why hadn't he already arrested him? Was he setting a trap? Robert wondered why he hadn't heard from the detective in four weeks. Now he knew. The man was investigating him. Lining up the evidence. Intending to spring it on Robert during the interrogation.

His heart was pounding like a drummer beating a bass drum. So many unanswered questions. The worst-case scenario was unfolding right before his eyes. He had to get it together. Caldwell told him to act like he wasn't surprised by any of the questions. How was that possible?

Could he ask for a break? Already? After only two questions?

No. He had to get it together. Answer the questions and hope for the best. Stick to the script.

Stop squirming!

"Who is the woman in Virgin Gorda?" Detective Ford asked a second time after Robert didn't answer.

"She's nobody."

"The concierge seems to think she was Mrs. Platt."

Robert was kicking himself. He should've kept Angel hidden from the hotel staff. But how could he explain that to Angel? He couldn't. He should've never gotten involved with her, to begin with. But that's water under the bridge now. He had to keep a cool head. Breathe and answer the questions.

What a friggin' nightmare!

"I never told the concierge that she was my wife," Robert answered.

That question hadn't been part of his preparations, so he was winging it. How could they have possibly known that Ford had talked to the concierge.

"Then why did she think she was?" Ford asked sternly.

Caldwell interrupted. A good thing because Robert was reeling. "How could Mr. Platt possibly know what the concierge was thinking?"

"What's Angel's last name?" Ford asked.

"I don't know," Robert said.

184

Why did Ford ignore his attorney? Doesn't he have to answer his attorney's questions?

"You spent the week with her, and you don't know her last name?" Ford continued with blistering questions.

"It wasn't serious. I met her in the bar. We had a little fun."

"I thought you said you were devastated that your wife was missing."

"I was."

"You were so devastated that you jumped into bed with the first woman you met in a bar? Is that what you want me to believe?"

Robert didn't answer.

Caldwell warned him not to take the bait. To keep his cool. Don't let the detective goad him into responding in anger or answering rapid-fire questions. The detective's job was to frazzle Robert and get him to say something stupid. To let the truth slip out. Something Robert could not let happen.

He hadn't been read his rights, but the interrogation was being recorded and Caldwell said it could be used against him in a court of law. He had to keep it together.

"Your dead wife's lying in a morgue and you're off on an exotic island having an affair two days into your marriage. How do you think that looks?

Fortunately for Robert, Caldwell intervened again, "I'm going to have to object to this line of questioning," he said. "Having an affair is not a crime."

Ford ignored his attorney's objection again.

Is that legal?

"Did you know this woman before you went to Virgin Gorda?" the detective asked accusingly.

"No. I said I met her at the resort. In the bar."

"Did the two of you conspire to kill your wife?"

"No!"

"Detective Ford. Is this necessary?" Caldwell asked.

"I want to know who this woman is."

That was good information. Ford knew about a girl but didn't know anything about her.

Neither did Robert, really. Which should make it easy to answer his questions as long as he didn't dodge them.

Robert squirmed in his chair again. He wanted some water. Shouldn't there be water in the room? Did Ford not put any there on purpose? His throat suddenly felt like he was in the middle of the desert. He didn't remember ever feeling this uncomfortable.

Caldwell saved Robert's skin. "He already told you who she is! She's a woman he met in a bar. They had a fling. It's over. Mr. Platt thought his wife abandoned their marriage. He didn't know she was dead or lying in a morgue. He was devastated and despondent. He fell into the arms of another woman to seek comfort. It's a story that's been written about for years, in thousands of novels."

It gave Robert time to regroup. Caldwell's retort about affairs not being against the law gave Robert time to catch his breath. It reminded Robert of the script. He needed to stick to it. The detective didn't have anything. If he did, he would've been more specific. He clearly didn't know who Angel was or what had happened between them. Because there was nothing there. Angel had nothing to do with Sylvia's murder.

Ford was grasping at straws. *Let him.*

"Do you know Angel's phone number?" Ford asked.

"No."

Robert liked those questions where he could tell the truth.

"Address."

"No. I told you I don't know who she is. Just her first name."

"Why did you tell me that your wife was asleep in the bed when she was lying dead on the sidewalk right outside your room?"

"Asked and answered!" Caldwell said.

"This isn't a trial," Ford responded. "I'm entitled to ask a question more than once."

This was good. The more the two of them argued, the less time Ford had to question him. Robert was more than ready to be done with the interrogation. Let Caldwell talk for them both. That's why he was paying him the big bucks. It's a good thing he had access to the joint checking account Sylvia had set up, or he wouldn't have the money for a heavy hitter like Caldwell. Right now, all Robert wanted was to get up and go to the nearest bar for several whiskey sours. To forget this whole mess.

Caldwell kept it up. "He told you he doesn't remember talking to you that night. I'm not going to let you badger my client."

Robert was so glad Caldwell was in the room with him. He had intended to go it alone. He was glad he put his cockiness aside for once in his life and erred on the side of reason. Not having Caldwell on his side would've been a colossal mistake. Ford was good. Far better than Robert gave him credit for in the beginning. Underestimating Ford was a mistake. He wouldn't make that same mistake again.

"When did you discover your wife was missing?" Ford asked roughly.

Robert didn't like the detective's tone.

"The next morning."

"Where did you think she went?"

"I didn't know. I searched the hotel. She wasn't anywhere."

"Were her things still in the room? Clothes? Toothbrush? Luggage?"

"Yes."

"You didn't find it strange that she left without taking her stuff?"

"The whole thing was strange."

"Why would she leave?"

"I don't know."

The rest of the interrogation followed the same line of questioning Caldwell prepared him for and went on for more than two hours with no break. Robert could've asked for one but wanted to get it over. There were no more surprises. The questions were tough, but Robert already had the answers memorized and regained his composure. He was even able to lead the detective on a trail. To the security cameras in the hotel. The security camera at the guest house. Robert told the detective he left Sylvia's things at the guest house. Left her messages on her phone.

That'd keep the detective busy.

"Where's her phone?" the detective asked.

"I don't know."

Robert tried to keep from smiling. The phone was on silent in his wife's luggage.

"Is it in her luggage?"

He almost said yes but caught himself.

"I don't know. I never looked in her bags."

The questions started to wind down. At the end, Detective Ford asked, "What do you think happened to your wife?"

"He doesn't know!" Caldwell interjected. "Maybe she committed suicide. She could have jumped off the balcony. Maybe she was drunk and leaned over too far and fell. I'm not going to let my client speculate about things beyond his realm of knowledge."

Caldwell was basically laying out his defense. A good tactic. That would scare Ford off. He'd never arrest Robert if he couldn't prove his guilt beyond a shadow of a doubt. Caldwell just raised all kinds of feasible alternatives.

Robert was asked to submit to fingerprinting and to provide a DNA sample. He agreed to it. Caldwell warned him to submit to them voluntarily. The detective would serve him with a warrant if he refused, and it would make it look like he had something to hide. Since the detective would get the samples eventually, there was no reason to resist.

Robert gave the samples, and they left. Once outside the building, Robert asked Caldwell, "How did I do?"

"You did okay. A little defensive. A jury would not be sympathetic."

Caldwell didn't seem as happy with Robert's performance as he had been. He thought he did pretty good, considering the toughness of the interview. But Robert always thought pretty highly of himself.

"I thought your job was to keep it from going to a jury," Robert said.

"It is. But I feel that Detective Ford isn't going to let this drop. He's a bulldog. He didn't believe you. I could tell. If there's something to find, he'll find it. He might even bring charges without any real evidence. He has a circumstantial case. That's the kind of detective he is. He might take his chance with a jury. You've got a dead woman. You were just married the day before. Not to mention she was from a northside Jewish family with a lot of money. A fortune by almost anyone's standards. The kind of money people kill for. You spent your honeymoon with another woman. The jury is going to want to blame someone. Ford will know that. You aren't out of the woods yet."

That wasn't what Robert wanted to hear. He wanted this interview to be the last of it and for the whole thing to go away. He wasn't naïve enough to believe that the detective wouldn't keep investigating. He would. But Robert's story was airtight. There was nothing to find. Robert had been too careful. Maybe it wasn't the perfect crime. Angel was a slip-up. Everything else went as planned.

"Prepare for the worst-case scenario," Caldwell said.

Robert would. But not in the way Caldwell was thinking. Robert was confident.

He'd killed before. Sylvia wasn't the first time and wouldn't be the last. He killed the others for the way it made him feel. For the thrill. He killed Sylvia for the money. Hopefully, there'd be a big payoff at the end.

He'd kill Ford, too, if he had to. He'd never killed a man before but wasn't opposed to it.

Worst-case scenario.

26

Cliff was starving after he finished his interrogation of Robert Platt. He went into the breakroom and got the lunch out of the refrigerator that Julia packed for him. Inside was a note, but not the one he was expecting.

So proud of you. You're such a great detective. Enjoy your lunch. I can't wait to see you tonight. Love, Your Julia.

Julia was messing with him. She was a prankster. He knew that about her. She even faked being upset when he pranked her about Big Al eating his lunch. Well, the joke was on him. That made him laugh which was a good thing considering how intense the interrogation had been. While he was disappointed the note wasn't as promised, the lunch and the note hit the spot, and he felt much better afterward.

Interrogating Robert Platt took up most of the afternoon. The man was like a greased pig. Cliff could never quite get a good grip on him and shake his story. Cliff certainly had a challenge ahead of him. While he had a good circumstantial case, it wasn't airtight. Robert had explanations for everything, thanks to Caldwell, his highly skilled attorney. Caldwell wasn't new to this arena. He knew how to protect his client and how to play the jury. And unfortunately, he was a man juries liked.

Getting a conviction with the information he had at this point wouldn't be easy. Cliff barely had enough particulars to take to the D.A. But with the revelation of Robert spending his honeymoon with

in Virgin Gorda, he might very well have enough.
d a tropical island on excursions, drinking and dining,
together in the arms of a woman you're not married
eymoon was the type of evidence that would inflame

Thank , Julia.

While he couldn't condone Julia calling the hotel in an under-cover sort of way, he wished he'd thought of it himself. He gave her points for ingenuity. It certainly changed the trajectory of the interrogation. Seeing Robert Platt's mouth drop open when he asked about the woman was priceless.

But he still felt like he needed more. He didn't want this guy to walk. Robert's cocky attitude bothered Cliff. Not to mention the fact that he was driven to get justice for the beautiful woman lying in the morgue. Whose life was prematurely taken from her. If his theory about Robert was correct.

Back at his desk, he contemplated his next move. Before he had a chance to come up with anything, his phone rang.

He answered with the usual greeting. "Ford."

"Detective Ford, this is Josef Goldman."

Was it Josef the first or Josef the second? Sylvia Platt's dad or brother? Cliff fumbled around his desk to find a piece of paper and pen to take notes.

Pen poised, he was ready.

"Our housekeeper said you wanted to speak with me. Something about my sister, Sylvia."

The man on the line was her brother.

"Mr. Goldman. Thank you for calling. I'm afraid I have bad news regarding your sister."

He paused for a moment to let that sink in. To give the brother a chance to absorb the shock. Usually, he liked to notify the next of kin in person. It couldn't be helped in this instance. He had a family member on the phone, and they needed to know right away. Also, Sylvia had been lying in the morgue for four weeks. Cliff didn't want her to have to spend one more night in that place.

"Your sister has died," Cliff said, soberly. "My condolences to you and your family."

"That is horrible news. Do my parents know?"

"I don't believe so. I was hoping you could notify them."

"Of course. Where is Sylvia now?"

"She's at the city morgue. Is there a funeral home you'd like to have her body sent to?"

"Please have it sent to the *Heritage Funeral Home* on East Phillips Road in Vernon Hills."

"I'll have her there as soon as possible. It will probably be later today."

"Thank you."

Cliff had another question. "I understand your parents are on a cruise and are scheduled to arrive home tomorrow. Could you arrange for them to meet with me at their home as soon as possible? I have some questions for them. I'm sure they'll have some for me. I'll do my best to answer them."

"Would three o'clock tomorrow afternoon work for you?" Josef asked. "That's the earliest possible time they could meet based on their travel schedule."

"It would," Cliff replied.

"That should give them time to get home and get unpacked."

"Perfect."

"I assume you know where they live. Seeing as how you talked to the housekeeper."

"Yes, I do. Thank you. And I'm very sorry for your loss."

"Thank you, detective. Have a good day."

Cliff hung up. He hated that part of his job. Telling people that a loved one died was never easy. The response was always unpredictable and never the same. Sometimes the grieved were inconsolable. Other times they were as stone-cold as a marble floor. So shocked, they felt no emotion. The brother was the latter.

There weren't any rule books for proper reactions to grief and loss and Cliff knew not to read too much into it.

The most important thing was that he had a meeting with the parents, and he could get Sylvia out of the morgue. Hopefully, they could paint a better picture of their impression of Robert and the relationship he had with their daughter.

Did they think Robert was capable of killing her? He wouldn't come out and ask it in that way, but he'd find out a lot just from their demeanor and reactions to his questions.

Cliff suddenly felt pressed for time. He had a number of urgent issues to deal with. First and foremost, he needed to secure several warrants. Robert Platt had given him a number of leads to follow up on.

Robert said he dropped Sylvia's bags off at the guesthouse of her parent's estate. Cliff wanted to know what was in those bags. Probably her cell phone. While he assumed Sylvia's parents would let him search the guest house, he wanted the warrant just in case. If they were uncooperative.

Stranger things had happened.

The warrant would also provide cover for him. Doing everything by the book was critical, so there was no challenge to the gathering of evidence. Having pertinent evidence thrown out in court because procedure wasn't followed was a detective and lawyer's worst nightmare.

Another warrant application was for Robert's apartment and vehicle. Robert gave him his address during the interrogation when Cliff asked for it. In the warrant, Cliff specifically asked to seize Robert's computer and cell phone. Along with a number of other broad requests.

A third warrant was for the *Regency Hotel*. He couldn't wait to give that one to the hotel manager who kept demanding one the night Sylvia's body was found. The room had already been searched so the warrant was specific to security camera footage.

He'd like to get a warrant for the hotel in Virgin Gorda as well, but that probably wasn't going to happen. It required an international warrant. Lieutenant Louth would be against getting one at this point. Cliff needed something more solid. International warrants were time-consuming and expensive.

Since Robert already admitted the affair, Cliff wasn't sure what argument he could make or what new evidence would be uncovered.

The evidence in the states would keep him busy enough. If he found a link to the woman in Virgin Gorda on Robert's cell phone or computer prior to Robert going down there, he'd have reason to pursue that thread, and Louth would most likely back him.

Warrants could be filed electronically, and the paperback wasn't complicated. He just had to make sure he covered all the angles and thought through any possible objections from the judge. He had to submit an affidavit with each warrant. Under oath, Cliff had to state enough factual information to establish probable cause that a crime was committed, and that the person named in the warrant was the one who committed it.

At the very least, the target of the warrant had to be a person of interest which Robert was for reasons that would be obvious to the judge.

In Cliff's mind, Robert was more than a person of interest. Giving him the benefit of the doubt, he was, at the very least, a witness and potentially the last person to see Sylvia alive. In reality, Robert was a suspect. A slight nuance, but an important legal distinction, nonetheless.

A person-of-interest wasn't automatically assumed to be involved in the crime. A suspect was a person believed by police to have actually committed the crime and was ready to be taken into custody. Cliff wasn't there yet as far as the evidence went. He needed to talk to the parents. Hopefully, he'd get there after talking to them and could make an arrest.

Before that could happen, Cliff needed to solve the biggest hole in his case. A motive. The why.

Why would Robert kill his wife on their honeymoon?

With the warrants filed, Cliff allowed his mind to go there. Typically, there were three reasons a husband murdered his wife. Money was the most common motive in a case like this. Sylvia and her parents were wealthy.

But what did Robert have to gain financially from her death? It seemed like he already had an inside track on the money. He was her husband. Daddy had probably spoiled his little daughter all her life. That wouldn't stop now. Robert could ride her coattails for years and get half when they divorced.

Money probably wasn't the motive.

Another motive could be an affair. Thanks to Julia, that was now on the table. Although, why go through the charade of a wedding if Robert wanted to be with someone else? That brought him back to the money motive. Perhaps Robert and his girlfriend saw a way to go off into the sunset with Sylvia's money financing their future.

The last motive was a crime of passion. This was his weakest thread. There was no evidence that the couple had fought the night in question. No one heard yelling. The room didn't show signs of a struggle. Sylvia didn't have those kinds of injuries on her. Like hands strangling her neck or signs of blunt force trauma.

The interview with the parents would help clear up this area as well. Did the couple get along? Were there any signs of abuse? Erratic behavior? Did they argue? Does Robert have any history of violence in his past?

Cliff wrote down all the questions that were swirling around in his head like a tornado as he thought of them.

His stomach growled and he realized he was hungry again. The clock on the wall ticked five minutes past six. He had at least three more hours of work to do. He should call Julia and tell her not to expect him for dinner.

As if on cue, his phone rang again. Julia was calling.

"You lied to me," Cliff said when he answered. "My lunch *did not* have a dirty note in it."

"It was sweet though, wasn't it?" She giggled, clearly enjoying his reaction to the real note versus the note he expected to find.

"It was. I liked it almost as much as I would've liked a nasty note. The lunch hit the spot as well. Thank you."

"Are you done with Robert Platt?" she asked. Her voice was excitable.

"I am."

"I can't wait to hear about it. When are you coming home?"

"Why, because you can't wait to see me?"

"No. I mean... yes. I can't wait to see you. The main reason is because I've solved your case for you. I'll explain when you get home."

The line went dead.

Whatever work he was planning on doing at the office was now on the backburner.

He had to know what in the world his wife was talking about.

27

Julia had turned their dining room into a makeshift conference room. Papers were strewn on the table, and a whiteboard was set up on a stand-up easel off to the side of the table. A drawing of what appeared to be a balcony above a sidewalk was on the whiteboard. On the sidewalk was the outline of a body—presumably, Sylvia Platt and a re-creation of the crime scene at the *Regency Hotel*.

Cliff's interest in Julia's unusual statement, 'that she had solved the case,' was already a ten out of ten. Seeing the drawing set his curiosity shooting off the charts and fighting with his skepticism for dominance.

How could Julia solve the case? He was a trained investigator. There was no smoking gun apparent to him. But he was determined to humor her. She'd already been right a couple of times in this case, and it didn't hurt to hear her out.

When Julia saw him, she greeted him warmly. Kissed him on the lips, took his hand, and led him to a dining room chair at the head of the table and facing toward the whiteboard.

His favorite beverage was sitting on a coaster. He took a big gulp. His mouth was dry from the anticipation and from talking for several hours while interrogating Robert.

"What's this?" Cliff asked, directing his hand toward the whiteboard.

Julia started talking slowly and deliberately. "This is a crude drawing of the *Regency Hotel*."

"I gathered that," Cliff said.

"Tell me if I have everything right," she said. "Particularly the body. Is this the way Julia was facing on the sidewalk?"

Cliff studied the drawing and pictured the body and how it was lying when he first arrived on the scene. The drawing was correct. At least in how the body was facing. The configuration was slightly different, and the picture was obviously not to scale. That night, Sylvia's right arm was above her head. Her head faced to the right. Her left knee was bent. She was almost in a sleeping position, except that the body had contorted into that position.

According to the coroner's report, nearly every bone in Sylvia's body was broken. A sharp pain hit his heart. A sense of sadness on her behalf. It was quickly replaced with anger toward Robert Platt. Even if he didn't kill Sylvia, he was a cad. He couldn't imagine falling into bed with another woman on what was supposed to be his honeymoon with his new bride, even if she had left him. Not if he truly loved her.

He made a mental note to add that to his murder book. Not one time in the interview did Cliff feel like Robert loved Sylvia. Except for the breakdown at the beginning, he didn't appear heartbroken at all to learn about her death.

"That's basically how Sylvia was lying on the sidewalk," Cliff confirmed.

"Okay. To be certain, she's facing the hotel. On her stomach. Her legs are facing toward the parking lot."

"That's correct."

He still wasn't sure where she was going with this.

"How did Robert say she got on the sidewalk?" Julia asked.

"Robert said he didn't know what happened to her. His attorney speculated that she jumped."

"That's impossible! Do you want to know how I know?"

"I'm dying to hear this."

Cliff then resisted the urge to say, no pun intended. It didn't seem appropriate. Julia's tone and demeanor were as serious as a surgeon about to perform open-heart surgery. He didn't want her to lose the momentum she had going with a lame attempt to be clever.

Julia took the cap off her dry erase marker and pointed to the balcony. She drew a crude picture of a female stick figure standing at the railing of the balcony with her back toward the hotel, facing outward toward Lake Michigan.

"Pretend this is Sylvia," Julia said.

"I'm with you so far."

He'd never seen Julia quite so focused and intense. She was really into it. He'd need to be careful to let things play out. Not to immediately shoot down whatever it was she was going to say. Even if she was wrong. She wasn't overly sensitive, but she'd clearly put a lot into this. He didn't want to hurt her feelings by dismissing it out of hand.

And maybe she did have an idea that would help his investigation. He wasn't going to rule that out before he heard what she had to say.

With her marker, Julia simulated Sylvia jumping off the balcony by simply leaving marks from the balcony all the way down to the sidewalk.

"If Sylvia jumped headfirst," Julia said, "the body would land in one of two positions. If face down, she'd be facing toward the parking lot. If she was facing the hotel, which she was, then she'd be on her back, not her stomach."

Julia paused for effect.

Cliff started to respond but stopped himself. He thought it through. Then spoke his thoughts out loud. Not so much to her, but to himself.

"If she went over the railing face first, she would've either tumbled head over heels or taken a swan dive all the way to the ground. Either way, she wouldn't have landed in the position she did."

"That's what I thought," Julia said.

"If she landed on her back, her body could've bounced over to her stomach." Cliff speculated.

The excitement drained from Julia's face.

So, he corrected himself. "That's actually not possible. The balcony is twenty-three stories high. The body would be traveling at a high rate of speed when it hit the ground."

"I thought about that," Julia said. "Twenty-three stories are approximately 265 feet high. The body would hit the ground traveling at seventy miles per hour."

"I'm impressed. You've really done your research."

Cliff had intended to take another drink a minute or two before but forgot when he realized the direction things were headed. He held off now because he didn't want Julia to think he was disinterested in what she had to say about the case.

He was very interested.

"From what I've read," Julia said. "Bodies don't bounce off concrete. Not going at that rate of speed. Of course, deceleration is immediate. The body is like a dead weight smashing into the concrete sidewalk. It wouldn't bounce. The human body isn't elastic in that way. Not like a ball."

"Sounds logical to me."

Julia fiddled with the marker again. Cliff used the opportunity to take that drink. Then he stared admirably at his wife. She was wearing shorts and a baggy tee-shirt. He couldn't help but notice how gorgeous she was even though it appeared she hadn't taken a shower that day. She'd obviously spent a lot of time working on this presentation. And he was still impressed.

She continued. "So, we agree that if Sylvia went over the railing headfirst that she could not have ended up in that position." Julia pointed to the drawing of the body on the sidewalk facing the hotel.

"I think we can agree on that. A good defense attorney can hire an expert to refute just about anything. You can argue in court that the sky is blue. An expert will argue that it's not always blue. Sometimes it's red, or white with clouds. Anyway... you get the point. I think we can surmise that Sylvia didn't jump off the balcony headfirst."

He didn't think she jumped off the balcony, so it wasn't hard to agree with Julia's deductions.

Julia's jaw was clenched. Her shoulders were tight. Lips pursed almost into a fixed position. Her lips were barely moving when she spoke. Her arms were, though. Her hands were highly animated. That's how serious she was taking this.

"How do you think Sylvia went off the balcony?" Cliff asked.

"I'm getting to that," she said tersely.

For a second, Julia allowed herself a flash of a smile.

"Sorry to interrupt," Cliff said.

"It's okay. So... Oh yeah. I meant to ask you, were Sylvia's fingerprints on the railing? Or do you know?"

"I do know. They were not."

Cliff's mind had already started down this road earlier when he saw the coroner's report, but, with all the day's events, he hadn't had time to think about it thoroughly. Why were Sylvia's fingerprints not on the railing? They had to be if she jumped.

"One way Julia could've ended up in this position," Julia pointed at the board again, "was if she climbed over the railing and held onto it facing the railing and then let go. In that instance, she would have landed either on her stomach with her head facing the hotel or on her back with her head facing the parking lot."

Julia illustrated it on the board.

"Since her fingerprints weren't found on the railing, then that's impossible," Cliff said.

"Exactly. It practically rules out Sylvia jumping off the balcony. How does she do it without touching the railings?"

His mind already went there, but he didn't say anything to let her have her moment.

"She could stand on the chair and jump," Cliff blurted out, even though he didn't believe it.

"When we were on the balcony, the chair was several feet away from the railing," Julia retorted.

"You're exactly right."

"Good... Cause I know how Sylvia went off the balcony," Julia said emphatically.

"How?"

"Let me illustrate."

Julia pulled two dining room chairs together. Then stood behind them.

"Imagine that this is the balcony railing," she said.

"Okay."

Julia turned around, so her back was to the chairs.

"The only way to jump off the balcony is headfirst. Either forward or backward. You have no other choice but to lead with your head."

Julia turned back around and stuck her head over the two chairs and put her arms together like she was diving over the chairs. Then turned around and simulated throwing herself over the railing backwards.

"We already know that she couldn't have gone over head first facing forward. Otherwise, she'd have landed in a different position."

Julia turned around again so her back was to the chairs.

"That leaves backwards."

She simulated it again. Attempted to throw herself over the dining room chairs backwards without really doing it.

Cliff laughed. Not because of the way she illustrated it but how utterly impractical it was.

"The Fosbury Flop," Cliff said.

"What is that?"

"It's a high jump technique. The athlete flies over the bar backwards."

"Not a good way to kill yourself."

"Dang near impossible."

Julia went back to the board.

"Look at this!" she said excitedly. She erased the figure on the balcony and redrew it, so the person's back was facing the railing. "If Sylvia flew over the railing backwards, and landed on her back, then her head would be toward the parking lot. Away from the hotel. See?"

Julia didn't draw it but illustrated how the body would tumble and land on its back.

"If she landed on her stomach, she'd be facing the hotel!"

"Which is how Sylvia landed."

Cliff stood to his feet and walked over to the board and stared at it with his hand on his chin. Deep in thought. He tried to visualize how the body would fall. Julia was right.

"Sylvia didn't jump," Cliff said. His excitement mirrored hers. "She was thrown over backwards."

"Yes! By Robert."

"Probably Robert. Could be an intruder. I plan on checking the security camera at the hotel. If an intruder entered the room, snatched Sylvia out of bed, and then threw her off the balcony, it'd be caught on camera."

"There's no way that happened anyway."

"Still, as an investigator I have to consider all possibilities including that she was killed by a third party. That's easy enough to disprove."

"I agree."

"Come here," Cliff said.

He took her hand and suddenly swept her off her feet. He carried her to the couch in the living room and stood behind it.

"Pretend this couch is the railing," Cliff said.

Cliff was standing sideways to the couch. He resisted the urge to kiss his wife and focused on the point he was making. He swung her forward and flipped her over onto the couch.

Julia let out a playful shriek.

"That's how he did it," Cliff said.

He went back to the whiteboard and picked up the marker. Then drew the body of the stick woman all the way from the balcony to the sidewalk. He pressed the marker against the board at the point of impact for emphasis.

"Julia, you were right! I think you really did solve the case."

She was back in the dining room standing beside him.

Beaming with pride.

28

Vernon Hills, IL
Mr. & Mrs. Goldman's house
The next day

The aggrieved and confused looks on the faces of Josef and Emilia Goldman said it all. Cliff could only imagine what they were going through. Four weeks ago, they celebrated the lavish wedding of their only daughter. They followed that with a luxurious, international vacation, only to come home and have their world shattered.

An attorney was present. Jacob Rosenzweig. He introduced himself not only as their family attorney but also as a long-time family friend. Cliff handed him the search warrant, and he studied it closely.

"May we get you tea or a soft drink?" Mrs. Goldman asked Cliff. She was a thin lady, elegant and properly dressed to the nines. Cliff guessed she was always well put together, even if she had just arrived home on an international flight.

Mr. Goldman had dark hair and a short graying beard. He wore a suit and tie. Everything about him was manicured and appeared ready for business. In this case, an interrogation about their daughter's death. It amazed Cliff that some people could keep it together in the face of a loved one's death while others crumbled before his very eyes.

The housekeeper stood in the doorway awaiting her instructions. She was wearing a maid's uniform with her hair back and under a hairnet.

"No, thank you," Cliff said, passing on the drink. "I'm fine for now."

Mrs. Goldman respectfully dismissed the housekeeper and asked her to close the door on her way out.

The four of them sat in the library of the mansion. It was overstated and surrounded by cherry mahogany paneling on every side and the ceiling. Massive bookshelves lined the wall behind the desk and ran alongside the entire left wall. To say it was impressive would be a gross understatement. It must've cost ten years of his salary to construct this room alone.

Cliff sat in an oversized, red wingback leather chair. The Goldmans sat forward on the edge of a couch with a coffee table between them and Cliff.

Rosenzweig occupied the other red wingback chair.

The brother was not present.

"I'm sure you have a lot of questions," Cliff said. "I'll try to answer them as best as I can."

Rosenzweig interjected. "Mr. and Mrs. Goldman both want it clear that they will cooperate with you in every way possible. While I am the family attorney, I'm mostly here as an observer, and an old family friend, and for support."

The message was clear. Cliff took it at face value. The Goldman's hadn't lawyered up. An attorney being there wasn't to send any message.

"Thank you for your cooperation," Cliff said. "Let me express how sorry I am for your loss."

The Goldmans both nodded.

"The search warrant looks to be in order," Rosenzweig said. "And feel free to ask any questions you'd like."

"Perhaps you could start by telling us what happened to our daughter," Mr. Goldman said. "We just heard about it after we landed. A couple of hours ago. We know nothing. As you can imagine, we're in a state of shock. We thought she went on her honeymoon and would be home when we got back in town. My understanding was that she died four weeks ago. Why weren't we notified?"

Cliff changed positions in his chair. He wished he'd taken them up on the offer of tea. His throat was suddenly parched. He really didn't want to tell them she had been lying in the morgue this whole time.

"Your daughter was found dead on the sidewalk outside the *Regency Hotel* around ten-thirty on the evening of the wedding. She was only wearing lingerie and was barefoot. She had no identification on her. It took us some time to figure out who she was."

Mrs. Goldman clutched a tissue and let out a soft moan.

"What happened to our daughter?" Mr. Goldman asked.

"We believe she fell from the balcony of the honeymoon suite."

Cliff didn't want to say thrown from yet.

"That's impossible," Mrs. Goldman said. "My Sylvia was terrified of heights. She never would've stepped out on that balcony on her own accord."

Good information to know.

"Did Robert kill her?" Mr. Goldman asked. His fists were balled, and his jaw clenched as he asked the question.

"Do you have reason to believe that Mr. Platt is capable of killing your daughter?" Cliff asked.

He shook his head no. It seemed, reluctantly.

"I made no secret that I never liked Robert," Mr. Goldman said. "But I didn't think he was violent or capable of murder. Did he report my daughter missing to the authorities? If so, why would it take three weeks to put the two things together."

"He did report her missing. Four weeks later. That's part of what took so long."

"Four weeks! Why did he take so long?"

"He claims he didn't know she was dead. His story is that he thought she left him. That he woke up the next morning and she was gone."

"I don't believe that for a second," Mr. Goldman said bitterly. "Why would my daughter marry him and then up and leave him on her wedding night?"

"I have the same questions. I want you to know that I'm treating your daughter's death as suspicious."

"Darn right it's suspicious."

Cliff didn't want to go much further than that with the details. The purpose of the meeting wasn't to fill them in on everything he knew, but to learn what they knew.

"Tell me about Robert and Sylvia's relationship," Cliff said. "When did they meet?"

"About six months ago," Mrs. Goldman said. "They met at my son Joey's birthday party. Sylvia was smitten with Robert from the get-go. She fell for him right away. Robert can be very charming."

"I never trusted him," Mr. Goldman said. "But he made my daughter happy from what we could tell. I never thought he was good enough for her, but she was a grown woman and after all was said and done, we tried to respect her decision."

Mrs. Goldman filled in more of the details about their relationship. They talked for a good twenty minutes, sharing what they knew about the situation. They didn't know much except what they observed from afar. Sylvia was an adult who obviously didn't tell her parents everything.

Cliff waited for an opening and then asked the million-dollar question.

"Did Robert stand to gain financially from the death of your daughter?"

"He did not!" Mr. Goldman said vehemently. "That's what makes this so confusing. They had a prenup. I insisted on it and Jacob drew it up. Sylvia tried to talk us out of it but acquiesced after numerous conversations. We convinced her it was in both of their best interests. And it was ironclad."

He pointed at his attorney who nodded.

"What are the terms of the agreement?" Cliff asked.

Mr. Goldman raised his hand toward his attorney in a gesture signaling that he wanted him to answer Cliff's question.

Mr. Rosenzweig hesitated.

"It's okay," Mr. Goldman said. "We're an open book. Tell Detective Ford whatever he wants to know."

"Sylvia has a sizable trust in her name," the attorney said.

"How sizable?" Cliff asked.

"Three quarters of a billion dollars."

Cliff choked back the frog that had suddenly jumped into his throat and was fighting to get out. He couldn't imagine being thirty-two years old and having nearly a billion dollars in a trust to use as you wanted. It was mind boggling to even consider anyone could have that much money at their disposal. Much less a young single girl.

It also confused him. Again, it seemed like Robert had an incentive to keep Sylvia alive. Not kill her. He was having a hard time wrapping his head around the scenario the more he learned.

"I gave both my kids the same amount of money," Mr. Goldman said. "But I made sure they couldn't access it all. You know how kids are. If they get too much, too soon, it can mess up their lives. Everyone has heard horror stories of trust fund babies going down the rabbit hole when they're given a huge lump sum of money all at one time."

Cliff nodded.

Rosenzweig continued. "In the event of divorce or death, Robert gets none of the trust money. He gets a one-time payment of fifty thousand dollars. And fifty percent of whatever assets the two of them accumulated during their marriage. Of course, they were only married for less than twenty-four hours. Robert will get his fifty-thousand dollars, but that's it."

Mr. Goldman had a satisfied look on his face as he nodded and set his features into a stern resolve. "If that man had anything to do with my daughter's death, he'll never see a dime of that money," he said. "I can assure you of that."

"Did Sylvia have a life-insurance policy?" Cliff asked.

"Yes," Mr. Goldman answered. "A small one. Five million dollars."

A five-million-dollar life insurance policy wasn't small in Cliff's world.

"Who is the beneficiary?"

"Her trust."

This line of questioning wasn't going anywhere. Cliff was disappointed. He'd hope to find a motive in the money angle. It appeared to be a dead end. He asked several more follow-up questions, but those didn't lead anywhere either.

After a little over an hour, Cliff said, "I have no further questions for now. Thank you for meeting with me. With your permission, I'd like to conduct my search now."

"Where would you like to begin?" Mr. Rosenzweig asked.

"The guesthouse please. I understand Sylvia's bags are still there. Unopened. Has anyone touched them?"

"No," Mrs. Goldman said. "No one has even gone into the building. I'd also suggest that you take a look in my daughter's bedroom. It's upstairs."

"Can you think of anything that might be useful to my investigation? Did your daughter keep a diary or a journal?"

"Not that I know of."

"I'd like to look at her computer, emails, and cell phone. Do you know her passwords?"

"I have them written down in my office. I'll go get them for you right now."

Mrs. Goldman disappeared for about two minutes.

While she was gone, Mr. Goldman asked barely above a whisper, "Do you believe my daughter was murdered?"

"I cannot comment on the investigation other than to say that I'm treating it as a potential homicide."

"I assume Robert is the target of the investigation."

"I can't comment other than to say that he is a person-of-interest."

"Promise me you'll get this S.O.B. Do whatever it takes Detective Ford, to find out why he did this to my daughter."

"If Robert Platt killed your daughter, I will do everything in my power to have him held accountable for his actions. I can assure you of that."

Mrs. Goldman returned with the passwords to Sylvia's computer and cell phone. Robert found the computer in her room and her cell phone with a dead battery in her luggage in the guesthouse. He put both into evidence bags and left the luggage and other items. Nothing else of notable interest was found.

The Goldmans walked Cliff out to his car.

"Again, I'm very sorry for your loss," Cliff said sincerely.

Mrs. Goldman began to tear up again. She had held herself together during the interview which couldn't have been easy.

"You had a lovely daughter," Cliff added. "I take my job seriously Mr. and Mrs. Goldman. I'm determined to find out what happened to her. I'll be in touch if I have any other questions for you."

"Thank you, Detective Ford," Mr. Goldman said. "If we can help in any way, don't hesitate to call on us twenty-four seven. We're here to help you."

Cliff opened the door to his car, but then thought of one more question.

"What happens to the money in Sylvia's trust account?" he asked.

"It all goes to my son," Mr. Goldman said. "In the event of the death of either of them, whatever is left in the trust goes to the surviving sibling."

Cliff nodded, told them thanks again, got into his car and drove away.

He was far less optimistic about making a case against Robert than he had been when he first arrived.

29

Two weeks later

Cliff was at a crossroads. A decision point. Arrest Robert Platt and make his case before the D.A. or keep digging. He'd built a strong circumstantial case. The evidence pointed indirectly toward Robert's guilt, but he hadn't conclusively proved it.

The one thing he lacked was a motive.

After attending Sylvia Platt's funeral, Cliff and Julia were driving home. He decided to get her advice. She'd been a tremendous help in the investigation from the beginning. He was waiting for the right time to bring it up and discuss the dilemma with her for several days. With both of their busy schedules, he hadn't had the chance.

They had a thirty-minute drive home. It seemed like as good a time as any.

She beat him to it.

"I didn't see Robert Platt at the funeral," Julia said.

"He wasn't there. Apparently, word got back to him that he wasn't welcome."

"I don't blame the Goldmans. I'd feel the same way if it was our daughter."

"They're convinced Robert killed her."

"Aren't you?"

"I think so, too." Cliff paused as he changed lanes. "But it doesn't matter what I think. It matters what the D.A. thinks. Well... ultimately, it's up to a jury. But it'll never get to trial if the D.A. refuses to prosecute the case. Right now, I'd say the odds of that are fifty-fifty. Maybe not even that good."

"What if Robert took a lie detector test?" Julia asked.

"It's not admissible. Besides, I asked Robert's attorney and they refused to take one. Obviously, at the advice of his attorney. Even if it's not admissible, everyone would know the results. His attorney doesn't want that on record."

Julia shrieked as a car next to them suddenly swerved into their lane. Cliff reacted in time to avoid a crash.

"Get off your phone!" Julia shouted at the other driver and then glared at him as Cliff sped up to get away from the careless buffoon. The highways were getting more and more dangerous.

Julia let out another yell when the car in front of them stopped abruptly. She slammed her foot into the floor, as if her braking would magically will the car to stop. Cliff jumped from her reaction even though he was paying attention and had plenty of time to stop.

"Too bad you can't arrest someone for being an idiot," Julia said.

"I'd have to arrest half the city of Chicago. We don't have enough jails."

Things calmed down for a couple of miles, three exits, and their conversation resumed.

"Why don't you think you have enough evidence?" Julia asked. "I already proved to you that she was thrown off the balcony backward. What more do you need?"

"A motive."

"Who knows what's in someone's heart?"

"The D.A. is going to want to know."

"I suppose. I can't tell you why he killed her. I just know that he did."

The traffic suddenly ground to a halt. They were now bumper-to-bumper and barely moving. It looked like they'd be there for a while.

"I have to look at it from the defense's standpoint," Cliff continued. "How is Robert's attorney going to rebut my evidence? I'll be put on the stand to testify. I'm going to have to be able to explain everything. I don't know if I can."

"What about his behavior afterward? It seemed like he was acting like a guilty man. He lied and told you she was sleeping beside him. He didn't file a missing person's report for four weeks!"

Cliff was impressed by Julia's knowledge of the case. She knew almost as much as he did.

"All valid points."

"That's not enough, is it?"

"I'm afraid not. His attorney will argue that his behavior the next morning was consistent with a husband desperately searching for his wife. I have Robert on the hotel security camera looking all over for her. I've got a dozen or so phone messages from him pleading for her to call him back."

"That sounds to me like Robert covering his tracks. The whole thing with the phone seems suspicious. Why was her phone in her luggage and on silent? I bet Robert turned it off on purpose. So, when he called it, he could say he didn't hear the phone ring."

"That's plausible, but I have no evidence to prove that. It was their wedding night. Sylvia could've put it on silent so they wouldn't be disturbed. I don't think that's what happened, but who knows that it didn't."

"Robert knows."

"Yep. He does."

The traffic started moving. Slowly, but at least it was moving. No sign of the idiot driver who had cut them off. Another one would probably rear his ugly head soon enough. Some were already honking at other drivers. As if anyone could go anywhere.

Cliff let out a huge sigh. Partly because of the traffic and partly because of the frustrating conversation. "I hate to say it, but I have to hand it to Robert. If he did kill his wife, he sure covered his tracks well."

"Except."

"Except what?"

"Except that he flew to Virgin Gorda without her. And spent the entire honeymoon with another woman. In the same suite he was supposed to be sharing with his wife!"

"There is that."

"If I was on the jury, that's all I'd need to hear. To me, that makes it an open and shut case. It's just unbelievable that he would shack up with some random woman he met at a bar at the hotel when he was supposed to be on his honeymoon with his wife. Who does that?"

Traffic was moving again. They passed a fender bender on the shoulder on the other side of the interstate. Traveling in the opposite direction. The traffic had slowed down because of the gawkers. A gawker's block was something that was a pet peeve of Cliff's. If the accident was minor, why bother looking at it? If the accident was serious, with injuries and fatalities, why on earth would anyone want to look at it and have those images seared into their brains? Cliff saw enough death as it was.

Julia's comment did make Cliff think of something. "My lieutenant thinks the whole affair in Virgin Gorda would be ruled inadmissible by a judge."

"Why?" she asked. "How can they not take that into account?"

"Too prejudicial. Like what you just said. That's all you'd need to hear if you were a juror. Having an affair doesn't mean he committed the crime. The only way it'd be admissible was if I had a way to tie the lady to the crime. Which I don't."

The last statement was sobering and the conversation ground to a halt. It resumed when the subject changed to what Cliff wanted for dinner. They drove the rest of the way with nothing but idle chit chat. Later that night, they were lying in bed when Cliff brought it up again.

"Do you want to hear something funny?" Cliff asked his wife.

"Always," she replied.

"Robert and his paramour ran up a huge bill in Virgin Gorda."

Julia turned toward him and rested her head on her hand propped up by her elbow.

"How much?" she asked.

"Guess."

"Twenty thousand dollars?"

"Too low."

Her eyes widened. "No way! I can't imagine what you would have to charge to have it amount to more than twenty thousand dollars. I mean I know spas at places like that have to be ridiculously expensive, but that's crazy. You've got my attention now. Ok, I'll bite. Thirty thousand?"

"Not even close."

" You've got to be kidding me. Are you messing with me Cliff? Seriously, how is that even possible?"

"I'm not kidding you. If you want to know, you'll have to keep guessing."

"Fifty thousand?"

"Higher."

"I can't even believe this. That's a down payment on a house for goodness sakes. What could they have been thinking? What kind of gifts was he buying her? That's flat-out insane."

"I'll give you one more guess, Julia."

"A hundred thousand?"

"Sixty thousand dollars," Cliff said. "Can you believe it?"

"You've got to be kidding me! I'm completely gobsmacked."

"What the heck is gobsmacked? Is it possible for us to have one conversation without you throwing out something that's not even a word?"

"Gobsmacked is a word."

"What does it mean?" Cliff demanded.

"It means hoodwinked. Deceived. Hornswoggled."

"Horns what?"

"Woggled. That's a word, too."

"You are a piece of work."

"Thank you."

"I'm not sure I meant it as a compliment."

"I took it as one. That's the most important thing. Anyway. . . How could Robert afford a sixty-thousand-dollar honeymoon? Let me guess. Sylvia's dad paid for it."

"Bingo!"

"No way!"

"How did Robert pull that off?"

"Mr. Goldman's credit card was on file. He paid for the room and the card was on file for incidentals."

"Of all the nerve! Mr. Goldman must be livid. Bad enough that he killed the man's daughter but to also run up those charges. While with another woman who's not his daughter! That's unbelievable. What a low-life!"

"I know."

"What could cost sixty thousand dollars?"

"The room was four thousand dollars a night," Cliff replied. "For ten nights. The two of them ran up thousands of dollars in booze and fancy dinners. They went on excursions. A dinner cruise. He bought her clothes and jewelry at the resort gift shop. Massages. Like you mentioned. Mr. Goldman blew his top when he saw the charges on his card."

"I bet. Is that a crime?"

"That's what Mr. Goldman asked me."

"What'd you say?"

"I don't have jurisdiction in the British Virgin Islands. He'd have to take it up with the authorities there. But I don't think he'd get anywhere with it. How would you get Robert back to Virgin Gorda? Since, it wasn't a violent crime, I doubt the authorities there would touch it."

"So," Julia said, "he gets away with it. That's horrible. Just horrible."

"Mr. Goldman is going to dispute the bill with his credit card company."

"I don't blame him."

"That's not really fair though. It's not the hotel's fault. They shouldn't be out the money. The credit card was on file. Mr. Goldman gave it to the hotel voluntarily. I suggested that Mr. Goldman file a civil lawsuit against Robert. Even a wrongful death lawsuit."

"He'd win," Julia said.

"What if he did? Robert doesn't have any money. The only benefit for the Goldmans would be to put Robert Platt through the ringer. It would make Platt sweat, and he would have to come up with legal fees. Goldman could draw it out and make it more expensive for

Robert, and the Goldmans don't need more money. But some sweet revenge might make them feel a little bit better."

"That is the puzzling part of all this. Why would Robert kill Sylvia? She was his gravy train," Julia said. "Clearly he liked living the high life. Based on the charges on Goldman's card alone, I'd think he would be more than happy to have a ridiculously rich wife who didn't mind if he spent money like a drunken teenager. I just don't get it."

"That's the seven hundred- and fifty-million-dollar question I've been asking myself since I found out he had nothing to gain monetarily if she died. I don't get it either."

When he fell asleep several hours later, he still didn't have an answer.

30

Cliff took the Robert Platt case to the District Attorney, who declined to prosecute. His words were, "Bring me a motive."

One was never found, so the case went cold.

***

Three months later

Robert was late. He walked into the conference room of the law offices of his attorney, Thad Caldwell, and the other participants were already there.

Thad was sitting at the head of the table with a file in front of him.

Robert had been car shopping which was why he was delayed.

One of Thad's associates, William Williams, sat next to him. Williams specialized in contract law. Thad claimed he was the best in the state of Illinois. Williams's other claim to fame was having the same first and last name, which supposedly was rare in the United States.

Across the table from William Williams was Joey Goldman, Sylvia's brother, and his attorney, Rav Avinerq Piskei Shlomo, according to his business card. Robert assumed his name was even rarer.

After the obligatory handshakes, Robert sat down next to Williams, and Thad began.

"This shouldn't take long," he said. "Everyone has reviewed the agreement. It's to everyone's satisfaction. All we need is for the two parties to sign the documents."

Thad opened the file and pulled out two sets of papers. He pushed them across the table to Joey's attorney, who quickly scanned them. Satisfied, he gave them to Joey, who took a pen out of the holder in the center of the table, flipped to the last page, and signed on the line above his name on both copies.

Joey's attorney slid the papers across the table to Robert, who did the same thing, not even bothering to look at them. He knew what they were. A settlement agreement, an NDA, and a mutual release. The NDA was a non-disclosure agreement which meant the terms and conditions of the agreement could never be revealed to a third party. The mutual release meant that as of the date on the contract, neither party could ever bring a claim against the other for actions before that date.

When Robert was finished signing, Joey's attorney reached into the inside of his suit jacket and took out what appeared to be a cashier's check. He looked at it, smiled, then asked, "Who do I give this to?"

"That would be me," Robert said. "I want to see what a seventy-five-million-dollar check looks and feels like."

A wave of euphoria came over him when he saw all the zeroes and his name as the recipient on the check. Robert could hardly believe it was all coming together. He raised the cashier's check to his nose and smelled it. Then kissed it. After getting several curious looks, he handed the check to Thad, who put it in the file.

"My assistant will notarize the contracts," Thad said.

He called her in.

After checking the signatures with their driver's licenses, she filled in both lines in the notary book with the pertinent information. Took out her stamp and inked the signature page. She followed that with her signature and date.

"Please sign here, Mr. Platt," she said, indicating the correct line for his signature. She then did the same with Joey. The notary closed her book, returned the identification to Robert and Joey, picked up her stamp, and left the room.

"That's it," Thad said. "I think our business is concluded."

"Short and sweet," Joey's attorney said.

Joey and his attorney stood, and they headed for the door without the obligatory goodbye handshakes. Nothing but a nod of their heads. Thad stood to his feet as a courtesy. Robert and William Williams remained seated.

"Thank you," Thad said to them. Before they were out the door, he asked, "Did you park in our garage?"

"Yes," Joey's attorney said. He reached his hand into a different pocket and pulled out a parking ticket. Joey had one as well, which he waved in the air.

"Stop at the front desk, and our receptionist will validate it for you."

The men left, and Thad's tone turned as serious as a fire and brimstone preacher on Sunday morning. "We're not quite done here."

Thad sat back down and said, "I wish you'd waited a little longer to do this, Robert. It doesn't look good."

Robert replied. "You said the criminal case is behind us. That Ford isn't going to file charges."

"Let me give you a word of advice, my friend," Thad said. "This criminal case will never be behind you. There's no statute of limitations on murder. Just because the D.A. isn't willing to prosecute you now doesn't mean he might not in the future."

"They don't have nothin'," Robert said smugly. "And they won't find anything because I didn't kill my wife."

"Still," Thad said, "you need to be careful. I suspect Ford will still be watching you."

"I'm not worried."

"Be that as it may, you should wait a while before you start spending this money. Lay low with any exorbitant spending for now. It's in your best interest. You don't need to raise any red flags that Ford will pick up on."

"Why? It's my money. I should be allowed to spend it whenever and however I like."

"It's not that simple," Thad said, shaking his head. "If you start acting like you've come into a bunch of money, Detective Ford will be suspicious. I suspect the only reason they didn't file charges was because they couldn't find a motive. Seventy-five million dollars is a strong motive."

"I thought the agreement was confidential. That no one could say anything."

"They can't. But Ford isn't stupid. How hard would it be for him to put it together? All I'm saying is that it makes you look guilty."

William Williams was silent and hadn't added anything to the conversation. He was the one who drew up the paperwork.

"You know how that went down," Robert argued. "I called Joey and threatened to sue Sylvia's estate. Joey... Mr. Goldman settled rather than go through lengthy litigation. Seventy-five million was the agreed-upon amount. I should've been entitled to all of it."

"You were lucky to get any of it," William Williams said, finally joining the conversation. "The prenup was airtight. You weren't entitled to any of it. Except the fifty thousand dollars."

"Which reminds me!" Robert said. "I still haven't gotten that money."

"Mr. Goldman, Sylvia's father, refuses to pay it," Williams said.
"Why not?"

"He says you ran up a huge bill in Virgin Gorda. Apparently, you spent over sixty-thousand dollars at the resort. And it was on his credit card."

"He agreed to pay for our honeymoon. That was the deal. I can't help it that Sylvia didn't come. What was I supposed to do? Sit around moping. It was the old man's idea to have an open card available for my use on my honeymoon."

"When you were going there with his daughter!" Thad said frustratedly. "Not with some woman you met in a bar!"

"We should sue him for the fifty grand."

Thad glared at Robert. His look was worth a thousand words. A thousand angry words.

"Don't be ridiculous," William Williams spoke up. "You'd lose. You got your seventy-five million. Be thankful for that."

Robert conceded the point. He was tired of arguing about it. Even though he was still owed the money in his mind, he'd have to let it go. Caldwell would probably charge him a hundred grand to win it back in court. So what was the point other than to waste time and money. He could be doing something much more fun than dealing with the old man Goldman, lawyers, and the courts.

"I am thankful to both of you," Robert said, changing the tone. "When will the money be in my account?"

"It'll be wired this afternoon," Thad said. "Depending on the bank, it'll be in your account later today or first thing in the morning."

"Thank you for all you've done. I'm serious."

"Robert, I'm your attorney," Thad said in more of a fatherly tone. "You don't have to follow my advice. But I hope you lay low. Don't go out and buy a fancy car or a house. Don't go flashing your money around. Wait two years. After that, you can start to spend it slowly. Just don't do anything to draw the attention of Detective Ford. You don't need to be on that detective's radar. It wouldn't be in your best interest."

"Duly noted," Robert said. "Are we done here? I have stuff to do."

Thad let out a long-drawn-out sigh.

"I think so."

Robert stood to his feet and reached out his hand and shook each of theirs when they were offered. When he got to the door, he stopped and reached into his pocket and pulled out a parking garage ticket.

"May I get this validated as well?" Robert asked.

"Of course," Thad said.

Robert saw William Williams smirk.

They were probably thinking that he'd just gotten seventy-five million dollars and was worried about a twenty-five-dollar parking voucher. He didn't care. He could say the same about them. He'd probably paid them twenty grand to draw up that paperwork. They could afford to pay for his parking, although it'd probably show up on next month's bill.

After the receptionist gave him back his validated ticket, Robert caught the elevator to the parking garage and got out on the third level. He took the keys to his new car out of his pocket and hit the fob. He heard the beautiful sound of his Ferrari F8 Tributo beep and saw the pristine headlights flash.

His new baby. Just looking at the car made him smile like a kid in a candy shop. That's why he needed to know when the money was in his account.

He'd written a check for the car.

$277,173.43.

Robert couldn't wait to try out his new toy on the interstate. The salesman in the showroom said it could do one twenty. He'd test that number.

From behind the car stepped a figure. Someone Robert expected to be there.

"So," Joey Goldman said, "this is what my seventy-five million dollars can buy."

Joey walked around to the front of the Ferrari and then circled around to the back, admiring the car. The car was parked sideways in two spaces.

"You mean, my seventy-five million dollars," Robert corrected him. "I'd say I earned it."

Joey started laughing. Robert got closer and they hugged enthusiastically. Joey slapped Robert on the back. The two high-fived each other. Then they hugged again.

"We pulled it off," Joey said.

"My attorney says I should lay low. Not spend the money right away. Live like a pauper. Don't buy a house. Don't buy a fancy car. He must be out of his mind if he thinks I'm going to let this cash sit around."

His lawyer might mean well, but he was being ridiculous. Don't spend the money for two years! That was utter nonsense. Robert had no intention of waiting that long. Two years was crazy. He couldn't even wait two hours.

Joey was laughing and tossing around expletives like confetti to convey what he thought of the whole concept of waiting.

"Don't listen to him. Attorneys are conservative, man," Joey said, after bringing his laughter to a halt. "That's what you pay them for. To give you advice. That's all it is. It's your money. Do what you want

CLIFF HANGERS: MR. AND MRS. PLATT

with it. It's your dough, Schmo," Joey laughed. "Like you said, you earned it. Enjoy it!"

Robert saw some movement out of the corner of his eye.He was so excited to see his new car he hadn't even thought to see if anyone else was in the garage.

A person emerged from the shadows.

A woman.

Holding a cell phone up in front of her face. Like she was taking photos or shooting a video.

He recognized her.

Julia Ford.

Detective Ford's wife.

"What are you doing?" Robert shouted as he was suddenly filled with rage.

31

Earlier that day

Cliff had already left for work when Julia groggily made her way out of bed on her day off. In the dark recesses of her mind, she vaguely remembered him kissing her goodbye. A tinge of guilt hit her as she wished she were better at getting up early, cooking him breakfast, and sending him off to work properly.

But he was a morning person, and she was a night owl. Getting up before him would be next to impossible. Sometimes she turned over in bed as early as four in the morning, and he'd be gone. He never complained about her not being awake when he left, so she mostly put it out of her mind and tried to be a good wife after she'd had two cups of coffee up until the time he went to bed at night. Early. Usually between eight and nine.

This particular morning was a busy one. After a quick and fast-paced five-mile run, she skipped the shower, pulled her hair back in a ponytail, and ran a few errands. She was scarfing down a power bar and banana while on the go.

Around eleven, she started feeling lethargic and stopped into *Hipsters Coffee Shop* for a double shot latte, sans the whipped cream. As she was about to cross the road to go back to her car, a red blur came whizzing around the corner and nearly hit her causing her to drop the coffee out of her hand. Although, she was thinking more about the near-death experience, than the lost caffeine.

Had she not stopped mid-step or had ventured onto the road seconds earlier, the driver would've hit her. At the rate of speed he was traveling, the outcome would not have been good for her.

She shouted and shook her fist at the driver, but he was already past her.

The red sports car screeched to a stop and turned on a dime into a parking garage next to *Hipsters*. The garage was attached to a six-story office building. The car stopped at the entrance, and the driver reached out his arm and took a parking ticket.

Julia couldn't believe her eyes.

Was it?

Could it be?

Robert Platt?

She had to do a double-take. On second look, it was. She'd recognize his smug pug face anywhere.

What was he doing in an expensive sports car?

The tires squealed as the parking garage gate arm rose in the air, and he sped up the ramp. Julia fumbled for her phone in the back pocket but couldn't get it out in time to take a picture.

Curiosity got the best of her, and she walked toward the garage. She hesitated before entering. Should she call Cliff? He'd definitely be interested in knowing that Robert had come upon some money. Four months had passed since Sylvia was murdered, and Cliff had never been able to bring a case against Robert even though he was certain he killed his wife.

Cliff never said, but she could tell it bothered him. Still. Even after all these months.

It'd been several weeks since he'd mentioned it. The D.A. refused to take the case because Cliff hadn't found a motive.

Was the car evidence? Was there a money trail that might lead back to a motive?

Julia had to know. That was her nature. She was inquisitive. She liked to know things. Cliff had included her in the Platt case to an extent. That made her feel good, and it brought new life to their marriage which had fallen into a routine. Cliff asked for her advice on more cases since then which made her feel good.

If she couldn't make him breakfast every morning, maybe this was one way she could help, by bringing him new information on a stalled case.

What could it hurt?

Julia walked up the ramp to the garage and went level to level until she found the car parked diagonally, taking up two parking spaces on the third floor of the parking garage. Julia could see the familiar Ferrari stallion on the front grill and back tailgate.

Nice car.

Robert was nowhere to be seen, so Julia pulled out her phone and took several pictures of the expensive vehicle.

The car looked brand new. Maroon red. Shiny and sleek. She searched on her phone how much one of those would cost and almost dropped her phone when she saw they were more than two hundred thousand dollars.

Where did Robert get that kind of money?

Then she began to doubt herself. What if it wasn't Robert? He didn't have any money according to Cliff. It had to be someone who looked like him.

Doubts began to click in. Maybe she was seeing things, imagining that the driver was Robert. She didn't actually get a good look at him. He went by the coffee shop too fast. The parking garage entrance was several hundred feet away. The car windows were slightly tinted.

Suddenly she felt embarrassed and had the urge to leave. But the confusion kept her from it.

What if it was Robert? She had to know.

A large pillar was across from where the Ferrari was parked. Several cars were in the spaces on that side. Julia took up position behind the pillar and leaned against it.

And waited.

A few people came out of the door to the office building, but none were Robert. After a while, she began to think this wasn't such a good idea, but she couldn't make herself leave. She'd wait all afternoon if she had to.

Then she realized that Cliff could run the temporary plates on the car and confirm that Robert owned it within seconds. She didn't need to stay. The pictures would be evidence enough.

As she started to leave, the door to the parking garage opened. A man walked out. Julia ducked back behind the pillar and carefully peeked around it.

The man walked toward the sports car. When he got to it, he walked around it, checking it out. That seemed normal. Men were always interested in other men's toys. Like women who checked out other girls in a bar. More than they checked out men. Women wanted to know what purse other women were carrying or what shoes they were wearing.

Then it hit her. Something about the man seemed familiar.

She remembered.

Joey Goldman.

Sylvia Platt's brother. She saw him at the funeral. He said a few words.

What was he doing there? This couldn't be a coincidence. That meant Robert had to be the one in the sport's car. She wasn't seeing things.

After Joey was done ogling the car, he got in a car two spaces over, but didn't leave. Julia's heart started racing, and she took in a massive gulp of air when she realized she'd been holding her breath. The pillar was between her and Joey Goldman, so he didn't know she was there, and she planned to keep it that way.

About ten minutes later, the door opened again. Another man appeared.

Robert Platt!

Was she about to witness a confrontation? A killing? Was Joey Goldman there to avenge his sister's death?

Julia peered around the pillar. She had to see what was happening. Robert was at the Ferrari now. She heard the beep as he unlocked it.

Joey stepped out of his car and walked toward Robert. She looked to see if he had a gun or knife in his hand.

To her shock, the men embraced. Started high fiving each other. Laughing. She thought she heard one of them say, "We pulled it off."

Julia fumbled with her phone. Her hands were shaking. She found the camera and hit video, then pushed the record button.

Emboldened, she stepped out from the pillar and pointed the camera at the two men. They were oblivious to her. They were looking at the car.

"Don't buy a fancy car," she heard Robert say. Something about his attorney not wanting him to buy it.

Her hand was now as steady as her resolve.

"Don't listen to him," Joey Goldman said. "Attorneys are conservative, man. That's what you pay them for. To give you advice. That's all it is. It's your money. Do with it what you want. Like you said, you earned it."

What did he mean by he had earned it?

She raised the camera higher and stood closer to them.

Robert saw her!

Only because she wanted him to.

"What are you doing?" he said.

She kept the camera pointed at him.

He started toward her. Julia kept filming but backed up. He kept coming, closer, closer still. He wasn't stopping.

She bumped into a car, which kept her from backing up further.

"You're Julia Ford," Robert said. "Cliff Ford's wife."

How did he know her name?

He must've seen the surprised look on her face because he said, "Yeah. I know who you are. Are you surprised? I know all about you. I know where you live. I know you work at a women's shelter. You're his second wife. You don't have kids. How does a loser like Cliff Ford end up with a knockout like you?"

"My husband is not a loser," Julia said angrily. "He's the one who's going to haul you off to jail in handcuffs!"

Robert's eyes were suddenly blazing on fire like embers of dark coal. It caused her to gasp when he lunged for her.

He grabbed the phone from her hand and threw it to the ground.

"Robert, don't," she heard Joey Goldman say. "She's not worth it. Let's get out of here."

Robert didn't stop. He had one hand on her neck. Not choking her but holding her in place. He was pressing his body against hers. She was trapped between him and the car.

His grip was strong. The look in his eyes was pure evil. It felt like he was going to kill her.

Julia knew martial arts and self-defense, but her training had left her now that she was in a life and death situation.

She was frozen in fear.

"Robert, don't," Joey Goldman said a second time.

"Shut up! Grab her phone."

Joey Goldman reached down and picked her phone up off the ground.

"Destroy it," Robert said. "She's got pictures of us on it."

Joey sat it on the ground and began to stomp on it.

Julia would've shouted an objection but the hand on her neck was now cutting off the air and hurting her throat.

It burned from the pressure.

She had to do something soon. If she was deprived of too much oxygen, she wouldn't be able to fight back.

He released his grip slightly. It appeared that he wasn't going to try and kill her after all. Not in the parking garage. Where there were cameras.

"If you're not careful, you're going to end up dead like your husband's first wife," Robert said with vitriol.

How did he know about Cliff's first wife who was shot and killed by a gang member? The words infuriated Julia and she felt a sudden bolt of strength. She shot the palm of her hand upward and connected just below Robert's chin. He saw it coming and turned slightly to avoid the direct hit. It had some effect as he staggered slightly.

He recovered quickly. Robert moved his right arm across his body and then backhanded her, right across the mouth.

She tasted blood.

Saw stars for a moment.

He was on her again. Pressing her back against the car. The tailgate pushed against the small of her back and was hurting her.

This time she wasn't frozen.

Julia's knee met his groin just as he was about to press himself against her further.

Robert let out a burst of air and a loud yelp.

He released his grip and doubled over in pain. Then fell to the ground.

Julia took off running.

Joey followed her for a few hundred feet but then turned back around and went back in the direction of the car. Julia was sprinting now. Her lungs were burning as she ran as fast as she could down the ramp. Out onto the street and to her car.

She fumbled for her fob. Her hands were shaking so hard she almost dropped it. She glanced back at the garage but neither Robert nor Joey had come after her.

Once she got the car door opened, she jumped in the car and started it.

She struggled to catch her breath.

What do I do now?

She needed to talk to Cliff.

My phone!

How could she call him? If she went home, she wouldn't find one there. They didn't have a landline at the house.

She looked in the rearview mirror. Her lip was bleeding slightly and a little welp appeared. She had to get out of there. Before Robert and Joey came out of the garage. She sped away. The only thing she knew to do was drive to the police station. Once there, she ran into the building and into the bullpen where the detectives were.

Cliff was at his desk.

She was still breathing hard.

"Honey what happened?" he said with eyes widened in disbelief.

"I was attacked."

"By whom?"

"By Robert Platt and Joey Goldman."

32

Big Al handled taking Julia's victim statement for obvious reasons. Cliff couldn't go anywhere near whatever case they might have against Robert or Joey Goldman. In fact, as soon as he heard a crime was committed, he took Julia to an interview room, and instructed her not to say anything to anyone but Big Al.

His curiosity was through the roof—more like into the stratosphere. Robert Platt and Joey Goldman attacked Julia. He had no idea how that happened or was even possible. How did she come into a confrontation with them?

When Big Al finally emerged from the room, Cliff's anxiety was as high as a mouse in a room full of mousetraps.

"How's she doing?" Cliff asked.

Big Al motioned him to step out of the bullpen, through the door, and down the hall to the conference room so that they could talk privately.

"Is Julia okay?" Cliff asked a second time.

"You know Julia. She's a trooper. She's in better shape than Robert Platt. I guess she kneed him in the private parts pretty hard," Big Al said during a deep chuckle. "She did alright. You should be proud of her, Cliff."

"What happened?"

Big Al filled Cliff in on the details.

When he finished, Cliff asked, "Are you going to charge them?"

"I'm going to throw the book at them. Minimum... assault. I might add, battery. Theft of her cell phone for sure. But that's only a misdemeanor."

"If the theft results in bodily harm, then it goes up to a felony."

Of course, Big Al already knew that. From the sound of it, they were right on the line between charging them with a misdemeanor or a felony.

"I'll add disorderly conduct. Failure to use a proper turn signal. Driving without a license. Being ugly."

Cliff knew he was kidding.

Then Big Al's eyebrows narrowed, and his tone became more serious.

"Julia's got some information that'll help your murder case. You know. Sylvia Platt."

"What's that?"

Cliff's mind was already churning in that direction. He wondered if they were connected.

"Robert Platt was driving a Ferrari."

When Big Al related the details earlier, he'd said a sports car. Cliff didn't know he meant a car as expensive as a Ferrari.

Big Al smiled and said, "From what Julie said, it looked new and shiny. Where did Robert Platt get that kind of money?"

"Good question. He was with Joey Goldman. That parking garage is owned by Thad Caldwell. Robert's attorney. They must've made a deal."

"A payoff."

"Are you saying Joey is in on his sister's murder?" Cliff asked. He had to admit to himself that he had considered it.

"Julia overheard Joey say, 'I can't believe we got away with it.'"

Cliff just nodded as the information started to sink in.

"Robert said something like, I've *earned* that money," Big Al added.

"Earning, meaning, he killed Sylvia for it."

"Kind of sounds that way to me," Big Al replied. "And Julia said Robert and Joey were all chummy. Not how you'd think a guy would respond to someone suspected of murdering his sister."

Things were coming together. Cliff began to verbalize them.

"Joey got Sylvia's trust when she died. Seven hundred and fifty million dollars!" Cliff knew when Big Al heard that number, he would flip a biscuit.

"No way, man. That's some serious change. We both know there are low-life scum bags that will kill someone for a couple of Gs. That amount of money would make a lot of unscrupulous people step up to the plate to help."

"It sure is. Enough money that it'd be worth it to Robert to off Joey's sister for part of it."

Cliff pulled out his cell phone and made a call. He hated to interrupt the conversation, but it couldn't wait.

Mr. Josef Goldman, Sylvia's father, answered the phone.

"Mr. Goldman, I'm sorry to bother you at dinnertime," Cliff said. "I have a question. Are you aware of your son making a payment to Robert Platt out of Sylvia's trust?"

"I most certainly am not! That's not possible. Joey can't stand Robert. Why would Joey pay Robert any money?"

"I have some good evidence that it did happen. Can you talk to your son and get back to me?"

"Trust me. I'll get to the bottom of it as soon as we get off the phone."

"Thank you."

"Let's get Robert and Joey in here A.S.A.P.," Cliff said after hanging up with the father.

"I'm a step ahead of you. I've already put out the word to have them brought in. They'll spend the night in jail. Unless their attorneys can pull some strings."

"I'm sure they will."

When they were done talking, Cliff went to check on Julia. She had an ice pack on her lip and had an unfinished soda on the table.

When she saw him, she bolted out of the chair and was in his arms in a flash. They hugged for a moment before Cliff pulled back to look into her eyes and assess her injuries.

"I'm so sorry this happened to you," Cliff said to her. "Are you okay?"

"My ego's bruised a little bit. I kind of froze when he first came after me. I should have beat the 'you know what' out of him as soon as he got near me. At least I got in a good knee to his groin. He might have trouble walking for a few days."

"I'm just glad you're not hurt."

Julia's eyes widened. "Did Big Al tell you what they said? They did it! The two of them killed Sylvia. Can you believe it?"

Cliff nodded. He couldn't really discuss it.

Not yet. Julia had gone from anonymously helping him on the side to being a witness to a crime. If he wasn't careful, he could get thrown off the case altogether. A conflict of interest would mean that another detective would get assigned to the case. He would do everything he could to make sure that didn't happen. These guys were going down, and he wanted to be the one to put handcuffs on them.

For Sylvia, and for his wife too, who was now a victim of their evil.

"Can I go home?" Julia asked in a tired voice.

"Are you sure you don't need a doctor?"

Julia turned her head to the side and gave him one of her patented looks.

"I'm just worried about you," Cliff said. "I feel horrible that you were assaulted today. And because of a case of mine."

"They took my phone," Julia said.

"I know. Go by the cell phone dealer and pick up one. Just pay for it. We'll get insurance to reimburse us for the cost. Actually, I think we have insurance on a lost or stolen phone. Either way, they'll get you a replacement phone before you leave the store. And please call me after you get your new phone, so I know you're all set."

Cliff walked Julia out to her car and kissed her goodbye. He also made a mental note to have a policeman drive by their house and check on her. That'd make her mad, but he'd rather have her safe than alone at home.

Robert and Joey still hadn't been picked up according to dispatch. Cliff was starting to worry.

So, he picked up his phone and called Robert's attorney's cell phone expecting it to go to voicemail. To his surprise, Thad Caldwell picked up the phone on the second ring.

"Detective Ford. I was expecting your call."

"Do you want to bring your client in voluntarily, or shall we do the perp walk and drag him in?"

"The way I see it, your wife is the one who assaulted my client."

"Feel free to make that argument before a judge."

"She was in my parking garage. That's private property. I own it."

"Nice try, counselor. The public can use that parking garage. That makes it public property."

"Mrs. Ford stalked my client. She pursued him. Your wife hit him in the chin and kneed him between the legs. He's still walking funny."

"Is there a security camera in that garage? I'd love to see how all this went down."

"There is, but it wasn't working at the time."

"I bet it wasn't. How convenient for your client, Counselor Caldwell," Cliff retorted.

"Sounds like a case of he said, she said," Caldwell volleyed back.

"Why was Joey Goldman in the parking garage?"

"He had business with my firm."

"What kind of business?"

"You know I can't answer that. We respect clients' confidentiality."

"Did you know Robert Platt was driving a Ferrari? I'm sure you're aware that those are high-end cars. A person has to have a lot of money to drive one of those off of the lot. Did Robert get that money from Joey Goldman? Sounds like a hit-man for hire transaction."

Caldwell ignored the last comment and Cliff regretted saying it. Playing his hand too soon could be a mistake.

"I did know that Mr. Platt was driving a Ferrari. I prefer a Porsche myself. Less trouble. Easier to repair. More of them on the road. I think a Ferrari is a little flashy. Draws attention to it. Criminals and such. But to each his own."

Cliff didn't appreciate the humor the counselor was trying to interject into the conversation in an effort to protect his client. Acting flippant on behalf of Robert Platt chapped Cliff's hide. He almost wished he could reach through the phone and grab him by his collar. Slap some sense into him. But he knew this guy didn't get rattled easily.

"Did Robert get that money from Joey?" Cliff asked again.

"You know I can't answer that."

"Denial. That's as good as a yes. It doesn't matter. I have other ways of finding out that information. I ask again. Are you going to bring your client in, or shall we put out an APB on him?"

"What are you charging him with?"

"He stole my wife's cell phone."

"I have her phone in my possession. She dropped it in my garage. It'll be returned to her. Surely you're not going to arrest Robert for a few hundred-dollar cell phone. The judge will laugh you out of court. Maybe even fine you for wasting his time."

"Counselor, you're wasting my time. Which will it be? The hard way or the easy way?"

Caldwell let out a huge sigh.

"Okay. We'll come in. He'll be out and back home before dinner."

"Don't count on it."

Cliff hung up the phone, spitting mad. Attorneys, in general, rubbed him the wrong way. This one, in particular, was as cocky as his client. If that were even possible.

His phone rang, and Cliff was thankful for the distraction.

"Detective Ford, this is Josef Goldman."

"Yes, sir. Thank you for calling me back so soon."

"Turns out you were right. My son did pay Robert some money."

"Did he say how much?"

"He wouldn't say. We got in a huge row. He hung up on me before I got a lot of the details. I kept pressing him about how much he'd given Platt, and he said it was none of my business. Can you believe that? I worked hard for that money. And for my own son to give it to that murdering scumbag, Robert Platt, is infuriating. I can't imagine what he was thinking. His behavior is unconscionable."

"Mr. Goldman, do you know where your son is?"

"I do. Why do you ask?"

"There's a warrant out for your son's arrest. He assaulted a woman earlier today in a parking garage. Stole her cell phone."

"That's very disturbing news, detective. I wasn't aware."

"It just happened. We're looking for him. Any chance you could talk him into turning himself in?"

"Detective, he will be at your station within the hour. If I have to drag him there myself."

"Thank you, sir. You're a decent and honorable man."

The line went dead.

Cliff went back to his desk to prepare Robert's and Joey's arrival. Those interrogations would likely go well into the evening. The questions and timing had to be well scripted. Cliff went and grabbed his murder book for Sylvia's case. He started making notes about everything he had come to learn since Robert and Joey assaulted Julia. His focus was imperative. He didn't have time to let his feelings get in the way.

Less than an hour later, Robert and Joey showed up at the station and were put into different rooms. By that time, Cliff had made a decision. He was going to arrest them both for the murder of Sylvia Platt.

33

Robert Platt and Joey Goldman were put in two separate interrogation rooms. Both were brought in voluntarily, as promised, by Robert's attorney and Joey's father. Neither the father nor attorney seemed very happy with their client or son. They wore frustrated, upset looks on their faces.

Mr. Goldman seemed the most distressed. He pulled Cliff aside and said, "I want to apologize to you for my son's behavior. Also, please apologize to your wife on my behalf. This is not how Goldman's are taught to behave. It's unacceptable and shocking, not to mention scandalous. We never brought up our children to act in such a disgusting manner. Again, my apologies."

"I will tell her," Cliff said. "That'll mean a lot to her coming from you."

"I've told my son to cooperate fully," Mr. Goldman said. "He's been instructed to tell you the truth. I've told his lawyer the same thing. They've been directed, in no uncertain terms, that they aren't to do anything to obstruct your investigation. If Joey doesn't cooperate, you let me know. I'll yank that trust fund away from him so fast, he won't know what hit him. Please tell me if he doesn't cooperate."

"I will."

"By the way, Joey told me how much he paid Platt. Seventy-five million dollars! I came unglued. This was the man who killed his sister. Can you believe that? What would make my son do something so unimaginable?"

Cliff didn't have the heart to tell Mr. Goldman that he suspected his son was involved in the killing of his daughter, and the money was tainted. Blood money. The whole murder for money scheme might've even been Joey's idea. Probably was. Cliff didn't think Robert Platt was all that smart.

He could see Robert going along with being the husband of a wealthy debutante, having an exorbitant monthly allowance, going to luxurious galas and balls with Sylvia on his arm. But Sylvia controlled that money. Having an enormous lump sum of cash dangled in front of his nose must have been more appealing for the lowlife scumbag—more than he could pass up. Especially, since Cliff was starting to get the idea that Robert couldn't stand Sylvia.

Mr. Goldman may regret wanting Joey to tell the truth. He'd be devastated if Cliff's hunch was correct. The thought of a brother hiring someone to kill his sister was not beyond Cliff's comprehension but would be beyond Mr. and Mrs. Goldman's.

Cliff had seen worse things in his years as a detective. People had done a lot worse for a lot less. Parents usually assumed the best when it came to their own children. Even if the evidence was as clear as a morning sunrise.

Big Al and Cliff huddled before going in. They had to make sure they were on the same page.

"Do you want to take the first crack at them?" Big Al asked.

"Oh, yeah! I intend to go in there and scare the living daylights out of both of them."

"How are we going to play it? Who do you want to start with?"

"How long have they been in there?" Cliff asked.

"Platt is going on thirty minutes. Goldman roughly fifteen."

"Perfect. Let's let them both stew for another ten minutes. Let 'em squirm. I want them to worry about the possibility that the other is talking. I think I'll start with Joey Goldman. His father told him to cooperate. He might give us information that'll make Robert believe Joey is ratting him out."

Ten minutes passed, and Cliff and Big Al entered the room. Joey was noticeably nervous. He looked like he was going to pee his pants when Cliff started by reading him his rights.

"I'm being arrested?" Joey pleaded. His eyes ping-ponged back and forth between his attorney and Cliff.

"What are the charges?" his attorney asked.

"To be determined. We can start with assault."

"I didn't lay a hand on that girl!" Joey was sitting on the edge of his seat.

"That girl was my wife!" Cliff said.

Joey slumped back in his chair. "I'm sorry. I didn't know."

"Why don't you tell me in your own words what happened in the parking garage."

Cliff was on thin ice here. Technically, his questioning needed to focus on his case. Sylvia Platt's investigation. When he strayed into talking about the incident with his wife, he was venturing smack dab into a conflict of interest.

Big Al wasn't going to stop him. Cliff needed to police himself, so to speak, and stay as close to the line as possible without crossing over it.

Joey described the entire confrontation in the parking garage. It mirrored what Julia said.

"See. I told you. I never laid a hand on her."

"You destroyed her cell phone."

"It all happened so fast."

"So fast that you don't know destroying someone else's cell phone is a crime. So fast that you didn't think hitting a woman in the face was wrong!"

"I didn't hit her in the face. Robert did. I'm sorry. I told him to stop."

Cliff was hot. The fact that Joey was genuinely remorseful didn't change his disgust for the two men's behaviors. Many murderers were remorseful afterward. When they thought they were about to be caught. When it was too late.

"Robert wouldn't listen to me."

"It doesn't sound like you tried very hard."

"I'll buy your wife another cell phone."

His lawyer interjected, "Detective Ford, I appreciate how angry you are about what happened to your wife. I can speak on behalf of my client and say that he's truly sorry for what happened. Are you really going to arrest him for a thousand-dollar cell phone? Especially since my client is willing to provide restitution."

"The cell phone is the least of your client's worries," Cliff said.

"I'm not following you," the attorney replied.

"You will in a few minutes. Mr. Goldman, why did you pay Robert Platt seventy-five million dollars."

Joey squirmed slightly in his seat. He looked at his attorney and squirmed some more. A small bead of sweat started to form on Joey's top lip.

His attorney spoke up, "The parties signed a non-disclosure agreement. Mr. Goldman is not allowed to disclose the terms and conditions of the agreement. I can tell you that it was a settlement to avoid a civil lawsuit."

"As you know counselor, Mr. Goldman can disclose the terms and conditions when asked about it in a criminal investigation. Although, I'm not really concerned about the terms. I'm more interested in the why."

The attorney continued. "Mr. Platt threatened to sue his wife's trust. Mr. Goldman is the beneficiary of that trust. He felt it was in his best interest to settle out of court and avoid lengthy litigation. Especially considering that he might lose all of the trust if a court ruled against him. He wasn't interested in rolling the dice, so to speak, on such a large sum of money."

"Mr. Goldman, why did you say to Robert Platt, and I quote, 'We pulled it off'? Please elaborate."

More squirming. Eyes looking in every direction. A signal of lying. More an indication of trying to figure out how to tell a lie. Cliff saw it all the time when he was interrogating the guilty. No one was comfortable in an interrogation room, but innocent people behaved differently.

"I don't remember saying it," Joey stammered.

"The witness in the parking garage remembers it crystal clear. And she caught the whole conversation on her phone. If we were to play the recording back for you, would that help refresh your memory?"

A bluff on Cliff's part. They had the phone. Robert's attorney handed it over when they came in. The phone didn't come on when it was powered up, but they should be able to capture the video. That could take several weeks. Cliff was certain the video would show exactly what his wife had described.

Cliff didn't mind telling a white lie. Joey didn't need to know that Cliff didn't have the video yet.

Joey changed his story. "All I meant was that we pulled off the settlement. We got it done."

Cliff was always suspicious when, one minute, a suspect doesn't remember, and the next minute, when pressed, all the information miraculously comes back to him.

"What did Robert mean when he said he *earned* that money?"

"I don't know. You'd have to ask him."

"I intend to. But I'm asking you. You repeated it back to him. You said to Robert, 'you did earn it. It's your money. Do with it what you want?'"

"I may have said something like that."

"Why were you so chummy with Robert Platt all of a sudden?"

"We were friends before the wedding, and we remained friends after."

"Even though your family suspects him of killing your sister? That seems like an odd friendship to maintain."

"I don't believe he killed my sister."

"Then there's nothing I can do to help you here. We're done."

"Does that mean I can go?" Joey asked, eyes darting between Cliff, Big Al, and his attorney.

"Nope. You're under arrest."

"On what charge?" his attorney said.

"On conspiracy to commit murder!" Cliff looked directly into Joey's eyes as he said it.

"What?"

Joey almost came out of his chair.

"The seventy-five million was a payment to Robert Platt to murder your sister so you could collect all the proceeds of her trust, wasn't it?"

"Don't answer that," his attorney said.

Cliff ratcheted up the pressure, "You hired Robert Platt to kill your sister! He threw her off the balcony at the honeymoon suite of the *Regency Hotel*! You paid him seventy-five million dollars! To kill *your own* sister!"

Cliff was standing and leaning over the table. Joey was cowering back.

"I am advising my client to remain silent!" Joey's attorney bellowed.

Big Al had his big paw on Cliff's arm and was pulling him back. Cliff lowered his tone.

"Do you remember the first time we spoke?" Cliff asked Joey quietly.

He nodded.

"I told you that your sister was dead. Do you remember what you said?"

"No, I don't."

"That's right. That's because you didn't say anything. You didn't ask any questions. Nothing. No, how did she die? Car accident? Fall? Murder? You weren't the least bit curious. It's like you already knew. I thought it was strange at the time. But in thinking back at it, it makes sense now. You already knew what happened to your sister. You already knew Robert killed her!"

"I would like to confer with my client," his attorney said briskly.

"You didn't ask about Robert. Why not, Joey?"

"Don't answer that!"

"He doesn't need to. I already know the answer. Joey knows it. Because you already knew, didn't you Joey? You already knew what went down. The phone call notifying you of your sister's death just confirmed it for you."

"May I have a few minutes to consult with my client."

"Take all the time you need."

Big Al and Cliff left the room.

"That was intense," Big Al said. "You had him on the ropes. Did you see him squirming in his chair like a guilty greased pig about to be led to the slaughterhouse?"

Cliff nodded. He was elated with how well it went. While he didn't get a confession, Joey's behavior said it all. A good detective can often discern the truth in an interrogation, even if the suspect doesn't come right out and confess.

"What now?" Big Al asked.

"On to Robert."

"He'll be a tougher nut to crack," Big Al said.

"I think we'll use a different tactic with Robert," Cliff replied, smiling back at Big Al.

"What do you have in mind?"

"You'll see."

34

Being in the same room with the man who backhanded his wife across the mouth took all of Cliff's self-control. He'd like nothing more than to slap the smug look off of Robert Platt's face, so hard that he'd be sent flying across the room.

Since he couldn't, he did the next best thing.

"Mr. Robert Platt. You're under arrest for the murder of Sylvia Platt."

Robert Platt and his attorney Thad Caldwell reacted at the same time.

"What?"

"Whoa! Whoa!"

"What are you talking about?"

"Wait a minute!"

"Where did this come from?" Thad Caldwell said, when the din died down. "I thought we were here to talk about the incident in the parking garage."

"That bi" Robert started to say. He was clearly about to call Cliff's wife the b word but caught himself.

"That woman attacked me first."

"Robert shut up," Thad Caldwell said.

"You have the right to remain silent," Cliff continued. "Anything you say can and will be used against you in the court of law. You have the right to an attorney."

Cliff pointed toward Caldwell.

"Although, you might want to consider another attorney," Cliff said. "Your attorney should've told you not to go off and buy a Ferrari. You've just given me motive."

Robert's head sank. Caldwell gave Robert an almost indiscernible scowl. Clearly, Caldwell had advised him not to buy a fancy car, and Robert had ignored his advice.

Cliff couldn't help but rub it in.

"That borders on malpractice, Mr. Caldwell. I expected more out of you. We wouldn't be here if your client hadn't gone out and started spending all that money like a drunken lottery winner."

Caldwell bit his lip and resisted what was clearly the urge to respond.

"Anyway. If you can't afford an attorney, one will be appointed to you. Do you understand these rights?" Cliff asked.

Robert didn't respond.

"Do you understand your rights, Mr. Platt?" Cliff demanded.

"Yes! I understand them!" Robert growled. "I didn't kill nobody."

"Joey Goldman says otherwise."

Robert's eyes widened.

"Why do you think you've been waiting so long? Joey's in the other room. And he's talking like a parakeet in a zoo. He has a lot to say. Like the settlement. He said he paid you seventy-five million dollars. To kill Sylvia."

"That's a lie!"

It was.

Detectives were allowed to lie in an interrogation. Cliff had more lies for him. And he couldn't wait to serve it up on a silver platter with handcuffs on the side.

Cliff was now the one who was smug and was enjoying every minute of it. "That's right. Your payout. Your golden ticket. That's a hefty participation award, I'd say. Although, I have to question Joey's judgment. Usually, hitmen in Chicago charge seventy-five hundred dollars. Not seventy-five million. You got a good deal."

Cliff was glad he knew that figure. It gave him credibility. That information could have only come from Joey.

Robert gathered his composure and said, "That money was for a settlement. I thought Joey wasn't allowed to discuss the agreement."

Robert looked at his attorney when he said it. Caldwell sat stoically, listening. Putting on his best poker face.

Finally, Caldwell spoke up. "Detective Ford, you know my client nor Mr. Goldman can discuss the terms of the settlement agreement."

"Joey's allowed to talk about it if we offer him an immunity deal," Cliff retorted, staring right at Robert for a reaction. He was avoiding eye contact with Cliff.

That got Caldwell's attention. He sat up and asked, "Did Mr. Goldman take a plea deal?"

"You know I can't discuss the terms of an immunity agreement," Cliff said sarcastically.

Cliff was badgering the attorney but couldn't help it.

"Do you want to know what else Joey said?" Cliff asked. "It's very interesting. He said killing Sylvia was your idea."

"That son of a b."

Robert caught himself for the second time.

"Book him!" Cliff said to Big Al and then abruptly stood and walked out of the room.

Cliff slammed the door for dramatic effect. Then went directly into Joey Goldman's room.

"Mr. Goldman, I just had an interesting conversation with Robert Platt," he said. "According to him, killing Sylvia was your idea."

"My client has no comment," his attorney said.

Cliff now knew what advice his attorney had given Joey. Advice which trumped the orders from his father.

"That's fine," Cliff said. "Joey Goldman. You're under arrest. You have the right to remain silent. Anything you say can and will be used against you. You have the right to an attorney. If you can't afford one, the court will appoint one for you. Do you understand these rights?"

"You've already read him his rights," his attorney said.

"Oh yeah. That's right. Never hurts to read them to him again."

Joey's eyes were burning with fear. He was tearing up. Starting to lose it. His lip was quivering, and his hands were shaking.

"Please stand."

Joey stood to his feet. His knees were wobbly as he reached out to brace himself on the table.

"Put your hands behind your back," Cliff instructed. He took a pair of handcuffs out of his back pocket and slapped the cuffs on him. Next stop was processing. Then a holding cell. Probably for the night.

Joey Goldman began to cry. Snot was starting to run down his face, and he couldn't even wipe it off because he was cuffed.

"Don't say anything to anybody unless I'm present," his attorney said to him. "We'll get you out of here on bail. Probably not tonight. But we'll get you out first thing in the morning."

It'd probably be two to three days. Cliff had seventy-two hours before he had to formally charge Joey or Robert. He needed the time to get his facts in a row so he could present the case to the district attorney.

The settlement agreement should be all he needed to get the DA to proceed against Robert. It had motive written all over it. Coupled with Julia's testimony, Cliff felt good about his case.

The evidence against Joey was flimsier. The only thing he really had to go on was Julia's testimony. The 'We pulled it off' comment. There wasn't any other corroborating evidence. Like Joey said, those words could be twisted to mean almost anything. He needed a connection between Robert and Joey. Cell phone communications. A witness who saw them meeting before the murder. He had money-changing hands, which was persuasive but maybe not beyond a reasonable doubt.

Cliff led Joey away to the same place Big Al was in the process of booking Robert.

The two suspects glared at each other, which gave Cliff an idea.

He pulled Big Al to the side out of earshot of the two suspects.

"Brilliant move telling Robert that Joey was talking," Big Al said. "It's got him scared to death."

Cliff nodded. "I told Joey the same thing. That Robert was talking."

"Oh, man. That'll give them both something to think about tonight."

"That's what I'm hoping for. Listen. Put Robert and Joey in the same holding cell. Just the two of them. Make sure everything is caught on camera and recorded. I want to see if they say anything to each other."

"They might kill each other."

"We should be so lucky."

As Cliff was leaving, he said, "Don't stay in the office too much longer, Al. Big day tomorrow."

"I guess you've got a long night ahead of you too."

Cliff should really start working on his presentation to the DA. He decided against it.

Tonight, he needed to go home and comfort his wife.

35

The next morning

Louth called Cliff into his office. He'd only been at his desk for less than a minute.

"Have a seat," Louth said, pointing to one of the two chairs across from him. That usually meant that Cliff was going to be there for a while.

"Congratulations on your two arrests last night," the lieutenant said.

"Thank you."

Louth was probably about to ask him what he had on Robert and Joey. If past conversations were any indication of present behavior, the lieutenant would poke a thousand holes in his case. Tell him everything he did wrong. Cliff needed more time before he had this conversation with his boss.

"Which one do you want?" Louth asked out of the blue.

"Pardon?" Cliff didn't know what he meant.

"Who do you want more? Robert Platt or Josef Goldman?"

"I want both. I don't understand the question."

"I talked to both of their attorneys this morning."

"Okay."

"They want to deal."

"Both of them?"

"Yes. Apparently, Platt is prepared to testify against Josef Goldman. For a reduced sentence. Josef is prepared to rat out Platt. Tell us everything that happened. From start to finish."

"I assume Josef wants a deal as well."

"You got it."

Deal or not, it meant Cliff was right. The two of them conspired to kill Sylvia. The lieutenant wouldn't be poking any holes in his case. If they both wanted a deal, it meant they were both guilty of a crime.

"Have either of them proffered their testimony?"

In a plea deal, the suspect's attorney gives a proffer as to what evidence his client will provide against the other suspect. So, the investigator can know if the testimony is worth giving a reduced sentence. The condition is that the proffer can't be used against the suspect in court if the deal is rejected.

"No. I need to know who you want to nail the most," Louth answered.

"What do you think?"

"I don't have an opinion. You're closest to the case. I'll defer to your judgment."

"Let me get back to you."

"Make it fast. While the proverbial iron is hot."

Cliff left his office stunned at the sudden turn of events. He walked back to his desk and knew exactly what to do. Call his wife and get her advice.

Julia answered her phone on the first ring.

"Hi, honey," she said. "Is everything okay?"

He didn't usually bother her at work.

"Can you talk?"

"Let me close my door."

He heard her footsteps and then listened to the sound of a door closing. She was probably in her office at the women's shelter.

"What's up?" she asked.

"I need your advice."

"Okay."

Asking for it would make her feel good. He also genuinely wanted it.

"Turns out you were right. Robert Platt did kill his wife. Joey Goldman was in on it."

"That's huge! Congratulations Cliff. I'm thrilled for you. That's a big arrest."

"I couldn't have done it without you. That whole incident in the garage broke the whole thing wide open."

"I'm glad I could take one for the team. My jaw and lip are swollen and sore, but if my face helped you solve your case, then I'd do it again."

"Let's hope you never have to."

"You said you needed my advice. It sounds like you've got it all covered."

"Both of them want a deal. They'll testify against the other for a reduced sentence."

"Okay. That's a good thing. Right. What's the problem?"

"Who should I pick? Who do I do the deal with?"

"Hmmm. That's a tough one. I see your problem. Joey did it for money. Seven hundred and fifty million is a lot of cash. Still. That's his sister. His own flesh and blood. I can't even imagine doing something like that to Rita or Anna."

Cliff heard the pain in her voice when she mentioned her sisters.

Julia continued. "Well... on the other hand... Robert was the one who actually killed her. He's the one who threw her off the balcony. How could he do that? What kind of person would kill his wife? It's so cruel."

"Robert also did it for money. He got seventy-five million from Joey."

She didn't know those details. When Cliff got home that night, he didn't even bring up the case with her. He was more concerned about her mental and emotional state. Which was fine considering what she'd been through. The biggest issue to her had been how she looked with the swollen lip.

If the huge amount of money was a surprise, he couldn't tell it in her voice. "Robert also went to Virgin Gorda and hooked up with that floozy," Julia continued with her reasoning. "That's despicable. So... I don't know. I'm torn. What do you think?"

"I hate them both equally. Not them. We're supposed to hate the sin and not the sinner."

"That's hard to do sometimes."

"What they did is despicable. What's your advice?"

"My advice is to go with your gut. Trust your instincts. You'll do the right thing."

"Good advice."

He really couldn't expect her to make the decision for him. He hung up the phone and thought about it for more than an hour.

36

Cliff decided to make a deal with Joey Goldman. Joey seemed like the one most capable of remorse. Cliff also did it for Josef and Emilia Goldman's benefit. They already lost their daughter. Tragically. Now their son was charged with conspiring to kill her. They essentially lost both kids. According to the deal, Joey wouldn't be eligible for parole for twenty years. They'd both be in their eighties by the time he got out. That's if they were still alive.

Joey was already being punished to a certain extent. He would lose the trust fund. Spend twenty years in a concrete cell with bars. A lot different than the life he was used to. Twenty years was a long time. Losing the 1.5 billion dollars in his trust fund was punishment in and of itself. He'd have many long nights to think about it.

After the paperwork with Joey was signed, Cliff was tasked with giving Robert and his attorney the news.

They were rejecting his offer.

Cliff imagined that they were still holding out hope that the deal would be accepted. Caldwell was smart. He knew when he was dealt a losing hand which was why he recommended Robert take the deal. The death penalty wasn't on the table, but life imprisonment with the possibility of parole was.

Big Al was at his desk waiting for Cliff. As he started to go get him, the phone on his desk rang. He began to send it to voicemail but felt a compunction to answer it, so he did.

Cliff leaned back in his chair and said, "Ford."

"Detective Ford, my name is Leon Dispennette. I'm a homicide detective in East Lansing, Michigan."

"How can I help you, sir?"

"You recently arrested a man named Robert Platt?"

Cliff sat back up in his chair.

"Yes, sir."

"I've been working on several cold cases in East Lansing. They go back ten years or so. When Robert Platt was a student at Michigan State University."

Detective Dispennette got Cliff's attention in a red hot second.

A number of questions started swirling around in his head, but he didn't dare interrupt. The detective would get to them soon enough and Cliff didn't want to embarrass himself by having his hopes dashed.

"Anyway. We got a DNA hit. From your man."

"That was quick. We just booked him last night."

When Robert was arrested, his DNA and fingerprints went into a national database. DNA from unsolved cases was also in that database. Cliff knew from experience that the software sent an alert to the detective on record when there was a match. Most detectives didn't get to their emails that quickly.

"I've got him linked to five murders," the detective said. "I'm going to want to talk to him. Don't cut him loose."

"I can assure you that Robert Platt is not going anywhere."

They coordinated schedules. Cliff assured him that Platt would be held without bail for seventy-two more hours. That'd give the detective time to make flight arrangements.

Since Cliff's case was more current, he'd get the first crack at prosecuting him.

Dispennette would bring all the files from East Lansing for the district attorney in Chicago to review.

Cliff hung up the phone. Stunned. Five murders. He'd made the right decision taking the deal with Goldman. Robert Platt should never taste freedom again.

He filled Big Al in on the conversation. When finished, the two of them walked confidently into the interrogation room. Robert wasn't looking as smug as he had the night before. Lock-up often had that effect on people who had never been there before.

Caldwell had probably warned Robert not to act cocky. They wanted a deal. Robert was wearing the same clothes he'd been arrested in, so he looked disheveled. He was jail-cell-dirty. Unshaven. Hair mussed. Even though it was clear he had tried to comb it. He was a mess.

Cliff couldn't help but think of the verse in the Bible that said pride comes before the fall. Robert had no idea how hard and far he was about to fall.

Caldwell was his usual manicured self. Five-hundred-dollar shirt. Silk tie. Cufflinks. Rolex watch. He was probably relishing in his new client's misfortunes. Such was the life of an attorney. Caldwell prospered when people were murdered. Business was booming in Chicago.

"Do we have a deal?" Caldwell said.

Robert moved forward to the edge of his seat in anticipation.

"No, we do not, counselor. We made a deal with Joey Goldman."

Robert slumped down in his chair. Caldwell had no reaction.

"Mr. Goldman has already given us a statement," Cliff explained. "He told us everything that happened. Admitted that it was his idea. Joey had Sylvia killed so he could get access to her trust. Ten percent was the agreed upon price. Seventy-five million dollars and change. Blood money."

"I guess we'll see you in court," Caldwell said.

"Not so fast," Cliff said.

"Robert. Tell me about the girls you killed in East Lansing, Michigan."

Robert's head slumped to his chest. He began to sob.

Pride comes before the fall.

Indeed.

***

Afterwards, Cliff called Julia.

"Cancel all your plans for tonight," he said.

"Let me look at my calendar," she said teasingly. "Oh, that's right, I have no plans. Tonight. Tomorrow night. Or any night for the next fifty years. They're all free if you want them."

"I do."

"What are we doing?"

"Celebrating!"

"What are we celebrating?"

He told her.

All about Robert. His decision to take the deal with Joey. East Lansing, Michigan, and the look on Robert's face when he confronted him. Five women.

Robert was a serial killer.

"That's something worth celebrating," Julia said. "Do you want me to wear my sexy red dress or my LBD?"

"The little black dress sounds perfect."

"Where are we going?"

"You choose. Price is no object."

"The pizza place in Naperville."

"Andiamo's? You're going to get all dressed up to go to a pizza place."

"They have the best food in all of Chicago. They put sugar in their dough. It's like eating cake."

"Woo wap da bam."

"What did you just say?"

"You've never heard that before?"

"No! Did you make it up?"

"It's a phrase. A Chicago idiom."

Cliff switched the phone to his other ear. It felt so good to solve the case. Even better to have someone to celebrate it with.

"Say it slower."

"Woo wap da bam."

"What does it mean?"

"It means so on and so forth. Whatever. It's like saying yadda, yadda, yadda. I can't believe you've never heard it. It's common in Chicago."

"You made that up."

"I did not. Look it up."

"Don't think I won't!"

"Fine by me!"

The fake outrage from both of them warmed his heart. Tonight was going to be fun. In more ways than one.

Especially when Julia looked up the phrase on the internet. Cliff wasn't kidding. It was a real phrase.

That made him feel even better. It wasn't often he was right, and Julia was wrong.

Not The End

Thank you for purchasing this novel from best-selling author Terry Toler. As an additional thank you, Terry wants to give you a free gift.

Sign up for:

Updates
New Releases
Announcements

At terrytoler.com

We'll send you the first three chapters of The Launch, a Jamie Austen novella, free of charge. The one that started the Spy Stories and Eden Stories Franchises.

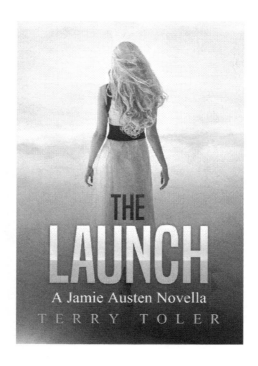

Want to read more Cliff Hangers
Book One: Anna

DO YOU LIKE THRILLERS

INTERNATIONAL #1 BEST SELLING SERIES FROM

TERRY TOLER

THE JAMIE AUSTEN THRILLERS

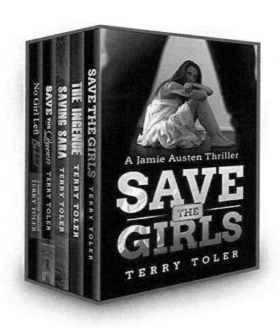

Made in the USA
Monee, IL
19 May 2024

58623912R00162